FLIGHT TO OPAR

Twelve thousand years ago Africa was not the continent we know now, not a land of waterless wastes, of infested jungles, and scattered villages. Great inland seas existed where now there is but desert, and along their shores rose mighty cities and high civilizations. One such was Opar, whose ruins and degenerate descendants were discovered in our century by the world-renowned Lord Greystoke, better known as Tarzan of the Apes.

Philip José Farmer, chronicler of the secret lore of Lord Greystoke and Doc Savage, historian of lost lands and unknown worlds, has, with the permission of Hulbert Burroughs, undertaken to recreate Opar in its golden days. In his novels of Hadon, outcast heir to the throne of that forgotten empire, he has created a new series to thrill the millions who seek after new marvels in the style of the master, Edgar Rice Burroughs, himself.

PHILIP JOSÉ FARMER

Flight to Opar

Methuen

Dedicated to J. T. Edson, Honorable Admiral of the Texas Navy, Honorable Deputy Sheriff of Travis County, Texas, and Thurston County, Washington, and creator of the epical Dusty Fog, the Ysabel Kid, Mark Counter, Ole Devil Hardin, and Bunduki.

A Methuen Paperback

FLIGHT TO OPAR

ISBN 0 417 01770 7

First published in Great Britain 1977
by Magnum Books

Copyright © 1976 by Philip José Farmer

Reprinted 1983 by
Methuen London Ltd
11 New Fetter Lane, London EC4P 4EE

Made and printed in Great Britain
by Richard Clay (The Chaucer Press) Ltd
Bungay, Suffolk

FOREWORD

Those unacquainted with *Hadon of Ancient Opar*, volume one of the Ancient Opar series, should refer to the map following. This shows the two central African seas which existed circa 10,000 B.C. At that time the climate was much more humid (pluvial) than now. What are now the Chad Basin and the Congo Basin were covered with fresh water, bodies whose area equaled and perhaps surpassed that of the present-day Mediterranean. The Ice Age was dying, but large parts of the British Islands and northern Europe were covered with glaciers. The Mediterranean was from one to two hundred feet lower than its present level. The Sahara Desert of today was then vast grasslands, rivers and freshwater lakes, and was host to millions of elephants, antelopes, lions, crocodiles and many other beasts, some now extinct.

The map also shows the island of Khokarsa, which gave birth to the first civilization of Earth, and the largest cities which grew around the Great Water, the Kemu, and the Great Water of Opar, the Kemuwopar. The prehistory and history of the peoples of the two seas are outlined in the *Chronology of Khokarsa* in volume one.

The map is a modification of the map in volume one. That, in turn, was a modification of a map presented by Frank Brueckel and John Harwood in their article: *Heritage of the Flaming God, an Essay on the History of Opar and Its Relationship to Other Ancient Cultures*. This appeared in *The Burroughs Bulletin*, Vernell Coriell, publisher, House of Greystoke, 6657 Locust, Kansas City, Missouri 64131.

This series basically derives from the Opar books of the Tarzan series, and the author wishes to thank Hulbert Burroughs again for the permission to write these tales.

There is a rumor that this series is based on the translation of some of the gold tablets described by Edgar Rice Burroughs in *The Return of Tarzan*. That speculation will have to be dealt with in an addendum to a later volume of this series.

Central Africa, 10,000 B.C.

1

Hadon leaned on his sword and waited for death.

He looked down the mountain slope from the mouth of the inner pass. Once again he shook his head. If only Lalila had not twisted her ankle, they might not be in such a hopeless situation.

The slope leading to the pass was steep, requiring a hands-and-knees approach during the last fifty yards. For a hundred yards from the inner pass, cliffs at least a hundred feet high and sixty yards wide walled the approach. These formed a sort of outer entrance. The walls went rapidly inward from that point, like the edges of an arrowhead. The slope and the walls met at the point of the arrow. Hadon stood now in the narrow aperture. Here the path began from a rocky ledge about ten inches high. It ran at a slightly less than forty-five-degree angle to the horizontal for a hundred feet, the cliffs that caged it rapidly dwindling in height.

It came out on the top of the cliffs, where the ground was fairly level. Beyond it was the vast oak forest.

The distance between the cliffs in the inner pass was just enough for a man to wield a sword. He had an advantage in that anybody trying to fight him would have to stand up before he could gain the less steep incline. That warrior would not have a stable footing. Hadon, standing on the ledge, would have a relatively firm stance.

The cliffs extended their high verticality for five miles on either side, however, so the pursuers did not have to attempt a frontal attack. They could go along the base of the cliffs until they came to a climbable part. Then they could ascend it and come back along the top of the cliffs. But it would take them about eight or nine hours to do this. They could not progress more than half a mile an hour on the steep rough terrain.

The soldiers would have their pride. They could not allow one man to scare off forty. In either event, direct or circuitous attack, they would be giving Awineth, Abeth, Hinokly, Kebiwabes and Paga time to get many miles into the forest. They would not know about Lalila's injured ankle and so would assume that he was making a stand just to give the refugees plenty of time to get lost in the woods. It would not take them long to know, however, that they were up against the man who had won the Great Games, who had been taught by the greatest swordsman in the Empire of Khokarsa.

Down on the slope, about twenty minutes away, the soldiers climbed steadily. In the lead were five dogs, straining at their leashes, digging their paws into the sparsely grassed dirt, slipping now and then. Three were keen-nosed tracehounds, belling as they sniffed the smells of the pursued. Two were wardogs. They were descended from the wild dog of the plains, bred to the size of male leopards, without the endurance of their ancestors but with no fear of man. Part of their training was the attacking of armed slaves. If the slave killed the three dogs loosed at him, he was freed. This seldom happened.

Some distance below and behind the dogs and their handlers was the lone officer. He was a big man, wearing a conical bronze helmet sporting a long raven feather from its top. His sword, still in its leather sheath, was the long, slightly curving, blunt-ended weapon of the *numatenu*. The same kind that Hadon was leaning on, which meant that the officer would be his first antagonist. The code of the *numatenu* dictated this. The officer would be disgraced if he sent in lesser men to face another *numatenu*.

Still, things were not always what they had been in the old days. Now there were men wearing the *tenu* who had no right to do so, men who often went unchallenged. The moral codes were breaking down, along with much else in these times of trouble.

Behind the officer, in straggling disorder, were thirty sol-

8

diers. They wore round bronze helmets with leather earflaps and noseflaps, leather cuirasses and leather kilts. They carried small round bronze shields on their backs and held long bronze-tipped spears. They dug these into the ground to assist their climb. Short stabbing swords were in their leather scabbards. On their backs, under the shields, were leather bags of provisions.

Behind the soldiers were four peasants clad in kilts of papyrus fiber. They carried round wooden shields on their backs and short swords in sheaths at their broad leather belts. Their hunting spears were in their hands, and slings and bags of sling-stones also hung from their belts.

They were close enough now for Hadon to recognize them. These were the sons of the farmer at whose house Hadon's party had stopped to get food. After a brief show of resistance, the peasants had fled. But Awineth, in a fury because they had refused hospitality, had indiscreetly told them who she was. They must have gone to the nearest army post to notify the commander. He had sent this small force after the daughter of Minruth, Emperor of Khokarsa. And after Hadon and the others too. Awineth, of course, would be brought back alive, but what were the orders concerning the others? Capture so they could be brought back for judgment by Minruth? The men would probably be tortured publicly and then executed. Minruth, who seemed to have a passion for Lalila, would keep her as a mistress. Perhaps. He might have her tortured and killed too. And he was insane enough to wreak his hatred on Abeth, Lalila's daughter.

The dog tenders were weaponless except for daggers and slings. That made nine slingers in all. These were the deadliest weapons he would face. He had no room to dodge a lead missile travelling at sixty miles an hour, but they would have trouble getting into the proper stance for action if he had his way.

Hadon turned to look up the steeply sloping pass at Lalila. She sat at its end, about two hundred feet away. The sun shone on her white skin and long golden hair. Her large violet eyes looked black at this distance. She was bent forward, massaging her left ankle. She tried to smile but failed.

He walked up to her and, as he neared, he was struck with

9

a pang of longing and sorrow. She was so lovely, he was so much in love with her, and they both had to die so soon.

"I wish you would do it, Hadon," she said. She indicated the long narrow dagger lying on the dirt beside her. "I would rather you killed me now and made sure that I died. I'm not sure that I'll have the strength to drive the blade into my heart when the time comes. I don't want to fall into Minruth's hands. Yet ... I keep thinking that perhaps I might escape later on. I don't want to die!"

Hadon said, "You may be sure that you'd never get away from him again."

"Then kill me now!" she said. "Why wait until the last possible moment?"

She bowed her head as if to invite him to bring the sword down on it.

Instead he dropped to one knee and kissed the top of her head. She shuddered on feeling his lips.

"We had so much to live for!" she murmured.

"We still do," he said after rising. "I've been a fool, Lalila. I was thinking of making a stand according to the dictates of tradition. One man in a pass, valiantly fighting, slaying until the warriors are piled before me, then dying when a spear drives past my arms, too weary to hold the sword up any more.

"But that's stupid. I can do other things, and I will do them. First, though, we'll get you away from here—not too far, since we don't have time. Come."

He raised her to her feet. She winced with the pain of the ankle but did not cry out. "It'd take too long for you to hobble there, even with me supporting you," he said. He put the sword in its sheath and picked her up in his arms. She started to ask him what he intended to do. He said, "Hush! I need my breath," and he hurried toward the forest. Coming to its edge, he halted a few seconds while he looked around. Then he plunged into the half-darkness under the great oaks, carrying her to the foot of a mottled white and brown giant.

The lowest branch was two feet above him. He lifted her up so that she could grasp it and then heaved her up. She stretched out on it face down, looking back at him.

"It may hurt you, but you'll have to do it anyway," he said.

"Climb up as far as you can and conceal yourself in the foliage. I haven't got time to wait here and see how you do while you climb."

"But what are you going to do?"

"I'm going to kill as many as possible. Then I'm going to run, drawing them away from you and the others."

"You'll leave me here to . . .?"

"To starve, possibly. Or be eaten by leopards or bears or be taken by the outlaws," he said. "That's a chance to be taken, Lalila. It's better than waiting for a sure death here. I'll be back for you. Somehow, I'll get back to you. But if I shouldn't, then take the same path the others took. It'll lead you to the temple, and you'll be safe in the sanctuary there."

Lalila smiled then, though it was certainly not with joy. The probability that he would return was small. She could not walk the many, many miles through the forest, up and down mountains. She could easily get lost, and there were bears, leopards, hyenas and many other beasts of prey hereabouts. Even if she somehow did find her way to the temple at Karneth, she might find that the sanctuary was no longer sacred. The followers of King Minruth, worshipers of Resu, would probably violate the temple.

She did not voice her doubts. Instead she said, "Go quickly then, Hadon! I will pray to my gods, and your goddess, that we will see each other again! And soon!"

She reached down and he kissed her hand, then turned without a word.

2

Hadon ran down the ancient hard-beaten path between the oaks for about fifty yards. Then he cut to his right, paralleling the path, and returned to the exit of the pass. If the dogs did track him to the oak where he had left her, they would smell only him. The trackers would see only his prints. The ground was not soft enough to show that his feet had sunk into the earth too deeply for one person. The dogs would follow his tracks down the path and then, hopefully, back to the pass through the forest ... if there were any dogs left by then, and there wouldn't be if he had his way.

There was nothing to stop the pursuers from just ignoring his tracks and following those of the refugees. He hoped that by the time they were through the pass they would be in a fury of vengeance, bent only on chasing him down and killing him.

He raced back to the pass. Instead of entering its narrow high walls, he went around its right side. He ran along it, going up a slope, and presently was standing on the edge of the cliffs. To his left was the wide mouth of the outer pass, a hundred feet below him.

He looked over the edge. The frantic barking of the dogs was loud now. The lead pair was only fifty yards from the mouth of the pass. But here the slope was even steeper and the going slower. He went back along the edge until he stood over the place where the narrow passage began.

He searched for rocks small enough to carry but large enough for the task he had in mind. By the time the lead dogs were several yards below the mouth of the slot, he had piled seven small boulders by the edge.

The officer had called to the dog handlers to stop, though he had trouble getting their attention. One of the tenders finally saw the officer's lips moving and spoke to the others who yelled at the tracehounds to keep quiet. This failing, they struck them with their hands. The animals yelped, but they obeyed.

The wardogs made no sound. They crouched low to the ground, their yellow eyes round, slaver dripping from long yellow teeth.

The officer gave a few orders, not quite loudly enough for Hadon to distinguish the words. The men kept looking up, but they were intent on the pass and so did not see his head further down the edge of the cliff. They would become aware of his location soon enough.

Two tenders suddenly released their dogs and spoke to their charges. These, breaking into a loud barking, bent like bows and then sped like arrows up the slope. Hadon waited. He could deal with them later. The dogs ran up the pass barking, while the men below listened carefully. As the clamor became fainter, they realized that no one was in the pass to oppose them. The officer smiled and said something to the other three handlers. These, still holding the leashes, urged their frenzied beasts ahead of them. Hadon rolled away so that no chance look would detect him. When a few yards from the edge of the cliff, he stood up. He picked up a boulder, heaved it above his head and walked to the edge. Just below him were the three dogs, in single file, each pulling hard on the leash held by its tender.

Hadon estimated their rate of progress, strained, holding the heavy rock, and then cast it out a few feet.

It fell true, driving in the bronze helmet of the man in the lead.

His dog burst loose, trailing the leash behind it. The other two men halted suddenly and looked upward. Their mouths were open and their faces were pale.

Hadon turned, picked up a smaller stone and hurled that down. The two men turned to run back down the pass, but the stone struck one on the shoulder, breaking it and knocking him flat on the ground. The survivor, crying shrilly, leaped out from the pass and rolled down the steep slope.

13

Hadon picked up another boulder, as large as the first, and moved to the edge of the cliffs. He looked over, saw that the rolling dog handler had knocked down the officer and two spearmen. All four were rolling out of control.

He gave a mighty heave, and the stone shot out, fell, hit the slope, bounded and shot into a group of four spearmen. One must have been killed by the impact; the others were hurled back down the mountains. One rolled into another man, knocking him off his feet.

The boulder, its rate of descent only a little slowed by striking the soldier, smashed into the legs of another spearman, knocked him down, rolled, leaped and slammed into the stomach of one of the farmer's sons. Then it continued on down the mountains. None of the men hit by the boulder got up or showed signs that they were able to do so.

Hadon, instead of running back for another boulder, returned to the point where he could not be seen by those below the pass. He dropped the sword, still in its sheath, over the edge. He let himself over the edge, clung to the rock a moment, then dropped. It was fifteen feet from the top to the bottom at this point, but he was six feet two inches tall, one of the tallest men in Khokarsa, and his arms were exceptionally long. He rolled without injury, rose and picked up the sword. After fastening the sheath to his belt, he ran down to the two fallen men. One was dead; the other was unconscious. He removed their slings and bags. Then he used the injured man's dagger to ensure that he would never be a danger to anyone again.

He unsheathed his sword, Karken, Tree of Death, and drove its blunt point into the thin hard earth. Within a few seconds, he had placed a biconical lead missile in its sling. He moved to the mouth of the pass.

The officer was on his feet by then, bringing the soldiers to order. He looked up while shouting and saw Hadon. Hadon grinned and began whirling the sling at the ends of its thongs in a horizontal circle over his head. The officer cried out, his face pale. Perhaps he was protesting against a *numatenu* using a sling against another, not at his being in peril. But Hadon believed that the officer had lost any right to individual combat when he had loosed the dogs. Besides, he had

14

decided not to play the game according to the rules. It would be stupid to give up his life for the code if it meant Lalila and the others would not escape. His highest duty was to Awineth, the high priestess of great Kho, now a refugee from the blasphemer Minruth. And also to Lalila and her child.

The angle was a difficult one for a slinger. It was not easy to estimate the trajectory of the cone. There was a tendency for a slinger in his position to underestimate, to cast the missile too low. But Hadon had given hundreds of hours to practice with the sling and he had hunted successfully in the jungle around Opar.

He released the end of the thong as it came down and the cone sped true. It was a blur on its way, but suddenly it bounced from the officer's nose. The nose disappeared in a gout of blood; the man was hurled back down the mountain. He fell on his back and slid for sixty feet downward, finally stopping when the top of his head was caught on a projection of rock.

The slingers had their lead missiles in their thongs by then and were whirling them. He stepped back, out of sight. Some missiles shot upward past the lip of the cliff. Others struck against the rocks below him, knocking off chips.

In those few seconds of observation, Hadon had seen that the other two dogs had been dragged back down the slope. One dog was in sight now, out of the pass, baying as it sped after Hadon's scent. It would follow his track into the forest, then double back and eventually find him. Hadon had some time, however, before he had to deal with it.

Suddenly the pass was loud with belling and growling. Hadon took a quick look over the edge. It was as he had thought. The *rekokha* or sergeant now in command had loosed the other dogs. Now he was shouting at the men, and they scrambled up on all fours. The noncom evidently hoped that the dogs would keep Hadon busy while they got through the pass. The sergeant was a good thinker; Hadon would have to eliminate him as soon as possible.

Hadon whirled around, placed another missile and spun the sling. Four dogs shot out of the end of the pass, the two swifter tracehounds in the lead, the two wardogs close behind them. The stone struck the rear dog in the left rear leg,

15

knocking him over. He got up, howling, his leg trailing, and tried to run after the others. He fell and could not get up again.

Hadon went to the edge of the pass, back from the edge of the cliff, however. In that glance, he had seen six slingers standing up, though with some difficulty, whirling their slings. They would throw at him if he showed himself.

Hadon pushed a boulder over the edge into the narrow pass. He dropped down after it, picked it up and staggered to the mouth of the slot. Easing it down to the ground, he waited, his sword in his hands.

Presently he heard a puffing. He crouched down. He held the sword above his head. Suddenly the hands of a man gripped the shelf of the entrance. The head of the sergeant followed. His eyes opened, his flushed skin whitened. He started to cry out, and his hands released their hold. The *tenu* whipped downward. The sergeant fell back, leaving his two hands on the rock, spouting blood briefly.

There were cries from below. Hadon stood up, heaved the boulder above his head, almost losing it because of its weight. He took one step forward and cast it outward. It hit a soldier who was on all fours, staring at the body of the sergeant just before him. It crushed in his helmet and then rolled over his body and continued down the slope. A man screamed and tried to roll out of the way, but the boulder ran over an arm.

Hadon ducked back as the slingers shot their lead at him. They struck the rocky walls above him, knocking off chips which cut his face and arms.

He ran back up the pass. It was not likely that the soldiers would be trying again very soon. He would have time to take care of the dogs. He hoped he would, anyway.

The animals were coming back. They burst out of the shadows of the oak forest just as he got to the exit. The tracehounds halted on seeing him. The wardog, growling, bounded toward him. Hadon dropped the sling. He waited and, as the wardog leaped toward his throat, swung his sword. The blade cut its head off, its impact driving the body to one side. He whirled and then stepped away, but the spouting blood covered his feet.

At that the tracehounds moved in. Though primarily bred for tracking, they had been trained to attack too. One sped in directly toward him, then stopped just out of reach of his sword. The other circled around behind to dash in and nip at his legs. Hadon shifted the *tenu* to his left hand, pulled out his knife and threw it. The tracehound dodged to one side, too late. The knife drove into its body just before the right rear leg.

Hadon whirled, shifting the *tenu* back to his right hand. The tracehound which had run in to bite his leg skidded to a halt. It bounced back and forth, sidewise, baying. Hadon backed up, keeping his eyes on the beast. He shifted the sword to his left hand again, bent down, quickly pulled the knife out, wiped it on the grass and waited. The dog moved too quickly to be a reliable target for the knife.

After a few seconds, Hadon moved toward the dog. It retreated, keeping a distance of about thirty feet, moving back and forth, in and out. Hadon kept walking toward the cliff's edge. Suddenly the dog realized what was happening. It was twenty feet from being backed off the top of the cliff.

As it ran at an angle away from Hadon, Hadon ran toward it. It was no longer shifting around; now it ran in a straight line. Hadon threw the knife, and the blade sank into its neck.

A moment later he peeped cautiously over the edge. Most of the group was gathered about thirty feet below the pass. Two men were almost at its mouth. They were on all fours but gripping spears. Evidently they planned to rise simultaneously just short of the mouth and cast their spears if Hadon was waiting for them.

He ran to the dog, picked its body up and ran with it to the top of the pass. Just as the two soldiers rose to their feet, he threw the carcass down. It struck one and knocked him back down the slope, into the knot below him. The other looked startled and for a moment did not seem to know what happened.

Hadon looked around. There were no stones handy for throwing, no boulders to drop. He rolled quickly over the edge and dropped to the floor of the pass. The soldier saw him then and scrambled upward, crawling into the pass. He

17

rose as Hadon ran toward him, raising the spear to throw. Hadon's knife flew, plunged to the hilt in the man's mouth, and the man fell backward.

His knife was gone, but the spear had fallen within his reach.

3

An hour had passed. Hadon crouched near the mouth, waiting. The soldiers had retreated to a distance of fifty yards down and about forty feet to one side of the pass. They were sitting down, talking among themselves. They seemed to be in disagreement. No wonder. Their dogs were dead, which meant they would have to do any tracking without their indispensable aid. Three of them were disabled, out of action. Eight were dead. That still left twenty-nine, but these could only get into the pass one at a time and their antagonist was better armed now than when the attack had started.

Hadon looked across the wide valley. To his right, far below, part of the road at the bottom was visible here and there among the trees. There were very tiny figures on it. Occasionally the sun flashed on a helmet, a spearpoint. Reinforcements were coming, with more dogs. It would take them until nightfall to get to the pass, but they would not wait for daylight, knowing that Hadon could slip away in the dark. Moreover, their main quarry, Awineth, would be getting further and further away.

They would light their torches and release the dogs. This time they would have too many dogs for him to handle, and they would storm the pass while he was occupied with them.

It seemed that the soldiers on the slope had not yet seen the men on the road. But they would. Then what would they do? Wait for the newcomers? Or continue the onslaught?

Far to the right, beyond the shoulder of the mountain across the valley, rose the Khowot, the Voice of Kho, the Great Goddess, Mother of All. Just past it was a dark splotch, all he could see of the city of Khokarsa. The Voice of Kho had discharged great quantities of lava and poisonous gases while he and Lalila and the others were fleeing Minruth's underground prison. It was fortunate for them that the earthquake preceding the eruption had opened the way for them, and the shaking of the earth had tumbled down buildings and panicked the city. Afterward, mighty Khowot had belched white-hot lava and huge chunks of stone and lava. In the chaos of the flight of the citizens, Hadon's group had managed to escape into the countryside.

Even then, Minruth's soldiers had been after them—and they might have caught up with them—but Kwasin, Hadon's herculean cousin, had leaped onto the boat full of soldiers. The last Hadon had seen of him, before the smoke veiled the battle, was Kwasin's tremendous ax rising and falling.

Hadon was grateful for Kwasin's sacrifice, though it had been motivated more by egotism than anything else. Kwasin thought he was the strongest man in the world—and probably was. But he hated Hadon, and he had promised to find them later and take Lalila away.

First, though, Kwasin would have to kill Hadon.

Fearsome as Kwasin was, he was going to have a battle he would never forget—if he survived. Kwasin was much larger and stronger, but he was not as quick as Hadon. Nor was he the equal of his cousin in swordsmanship. Yet that ax, that great ax made from a fallen star by Paga ... it was so heavy that only a giant like Kwasin could wield it as if it was fashioned from papyrus.

Hadon thought back to the time when he had left Opar for the Great Games at Khokarsa. Who could have foreseen the chain of events which would lead him to this mountain pass? Only Kho Herself, and She had let drop a few hints through the mouth of Her speaker, the oracular priestess in the cave near the top of the volcano.

Hadon had contested with the other ambitious athletic youths in the Lesser Games at Opar. Three had been chosen. Himself, his friend Taro and the surly, hateful Hewako. These and their substitutes had traveled on a galley through the Kemuwopar, the Southern Sea of Opar. They had gotten through the spooky Strait of Kethna and then had crossed the length of the Kemu, the Northern Sea, the Great Water.

Awineth, Queen of Khokarsa and high priestess, daughter of Minruth, wanted a husband, a king her own age. Minruth had asked her to marry him, but she had refused him. It was rumored that Awineth had taken her father to bed before making up her mind and had found him wanting. Hadon doubted the story because it was evident to all that daughter and father had long been hostile to each other. Another rumor had it that Awineth suspected her father of poisoning her mother. Hadon doubted this too, though Minruth was not called the Mad without good cause. But even he would not have dared to murder his wife, the high priestess, supreme vicar of Kho. Surely he would have feared the wrath of the Goddess too much. But then perhaps he *had* done it and, finding that lightning did not strike him, the earth did not open up beneath him, he had lost much of his dread of Her. It may have been that he dared to think of overthrowing Her, of making Resu, the Flaming God, the supreme deity. And with that the dominance of the kings in all matters, spiritual and temporal. And with that, a revolution in the role of the male in Khokarsa.

Minruth was not satisfied with being lord of the army and navy and in charge of the construction of roads and major buildings. He wanted to control the taxes, the postal system and the religious organizations. Above all, he wanted to finish the building of the Great Tower of Kho and Resu, that project begun five hundred years ago by King Klakor. The legend was that the king who completed it could ascend to the sky, to the blue palace of the Flaming God, and become immortal. It was half finished now, and Minruth was fifty-eight years old. He wanted to spend every cent possible, to draft an allout construction. But the priestesses had been interfering for half a millennium, slowing its construction. Times of troubles had also blocked its progress. The priestesses claimed that the Empire would be ruined if all efforts were directed to the tower's completion. That was obviously true. Additionally obvious was the fact that the structure could not take much more weight. The tower would have to be abandoned unless someone could invent a new type of very light-weight brick. Minruth had offered a reward equivalent to the annual taxes of the city of Bawaku to anyone who would come up with the desired construction material.

Hadon had won the Great Games, though he had been grieved when his friend Taro was killed. The proud victor, he had marched to the palace expecting to be proclaimed the husband of Awineth and Emperor of Khokarsa. Instead he was given news that staggered and outraged him.

The Voice of Kho, the oracle in the cave high on the volcano, had said that his honors must be deferred. First he must lead an expedition into the far north, to the shores of the Ringing Sea. There he must locate and bring back three people from beyond the Ringing Sea. These had been brought to the southern shores of the Ringing Sea by Sahhindar. But the exiled god of bronze, plants and time had left them there, sending Hinokly, a member of a previous expedition, to Khokarsa with his orders.

Why? Only Kho Herself knew. Hadon had suspected in his fit of rage that Minruth had somehow contrived to bring about this unjust deferment. But, cooling off, he had realized that he had been guilty of blasphemous thoughts. No priestess of Kho would dare speak falsely. Not when the commands of Kho were involved. The retribution would be swift and awe-inspiring.

Hadon had reluctantly led the expedition northward, past the Saasares Mountains and onto the vast savannas beyond. During the journey, he had run across his cousin Kwasin. The giant was fleeing from a tribe of wild men, and he had been saved only because Hadon's men fought the others off. Kwasin had been expelled from Khokarsa some years before because he had raped a priestess and killed some temple guards defending her. Ordinarily he would have been castrated and his body thrown to hogs.

But the Voice of Kho spoke, and his punishment was exile for an indeterminate time.

Kwasin accompanied them the rest of the way. The three strangers, Lalila, Paga and Abeth, had been located. Lalila claimed that Sahhindar had indeed brought them from across the Ringing Sea. For reasons known only to himself, he had then left them. They accompanied Hinokly's expedition back to Khokarsa, but savages had attacked them,

22

killing all but the three and Hinokly. The three had been separated from him, so he had made his way back to his native land.

Lalila, however, said that Sahhindar had disclaimed deity-ship. He was, he said, only a man. But he did admit that he had lived over two thousand years. And he had been born, he said, in a far distant future. Somehow, sailing in "a ship of time," he had traveled back to a period two thousand years before the present. And it was indeed he who had made the civilization of Khokarsa possible.

On the return journey, Hadon had fallen in love with Lalila. He was not the only one. She seemed to project an aura which drew men to her as the scent of the female moth drew male moths. She was undeniably beautiful, but there were many women in Khokarsa as beautiful. Paga had said that she carried a curse. It maddened men and at the same time brought them to death.

Hadon had not cared. He was in ecstasy when Lalila told him she loved him. She was ready to forget her grief for Wi, her dead lover.

Arriving in Khokarsa, they were greeted with shocking news. Minruth had imprisoned Awineth in her apartment and declared himself supreme ruler. Hadon, with the men in his party, was taken prisoner and conducted to Khokarsa, the capital city of the Empire of Khokarsa. Kwasin had escaped, but he was later retaken.

During the earthquake preceding the eruption, Hadon, Kwasin and Paga had escaped, rescued Lalila, her daughter and Awineth, and fled into the mountains northeast of the city.

Awineth and the others might still get away. Lalila might also escape, though her chances of survival in these woods infested with outlaws and beasts were few. More likely she would starve to death.

Still, he had done much better than he had expected. Now he permitted himself to hope, both for himself and Lalila.

4

The sun was in its final quarter. By then Hadon had rolled a boulder from the edge of the forest to the edge of the cliff about forty feet outward from the inner pass. He pushed it over and watched while it bounded down the slope. The men below, hearing the crash as it struck the bottom of the cliff, looked up. They rolled to one side, hoping to be out of the way of the bounding death, or got to their feet and ran. Some lost their footing on the steepness and fell.

The big rock struck a projection and leaped up, striking a dog handler full in the chest. He shot backward, sliding on his back for at least a hundred feet, then lay still. The boulder, only slightly checked by the impact, rolled and jumped the rest of the way down the mountain, lurching across a meadow at its foot and stopping when it struck the trunk of a tree.

Hadon had hoped to kill more than one. He was not, however, too disappointed. His main purpose had been to assure the soldiers that he was still in the area. He wanted them to think that he intended to guard the pass until nightfall and perhaps after that.

He was successful. The men went back down the slope to the meadow. Here they talked for a while, looking up at the pass now and then. They were evidently going to wait until the reinforcements arrived.

No, he was wrong. Now they were moving along the meadow. As he watched, they began climbing, this time at an angle. The end of their path was about five miles away, where the cliffs dwindled. They planned to ascend the climb-

able heights there and come back along the cliff's edge. At the
rate they were going it would take them at least nine hours.
Hadon went to the forest. He walked up the fallen tree supported by the two oaks. He called softly, "Lalila!" but got no
answer. He climbed to a branch just above the broad limb on
which she lay. She was on her side, sleeping, but she opened
her eyes when he called again.

He lowered himself from the branch, saying, "Don't be
alarmed." He explained the situation to her.

"What do you plan to do now?" she asked. Her violet eyes
were wide, showing the redness of the eyeballs. She looked
haggard; when she moved her foot without thinking, pain
shot across her face.

"We're going to leave," he said. "I'll carry you on my back
for a while, then I'll support you while you hobble. Do you
think you can make it?"

"I have to," she said, trying to smile. "There isn't any
choice, is there? But you were going to leave me here. . . ."

"I changed my mind because the situation has changed. I
may have to abandon you again for a while, if they get too
close. But the deeper I can get you into the woods, the less
distance I'll have to travel to come back for you. Besides,
there is the chance that we might lose them entirely. But . . ."

"But you'll still have to leave me," she said. "You can't let
them follow the trail of the others."

"If they find it," he said. "We will have to trust to chance
. . . and to Kho."

He helped her down from the tree, no easy task. When they
were on the ground, he shifted to his chest the pack of provisions he'd taken from a corpse. He bent down and Lalila,
biting her lip to keep from groaning, got onto his back. He
rose, placed his hands under her legs and started walking.
They were soon under the branches of the oaks spreading
above the trail. Hadon made no effort to go swiftly, since he
must not spend his strength. He had a long, long way to go.
Besides, the events of yesterday and today had weakened
him. He had not gotten much sleep, and he had used up
enough muscular effort and nervous tension for four warriors.

He kept his eyes on the trail, noting that the tracks of

Awineth's party were visible even to an untrained person. His own tracks were evident for a while; then they ceased. At this point he had gone off into the woods to double back. It had not been wasted time, though. It had led the dogs astray long enough for him to have time to handle them.

It was cool under the shade of the oaks. It was comparatively silent too, except for the croak of a nearby raven and the far-off chatter of some monkeys. After a while, he saw some of the oak-monkeys, creatures not much larger than the squirrels with whom they competed for nuts and berries. They were reddish except for faces outlined by a ruff of white hair. A small band followed him for a while, leaping from one oak to the next before losing interest. But he heard their cries for a long time.

From time to time, Hadon bent down and Lalila eased off his back. They would walk slowly while he held her and she hopped on one leg. When her good leg got too weak for her to proceed, they rested for about fifteen minutes. After that, she mounted him again.

The trail went steadily upward, though gently. By nightfall they were at the top of a saddleback with peaks on each side. Ahead, its snowy top illuminated by the setting sun, was a mountain twice as tall as the one on which they stood. The valley between was too dark for them to distinguish any features. They were surrounded by pines now; it was too cold for oaks here.

Lalila, sitting on wet leaves, shivered. "We'll freeze."

Hadon chewed on a piece of hard bread and even harder beef jerky. He swallowed and said, "It's not too cold to sleep. We'll get some rest until the moon comes up. That should be about two hours from now. Then we'll go on. Exercise will keep us warm."

"But you can't," she said. "You'll be too tired. Haven't we got a long head start on them? Couldn't we sleep until dawn at least?"

Before replying, he went to a nearby spring and scooped up some water in his hands. After drinking, he said, "It depends on whether they follow us in the dark or decide to wait until daybreak. Ordinarily, they wouldn't dare enter these woods now. It is said ..."

He paused. She murmured, "It is said...?"

Hadon bit his lip. He hadn't wanted to scare her, but if he was silent she would be even more frightened.

"It is said that this forest is haunted by demons. And then there are the leopards and the hyenas. The tale about the demons may be an idle one, something people like to scare themselves with. I have heard many; while it's true that I've never seen a demon, yet I've heard stories from those who claim that they have ... or knew people who claimed they had. But there is no doubt that the mountain forests of Khokarsa are inhabited by leopards, hyenas and bears. If we're moving, we're not likely to get attacked. But if we're sleeping, who knows."

He did not tell her about the *kokeklakaar*, the Long-Armed Killer of the Trees. This was said to be a hairy half-man creature which waited on a branch for the unwary traveler. When its prey passed below, it hung by one arm from a branch and reached down with the other and closed its crablike pincers around the neck of its victim. Snap! The pincers squeezed the breath out of the throat, cut through the flesh, half severing the head.

Then the thing threw the corpse up into the branches, clambered after it and settled down to sucking the blood through its trumpet-shaped mouth, formed of horn.

No, he would not tell her about that. She had enough to worry about.

"The men of Minruth may feel they are numerous enough so that even the demons will not dare attack them. If so, they'll light torches and follow the dogs. They can travel much more swiftly than we can. If they push themselves, they might be here by dawn. Or perhaps before then."

Hadon pointed out to her that the spring had become a small stream. It seemed to descend slantwise across the mountain, at least it did for as far as he had seen it in the light. Perhaps it became falls here and there later on. But they could proceed down it, allowing the water to wash out their tracks.

"Why didn't they"—referring to Awineth's party—"go down the stream too?" she said.

"I don't know. Perhaps they did further down."

27

"But won't the soldiers know that's what we did when our tracks disappear?"

"You're too logical," he said. "Of course they will. They'll send some men after us while the others follow the trail. But if we can lose those who'll be after us, I may be able to cache you some place. Then I'll come back and see what I can do."

The creek's water was very cold. They had not gone far before their feet were numb. Lalila did not comment on this until their feet slipped out from them and they sat down hard. Hadon, cursing, got up quickly. When he helped her up, she said, "I just can't feel anything below my knees."

"That's an advantage," he said. "You can't feel the pain of your injured ankle. You should be able to walk on it now."

It was true, but his own legs felt as stiff and dead as crutches. The loss of sensitivity made him unable to feel out the rocks and the holes in the bed of the stream. As a result, he fell now and then and was shocked by the ice-cold bath. He was shivering, sure that if he could see his skin, he would find it blue. Lalila's teeth were chattering, and he felt her body shaking when he supported her.

After an indeterminate, almost unendurable time, they came to a falls. It was too dark to tell how far it dropped. Not that that made any difference. They had to climb out and go through the woods where the slope was not too steep. Half of the time they slid on their rumps through the wet leaves and the mud. Bushes scratched them and stones cut their legs and buttocks.

The moon came out. It was not much help where they were because of the dense growth of trees. After a while they saw the water gleaming and returned to it. The stream allowed them passage for perhaps a mile, then became a cataract again. This was at the head of a deep but narrow gorge, compelling them to walk along its edges, though not too near. Once Hadon slipped on a patch of mud and both were nearly precipitated into the chasm. Lalila hurt her ankle again.

By the time they reached the valley, they saw clouds covering the stars to the west. Within fifteen minutes the moon was veiled, then shut out. A heavy rain battered at them a little while later. They took refuge under a tree, sitting with their backs against its trunk. Rain fell through the leaves and ran down the trunk against their back. It was cold, but not as cold as the mountain stream.

"If I had known that it would rain," Hadon said, "I would have gone on the trail. It's going to wash out all the footprints and the scent too."

"Then we won't be able to find Abeth!" Lalila cried.

"We can find the path and follow it. But if they had any sense, they will have gotten off it at the first place where they wouldn't leave tracks. Don't worry. If it's at all possible, we'll find them. If we run across a temple, the priestesses will help locate them for us. They know everything that's going on in these mountains."

He lifted her up, held her in his arms for a while as she clung to him. Then he broke the embrace and, speaking roughly to hide his own exhaustion and despair, said, "We don't want to go back to the trail yet. We'll cut through at an angle toward the gap we saw. The trail undoubtedly goes through it, but when we get to it, we'll see if we can't go higher somehow. And not leave any clues."

They reached the gap near dawn. It was about a hundred yards wide and walled with steep limestone. There were some ascendable places, however, and at the top of one was a ledge.

"We'll go up there and sleep, out of sight. The dogs won't be able to smell us if we're up there—I hope. And the rock won't leave much of a scent behind. It'll be gone by the time they get here, anyway." He silently added another *I hope*.

Normally they could have reached the ledge in fifteen minutes. Now they had to halt frequently to catch their breath, to still their gaspings and quiet the tremblings of their legs. Lalila had to ride on his back half the time. They pushed on and after a long while crawled up to the ledge. It was about fifteen feet long and ten deep.

"A cave!" Lalila said.

Hadon rose, drew his sword and advanced cautiously. When he was close, he could smell a fetid odor, the stink of hyenas, with which he had had extensive experience while on the expedition across the savannas north of Khokarsa. But no slinking, slope-backed, trap-jawed beasts rushed out at him. Peering within, he saw some crushed bones, hair and droppings. The latter were old.

He entered, still cautiously, until the ceiling sloped downward sharply. Getting down on his hands and knees, he looked into the darkness. More bones, and then what looked like rock.

Coming out, he said, "We can sleep here. But first..."

He looked out across the valley they had left. Tiny figures were crossing the bottom of the valley—a stream of figures. At a rough estimate, two hundred.

Lalila said, "I'm glad this ledge is on the sunward side. I don't think, though, I'll ever get warm again."

"They're coming," Hadon said.

She looked stricken. He hastily added, "But it'll be a long time before they get here. There's no use pushing on. We'd drop dead before we got to the bottom of the next valley. We'll sleep."

"And then what?"

"The dogs will make enough noise to wake us. Then, well, then, Lalila, I have to leave you. Just what I'll do after that, I don't know. Improvise. Pray to Kho to help Her devoted worshiper against the men of Resu."

He ate some more bread and jerky and insisted that she eat too. Then they lay down in the mouth of the cave in each other's arms. Hadon, feeling her naked breasts against his, was surprised by a stirring of desire. He had thought he was too tired to lift his head, let alone anything else. He told himself that this was no time to even think about such a thing.

And while he was thinking he fell asleep.

5

For some time he was vaguely aware that he was being disturbed. Suddenly he felt a hand tugging at his hair. He groaned "Go away!" then woke as he was slapped sharply. He sat up and looked at Lalila. "What...?"

The baying of dogs and the voices of men answered his question.

Grimacing with the pain of fatigue-rusted muscles, he rose. He crept out on all fours and peered over the edge of the ledge. Down below was a long procession, armored and armed soldiers. And at least forty dogs. Their clamor, if not enough to wake the dead, would quickly rouse the deadest of the tired.

Hadon withdrew his head. If one of those men should happen to glance up...

Lalila had crawled out to him. She started to look over the edge, but he pressed down on her shoulder.

"Wait until the last man has gone by."

He crawled back until he was out of sight from below. He rose, entered the cave and removed the provisions from the pack. He returned to Lalila and handed her her breakfast. While they ate and washed the food down with water from a ceramic canteen, he told her what she must do. It was simple: wait until he returned.

"I can endure being left here," she said. "But if you are not back in two days, I'll have only two choices, starve or kill myself. I can't climb down without your aid."

Hadon did not answer at once. He looked to the north. The valley there was much wider than the one they'd just left.

31

Even higher mountains walled it in. Because of the shoulder of the mountain they were on, he could only see the eastern half of the valley. It was heavily wooded except for the terminus of a lake at the west. If there were any villages on the lake, they must be out of sight beyond the shoulder. Suppose there were villages there? Could he trust them to take care of Lalila? This was an area dominated by the worshipers of Kho, and there were supposed to be several temples somewhere in these mountains. She could take sanctuary in one of them, except that what was once a sacred place, inviolate, untouched by even the most evil of men, might no longer be so.

He said, "Perhaps you are right, I'll take you to the bottom, and then you'll have to take your chances. Somehow I have to get them off the track of Awineth and the others, although it's possible they might have already lost their trail. But they are so numerous, they can split up and send parties all over the valley. I really don't know what I'm going to do—whatever one man can do against so many. But you'll be in more danger there than here."

"I want my daughter back," she said. "I'll do whatever you say. I just thought I should point out what will happen if . . . if you don't come back."

He had been looking at the valley to his left while he talked. Now he started and said, "Look there!"

Lalila began to crawl to him, but he lifted her up. She looked where he was pointing.

"More soldiers!"

"I don't think so," he said. "They don't seem to be wearing armor. They could be hunters. They might be traders; they're carrying big packs. They must know what they're doing, since the tracks of the soldiers must be plain. They're coming along very swiftly too. It's as if they're trying to catch up with them."

He paused. "This makes things different. I can't take you down after the soldiers are gone. These men would be too close behind us. They'd catch up with us."

Lalila said, "I'll do whatever you think is best, Hadon. I don't like to be stranded here, but I can take care of myself."

32

He permitted himself a quick look over the edge. The dwindling of noise sounded as if the soldiers had passed by. Yes, there went the rearguard with not a backward glance. He rose and said, "I don't like to leave you here, but there's no other way. And I have to get going at once. I must get into the forest before those men get here and see me."

"Very well," she said. "May you be back soon. With Abeth."

"Kho willing, I will be."

He leaned over and kissed her upturned lips. They were cracked and dry, but though she looked worn out and her mouth was arid, he felt desire stir again. He straightened up and, smiling, said, "You'll be able to rouse passion in men when you're on your deathbed."

"What?"

"I love you," he said, and he was gone.

Coming around the shoulder, he saw more of the valley. The end of the lake became large, oval-shaped. In its center was a small island, dominated by a building glittering white in the sun. It was round and topped by a dome. It would be made of limestone—it would be too difficult to ship marble in—and it would be a Temple of Kho or one of Her many daughters. Which meant that Awineth and the others would have headed for it.

That is, if they had gotten this far. It was possible that they were hiding in the valley behind him.

But the soldiers would have known that. They would have sent at least several small parties to hunt for them while the others continued. They had not done so, which meant that their commander knew of the temple, and that Awineth would know of it also. Like Hadon, the officer had calculated that the temple would be the refugees' goal.

Westward, the lake became a river, winding through the forest. He slipped into its safe shade and headed in as straight a line as possible for the nearest lake. There was some underbrush in the pines, but as he descended he entered the oaks. Their close-packed ranks and far-flung branches ensured that not much vegetation would grow beneath them. He walked swiftly, running now and then, working the stiffness and ache from his muscles. Though he was in rougher terrain than the soldiers, he was making better progress. The trail they were on wound to the northeast somewhat, then, he supposed, would cut back to the lake. Unless something happened, he would get to the lake first.

Twice he crossed creeks and stopped to drink. He finished the bread and jerky he'd brought along. It was not enough, but he did not have time to hunt. Besides, what could he catch with only a knife and *tenu*? The question was answered when, suddenly aware of his opportunity, he snatched out his knife and threw it at a monkey. This was a larger specimen than the small oak-monkey, and it had ventured to a low branch to scream at him. The knife caught it just as it turned to leap away and drove halfway through its side. It fell with a thump while its hundred packmates leaped around and hooted and screamed at him.

He stopped long enough to remove its head, tail, limbs and skin. Cutting out pieces of the flesh, chewing on them, he walked on. He would have preferred it cooked, but he had eaten raw meat as a boy in the jungles around Opar. He looked back once and saw several ravens settling down around the leavings. Perhaps the Raven-Goddess, M'adesin, would bless him for giving her charges food.

On the other hand, and here he almost lost his appetite, the monkey might be sacred to this forest. You never knew what the local taboos were until you asked around, and there was no one to ask.

"If I have sinned, O Goddess," Hadon said loudly, "forgive me! It was done out of need and ignorance. I needed sustenance to see me through this mission, which is to save the high vicar of Kho, to fight for Kho against Her enemies."

Actually he was far more concerned at this moment about his friends, Hinokly and Kebiwabes, and the manling Paga— so beloved by Lalila—and her daughter Abeth. There was no need to mention this, however.

Nor was there reason to comment that Awineth, though the chief agent of mighty Kho, was a bitch.

Hadon detoured to the creek to wash the blood from his face, hands and chest. He threw the rest of the carcass away and continued. He saw a number of deer browsing in the more open spaces between the oaks. Where deer were, there would be leopards. Of these he saw no sign, except for some pawprints in the mud near the creek.

Nightfall found him still far from the lake. He pushed on through the darkness, though he knew the absence of light would give him a tendency to circle. When the moon rose, he was still going, though more slowly than in the morning. His desire to lie down and go to sleep was counterbalanced by two motives. One, he had to get to the temple before the soldiers did. If their officers drove them, refusing to camp, then they would get there first. Second, he heard the roar of a leopard somewhere near. It would be hunting deer, but it might consider him for supper if it found him sleeping.

He murmured a prayer to Khukhaqo, Our Lady of the Leopard. But he could not help thinking that she could consider her first duty was to the leopard.

That thought hastened his pace. And then, after an hour or so—he wasn't sure of the time at all—he saw a light.

It was straight ahead and small, but within fifteen minutes it had gotten much larger. He was at the edge of the forest; the lake was before him, separated by a narrow dirt road and twenty feet of cut grass. The fire turned out to be three huge bonfires, all close together. They blazed in front of the white temple he had seen from the ledge. Shouts and screams traveled three-quarters of a mile over the stretch between the shore and the island, the voices of women mingled with the shrilling of trumpets, the beating of drums and the twanging of a harp. Now and then a bullroarer throomed.

The hair on the back of his neck seemed to rise; a chill raced over his neck and down his back.

The priestesses were holding one of their orgiastic rites. And he, as a man, was not even supposed to be looking at the fires and the tiny figures which danced before the flames. Any male passerby was obligated to avert his eyes and pass by swiftly. This road was probably forbidden to men at this time. The locals would be staying in their homes tonight and they would not venture out until dawn.

He looked down the road from behind a tree. About a hundred feet down, near the edge of the lake, a statue loomed. He could not make out its details; the light of the full moon and the glimmer from the fires did not furnish enough illumination.

Unable to repress his curiosity—pleading to himself that he had to investigate because of the urgency of his mission—he went along the edge of the forest toward it. Closer, he could see that it was about thirty feet high and was carved from wood. It represented a being which was half-woman, half-tree. Carved leaved branches crowned her head; her wide-spread arms were branches ending in gnarled fingers. Her breasts were huge; one suckled a squirrel. From holes here and there the heads of birds and animals protruded, civet cats, servals, deer, pigs, ravens, bustards, oak-monkeys and lemurs. The largest carving was that of a baby, extending halfway from the enormous vagina.

Hadon walked to the idol and made a closer inspection. The baby held an acorn in one hand, symbolizing, he supposed, the gifts of the goddess to the inhabitants of the oak forest.

The idol was of Karneth, deity of the oak. He did not know much about her, since there were no oaks around Opar. Though Opar was in the mountains, it was too far south and hence too hot for this tree to flourish.

So the temple was dedicated to Karneth, and the priestesses were conducting their secret ceremonies under the full moon.

Awineth and Abeth could be on that islet now. The male members of the group would be forbidden to touch the sacred soil of the isle. Where were they?

He looked up and down the shore. Nearby was a long wooden dock, but there were no boats tied to it. They had been taken to the islet to prevent any foolish—no, mad—males from using them to spy on the rites.

Hadon felt a chill again when he remembered tales of what happened to nosy men who had been caught where they had no business. They had lost more than their noses.

He sat down and considered the situation. If Awineth was on the island, she would have to attend the rites as the chief priestess. But Abeth, now that he thought about it, would not be here. Only adult women participated. She would be with the men. Since he could see no houses along the shore, it was reasonable to assume that the men had been sent, with the child, to the fishing village on the other lake.

That would be so if the group had actually arrived here. For all he knew, it had not.

He sighed and rose. There was only one way to find out. He must go the long way to the village. This road undoubtedly led to it, but it would take at least five hours to get there. And dawn would be here in two.

He was not about to swim to the island and ask Awineth. No excuse would be accepted for violating the sanctity of the temple.

At that moment he heard a noise to his right. He stepped out into the road and looked to the east. He groaned. A shadowy mass was moving along the road toward him. Faint voices reached him. As the dark bulk came closer, it separated into men. And dogs!

The dogs were silent, though, which meant they must be muzzled.

The soldiers had moved even faster than he had expected.

Now the moonlight flashed dully on spearheads.

Hadon froze into a half-crouch. The dogs would soon smell him. Their frantic whinings and growling would notify the men that someone was in the neighborhood. The muzzles would be taken off, the leashes unsnapped ... and the dogs would be after him.

He was too tired to outrun them. Even if he was fresh, he did not have a good enough head start.

He groaned again. There was only one escape route—the lake.

There was no time to lose. Still crouching, he entered the water behind the dock. It was cold, though not nearly as cold as the mountain stream. It lay at the bottom of the valley and had been soaking in the heat of the summer sun. But not nearly enough, not nearly enough.

For a moment he contemplated caching the sword under the dock. It was heavy, and he needed all the buoyancy he could get. It would be foolish to insist on taking it and then be dragged under, drowned, just because he could not bear to part with it.

Very well, so it was foolish. He did not want to be without

it when he got to the other shore. Who knew how soon he would desperately need it?

He began dog-paddling. He had to get far enough out so the soldiers would not see him. Using a fast stroke would disturb the water and possibly catch their eyes.

He went steadily, swimming at a northwest angle because the current would otherwise move him eastward toward its outlet. But his fatigue, plus the weight of the sword, slowed him down too much. He was being carried past the island.

Perhaps he was far enough away from the shore to swim now. He began using his arms to pull and his legs to propel. The moon shone whitely on the disturbed water, but perhaps the soldiers would think it was caused by fish leaping from the surface.

No. A shout carried over the water. He turned and treaded water to look at the shore. The men were on the edge and on the dock now, looking out at him, some pointing. They had spotted him. In this light and at this distance, however, they could not identify him. And even if they did, then what? He had a lead on them, and they would be just as tired. They had no boats, so they would have to shed their armor and all arms, except for daggers. That would take a few minutes, which would enable him to get even more distance between himself and them. They would never catch up.

Of course, they could send men around the lake to intercept him on the other side. He would still get there before they did.

Then despair seized him. He was not going to get to the other side. He was just too tired. His legs and arms felt like they were made of solid bronze, and he was breathing heavily. The sword was an arm reaching up from the bottom, trying to drag him down.

Though continuing to crab, heading to the northeast, he was actually going in a straight path to the island. After a few minutes he realized that this too had changed, that his course would take him past the island. That did have one advantage: if he could make it to the leeward side, he would find the current diminished.

He resumed dog-paddling, the water just below his nose,

sometimes above. As a result, he was swept ever more swiftly past the island, but he had no alternative. To continue his stroking was to exhaust himself utterly.

Soon he was about twenty yards past the islet. Summoning the last of his strength, he made progress northward and then was on the east side. The current was noticeably weaker here; it became even weaker as he neared the land. Then, during one of his exploratory ventures, his foot touched bottom. He managed to keep on going for a few more feet and he could stand up, the surface just below his chin. He stood there for several minutes until his gaspings eased off into heavy breathings. Then he pushed forward until the water was to his knees.

He sat down, feeling the cold ooze close around his buttocks. He would rest here, then continue to the other side. Why swim? he thought. He would steal—borrow, rather— one of the boats docked on the west shore. He would not even have to commit blasphemy, since he was not setting foot on the island. He would stay offshore.

When he felt that he had strength enough, he rose and trudged through the water a few feet from the grassy edge. The music and the shouts, screams and chants were loud. He kept his head turned away. As long as he did not see the ritualists he was not spying on them, so Karneth and her worshipers would have no reason to be angry at him.

He was about a hundred yards from the dock when he looked across the lake. He froze. There were boats on it. Six. Long craft with at least ten men in each.

6

Now he could see that a line tracing back down their path led to a shadowy clump under some trees on the south-east corner of the lake. There had to be buildings and a dock there, probably used by fishermen who supplied the temple with their catches. The soldiers had found them after sighting him. Or perhaps they had noticed them on the way in. It made no difference. They were coming after him.

Or did they only suspect that he was a refugee, their main purpose the seizure of Awineth? Would they be invading the island even if he hadn't been seen?

They must be driven by powerful motives. No man would venture on this taboo soil unless he was in great fear or in great desire of reward. In this case, the soldiers would be compelled by both. Minruth would brook no obstacles, accept no excuse. He would execute anybody who pleaded religious sanctity—after some suitable torture, of course. And he would have offered an enormous sum for the capture of his daughter. Given this double incentive, the soldiers were ignoring their fears.

He still found it hard to believe that anyone would deliberately violate a sacred isle and temple.

Yet here they came.

What was worse, personally speaking, was that he would be seen when he found a boat and rowed away. And those long-boats, paddled by ten men each, could catch up with him before he got halfway across the rest of the lake.

Gritting his teeth in frustration, he went under the shadow of a tree growing out over the water. He sat down, careful not to touch shore.

All was not lost—not yet.

The boats headed for the dock, passing within thirty feet of him. Each held eleven men, ten paddlers and an officer at the steering-sweep. The moon shone on strained faces. Though fatigue could account for part of their expressions, fear, Hadon was sure, made the other part. King Minruth proclaimed Resu the chief deity now and Kho his subordinate. But Minruth's men had been conditioned from infancy to worship Her as the Creator and the Replenisher of all things. That this island was not sacred to Her made no difference. Karneth was Her daughter. Besides, they were preparing to attack in the name of Resu and so were attacking Her.

Hadon wondered if these men had been ordered to man the boats or if they were volunteers. It was one thing to chase the high priestess and another actually to lay hands on her. The commander, if he was wise, had probably asked for volunteers. There were always some men who put greed above religion, and there were also men who had secret doubts about the reality of the deities.

Hadon watched them put up their paddles and allow the boats to ground gently on the beach. Then they climbed out and drew the craft up.

The commander, a tall man whose helmet bore three parrot feathers, walked to a tree which grew at the top of a stone staircase. He crouched by it, looking out from behind it at the spectacle.

Hadon looked also—he could not restrain his curiosity— and his eyes bugged. In front of the three fires was a weaving, dancing, leaping crowd of naked women. They ranged in age from twelve to a withered, shuffling crone who had to be at least eighty. Their faces were contorted, expressing savagery and ecstasy; black spittle ran down from their chins to their breasts. Their hair was unbound, flying every which way. Sweat polished their bodies, and they made frantic clawing gestures. They whirled and pranced and swung back and forth and forward and backward.

The musicians were naked also, the same dark saliva covering their mouths and breasts. One played a tortoiseshell harp of seven strings of goat-gut; three blew on brass trumpets; six beat on drums; nine twirled bullroarers over their heads.

The wind carried an acrid odor, which he supposed came from the stuff they were chewing. Some said this was laurel leaf, though others claimed it was ivy. Still others guessed it was something else. No man knew; they just speculated about this in guarded talk when women were not present.

Whatever it was, it was supposed to drive them into an insane frenzy, to enable them to see Karneth herself. It was also said that it gave them the power to detect male spies.

Thirty feet from the largest fire, the central one, was a cage of wooden slats. Inside it crouched a frightened male leopard. This, Hadon assumed, was to be the sacrificial beast. In the old days, over five hundred years ago, a man would have been in the cage, imprisoned until time for him to be torn apart by the nails and teeth of the worshipers. It was said that human males were still victims of such rites in outlying areas. Though the practice had been outlawed, not many had been executed as punishment for its infraction. Male police were forbidden to enter the site of the alleged crime, and investigating priestesses were likely to be lenient.

Except for the night's activities, no male animals were kept on such islands. But tonight, a male beast had been brought in, and would be ripped apart. The leopard would surely kill and injure some women, but they would be fearless, not caring about what happened to them in their frenzy.

The ceremony was going to be interrupted, which was, in a way, regrettable. As long as he was guilty of watching anyway, Hadon would have liked to have seen just how the leopard handled himself. How many would the cat take with him?

Hadon had expected the troops to spread out then, at a signal from their commander, to charge in on the women. But the officer apparently had different thoughts. He was still watching, waiting for something.

Suddenly Hadon knew what it was. Of course! Awineth was not present! There was no reason to attack if she was not there.

Where was she? Probably somewhere in the wilderness, perhaps in the fishing village, perhaps still in the valley beyond the western range. Or she might have continued with the others in the eastern mountains, but this did not seem likely. They would have left tracks, and the soldiers would have followed them.

The officer left the tree and went back to the beach.

Hadon looked back at the fires and saw why the man had acted. Awineth was now standing in front of the central fire, screaming so loudly it carried above the music and the cries of the others.

She was a wild but beautiful figure of medium stature, her hair long and jet black. Her face was striking and bold, her eyes large and dark gray but looking black at this distance. Her skin was white as milk. Her breasts were large but shapely and bore scarlet-painted nipples; her thick pubic hair was dyed green in honor of Karneth. Sweat filmed her; black spittle covered her face and breasts and thighs. Blood stained her hands, which meant that she had been making a preliminary sacrifice in the temple, attended only by the most select of the priestesses. The victim would be a raven, if what Hadon had heard was true.

Behind her were the high priestesses of the island, a young woman, a middle-aged woman with many birthmarks and an ancient, white-haired, wrinkled woman, her breasts hanging almost to her navel. Blood smeared her mouth; she must have drunk from the neck of the beheaded bird. Yes, she was holding the head in one claw.

The music stilled, the voices dying away as everybody turned toward Awineth. She continued her screaming chant, but Hadon, though he could distinguish the syllables, did not understand a word of it. She must be speaking in the secret ritual language, which his friend Hinokly had said was actually the language spoken when the hero Gahete landed on the then uninhabited island of Khokarsa.

Hadon moved closer to the soldiers, keeping within the shadows of the trees, floating, pulling himself along with handfuls of mud and weeds. He stopped when he was about forty feet away from the nearest spearman.

"We'll move in in ranks of six, running," the commander was saying. "We'll seize Awineth, and then you, Tahesa, and your squad will search the temple for the child. I don't think she'll be in there. It's not customary, as far as I know, to permit girl-children here. But she may have been locked in a room so she couldn't witness the rites. These women will attack you, so defend yourselves.

"After we've grabbed Awineth, we'll proceed to the temple itself and form a ring at the entrance while Tahesa looks for the little girl. I give you two minutes, Tahesa; it's not a big place. Then we move back to the boats."

Hadon, his ear close to the water, heard the man nearest him mutter, "I don't like it, Komseth."

Komseth said, "I don't either, but what the hell, we are under Resu's protection, aren't we? And what can naked, unarmed women do against us? Besides, look at the reward. We can retire, get out of this chicken army."

"It's still sacrilege," the first speaker said.

"Quiet back there!" the commander said. "Tahesa, get those men's names. No, never mind, they'd just deny it anyway. No time for that."

The soldiers stood up and waited for the order to charge. Hadon looked at the women. Awineth, wailing a chant, was walking to the cage. The women formed a circle around her, blocking her and the cage from view. The commander said, "Good! They won't even see us until we're on them."

Awineth had stopped chanting. There was silence except for the growls of the leopard, then a scream from Awineth and the women closed in on it, shouting, yelling.

The commander roared "Follow me!" He leaped forward, the soldiers at his heels, between the two oaks framing the top of the steps.

Hadon waited until the last six men had gone up the steps. He rose and ran to the beach—no way to work for Awineth and Kho unless he stepped on the soil, mighty Kho and Karneth forgive him—and seized the prow of the nearest longboat. It slid into the water, where he pushed it to set it adrift.

He ran back to the second boat and repeated the procedure.

Behind were screams, yells and the roar of the leopard, but he had no time to stand and stare.

By the time he had the sixth longboat into the lake, he was panting. The bedlam on the isle was frightening, but he did not once look away from his work. There were six rowboats to launch after the longboats and one to climb into. He pushed and hauled and, after what seemed a long time, he was rowing a boat around the island. When he got to the other side, behind the temple, he beached the craft.

Then he sat down to rest for a moment. For all he knew, the soldiers might have Awineth and be hustling her back to the beach. He hoped not. The longer the capture took, the more time the boats had to drift away.

From the noises, the soldiers were not having an easy time of it. Nor could they expect to. The women numbered about eighty, priestesses and women from the village in the western lake. They would be inflamed at this desecration. Their lack of weapons would not stop them from attacking the men. Crazed with the drug, they would launch themselves without fear of death. The men, though fighting for their lives, would still be inhibited. They couldn't overcome a lifetime of conditioning. Not at first, anyway. When they found themselves seriously threatened, then they would.

He rose and strode around the temple on a walk of flat round stones. Near the front, he peered around. There was no semblance of order among the soldiers now. They were milling around in the crowd, each man battling for himself. At least twenty of them lay on the earth in front of the bonfires. About the same number of women were dead. As Hadon watched three men went down, each attacked by two or three clawing biting, kicking females. A woman, eyes glazed, rose from one of them, holding in one hand the soldier's torn-out genitals. A trooper thrust a spear into her back and then he went down, his knees bending under as a screaming fury tackled him. He tried to pull his short sword, but a big beefy woman grabbed his ears, yanked his head against the ground and fastened her teeth on his nose. Both rolled out of sight.

The big cat, blood dripping from its mouth, was trying to get out of the melee. He ran through the swirl, was half flattened when a struggling couple fell on him, rolled away, got to his paws and was confronted by a man with a sword; the leopard crouched, leaped and fastened his jaws on the man's throat. The cat whirled away, reared up and swiped once with his paw. A woman crumpled, her breasts torn.

The leopard spurted through the human whirlpool,

dodging, weaving, and then found the walk leading to the beach. He disappeared through the archway of the oaks. Undoubtedly he would swim across the lake and into the forest.

Hadon ventured further around the curve of the building. Now he could see Awineth before the entrance, struggling with two soldiers. Arranged in a semicircle in front of her were the commander, helmetless, wielding his *tenu*, and five spearmen. They were hacking and thrusting at about twenty women. A woman seized a spear shaft and fell backward, jerking its holder forward. Two women grabbed him and the three spun into the crowd. Then Tahesa charged out of the doorway, two men following. Abeth was not with them.

Tahesa shouted at the commander, who partially turned to speak to him. A woman grabbed the commander's ankles and pulled his feet from under him. He fell hard on his back, striking his head on the limestone. Tahesa sliced the woman's skull open, but another woman grabbed his sword arm and he disappeared.

At that the other man lost all courage. They ran along the temple away from Hadon—he was glad of that—pursued by a howling, screeching mob.

Awineth leaned against the entrance, her mouth hanging open, her breasts rising and falling quickly.

Hadon glanced at the scene by the fires. The surviving soldiers were fleeing, throwing their weapons down, intent only on getting to the boats. Few of them made it to the oaks, and those who did would find themselves stranded. They would have to swim to get away, and it was doubtful that, burdened with leather cuirasses and helmets, they would elude the women.

Hadon ran quickly along the front of the temple to Awineth. She looked up when he stood before her, her face twisted and, screaming, she attacked him. This was not unexpected, since to her he would be merely another male intruder. Even if she recognized him, she might have attacked him. The last time he'd seen her, she had been very angry with him because he had stayed behind to protect Lalila. In fact, she had tried to knife Lalila.

His fist buried itself in her diaphragm. She bent forward,

46

vomiting black liquid all over him, and collapsed in his arms. Throwing her over his shoulder, he ran as fast as he could to the rear of the temple. There was some activity behind it, but at the other side. Hadon got to the boat without being observed and placed Awineth on its deck. He pushed the boat out, climbed in and began rowing. Just before dawn, he pulled into the narrow river feeding into the lake. The vegetation closed around them, blocking them from the view of the soldiers who had stayed on the mainland. Awineth had awakened, but she was too sick to do anything but moan and stare at him. Some time later, she had recovered enough to curse him.

He hadn't expected gratitude.

7

About three hours later, the boat left the river and entered the western lake. This was three miles wide. Judging from its shape as seen from the mountain the day before, its length was six or seven miles. The oak forest circled it; beyond that, higher up, grew the pines.

The sun shone on the square green sails of a number of fishing craft of different sizes. Here and there were boats propelled by paddlers, hauling seines behind them.

Hadon made for the island about a mile away, though he paused several times to answer the questions of the fisher-folk. They were almost pure Khoklem stock, descendants of those who had first peopled the great island of Khokarsa. They were short, snub-nosed, thick-lipped and straight of hair. Their skins were darker than those of the city-dwellers, who were mixtures of Khoklem and the later arrivals, the Klemsaasa. The men wore round wide-brimmed straw hats and loincloths; the women, conical brimless straw hats and loincloths. The children wore nothing. All were painted on the forehead with a blue stylized horned fish.

Hadon had some trouble making himself understood, since they spoke a dialect. Their vocabulary was different and they still retained some click-consonants which had dropped out of standard Khokarsan over a thousand years ago.

Awineth took over then. She understood them much better, though not wholly, since their tongue resembled the ritual language of the priestesses. When they learned that she was Queen Awineth, the high priestess, they broke into an uproar. They had known she was at the Isle of Karneth because, on

48

reaching the eastern lake, Awineth had sent the rest of the party on. Now, learning about the events of last night, the villagers were troubled. Several boats set off at once after Awineth ordered them to get their women off the island. They were to bring back the priestesses also, if they still lived and if they did not refuse to desert their posts.

Hadon and Awineth transferred to a seine boat, which took them to an island village, about a hundred feet wide and a half-mile long, dotted here and there with huts on the shore. The stockaded village was on the northern shore. Drums on their boat had notified the people of their coming, and so a crowd awaited them on the docks. This was mainly composed of children, men and some women too old to attend the rites.

In their front, smiling, were Hinokly, Kebiwabes, Paga and the child Abeth. Their smiles faded, though, when they could not find Lalila.

Hadon jumped to the platform of the dock and embraced each one. Abeth, beautiful, golden-haired, violet-eyed, threw herself into his arms and cried for her mother.

Hadon shouted to make himself heard above the gabble.

"Lalila is safe! I had to leave her in the southern pass! We'll go get her as soon as I've had some rest!"

Awineth climbed out, assisted by the chief, and she spoke rapidly to him. He turned and yelled until he had everybody's attention. He spoke quickly and fiercely, pointing to the east. A man ran into the largest building, a longhouse built of pine and oak, covered with the carved heads of beasts, birds, fish and spirits of the lake and forest. A minute later the man appeared on top of the hall and began beating on a large drum. Those boats still on the lake began to make their way toward the island.

Awineth summoned Hadon to her.

"The rest of the soldiers should be on their way here. They won't have boats, but they have axes, and they can build rafts. These people are peaceful; they know little of organized warfare. I think it best that we keep on going. The valley beyond the next valley is large and well populated with devout worshipers of Kho. In fact, there is a college of priestesses there, where we can be safe. The pass into the valley is trapped; it can be closed at any time. We would be safe for a long time, and I can conduct my campaign from there."

"Are you asking me or telling me?" Hadon said.

"I want your advice. After all, you are a soldier. And you would have been my husband ... if Kho had not dictated otherwise."

"Are you up to continuing?" he said. "You've been awake all night and must be terribly tired after the flight and the ... strenuous rites. As for me, I am too exhausted to walk, let alone run."

"If I can do it, you can," she said scornfully. "Besides, I was thinking of getting just far enough away so we can hole up some place and sleep. We don't want to be on this island when they come."

"We can't try for the main pass," he said. "For all we know, soldiers may have been sent there to hold it. Do the fishermen know of any other passes, ones which strangers would not be aware of?"

"The headman has told me there is one. It is difficult but it can be traversed. Some of his men will guide us."

"Then I think the other tribesmen should follow us, trampling our tracks to confuse the soldiers. When we get to a place where we won't be leaving tracks, a rocky place, for instance, they will go in a different direction, leading our pursuers astray."

"That is the kind of advice I want," she said. She looked into his eyes for a moment, then said, "I need you, Hadon. I want you to lead us, to guard your Queen and the chief agent of great Kho. So if you are thinking of going back to get that yellow-haired savage, that bitch Lalila, forget it."

"She can't walk!" Hadon said. "You know that! She will starve!"

"It's too good a death for her," Awineth said.

Hearing this, seeing her smile of triumph and hate, Hadon felt himself sway. A shock ran through him and for a moment everything became dimly red.

"Would you dare?" Awineth shrilled. He became aware that he had raised his fist, that Awineth had stepped back.

He breathed in deeply and lowered his hand. His voice

shook as he said, "This is not the order of a great ruler. To condemn a woman who has done you no harm . . ."

"No harm!" she shouted. "No harm! She stole your love from me; she bewitched you! She is indeed the Witch-from-the-Sea, Hadon! She took your senses away, she turned you into a traitor! And you know what happens to traitors, Hadon! And you are not just a traitor to the Queen, Hadon! You are a blasphemer, an infidel! To turn against the one who speaks for Kho is to turn against Kho Herself!"

"I have not betrayed you," he said. "I have fought for you, helped you escape from Minruth! Would you be free today if it were not for me? If I had not stayed to fight at that pass, would you be free?"

"You stayed because of Lalila, not because of me!" she yelled.

"I stayed for both of you," he said. "Even if she had been able to walk, I would have stayed!"

"Yes, so you could delay them long enough for *her* to escape!"

The chief said something to her. She turned and spoke rapidly. Then she said to Hadon, "He wants to know if you are friend or enemy. He said that you can be killed now if I so order."

Hadon forced back the words choking his throat. He said, "What are your orders?"

"That we leave at once."

She began speaking to the chief again. Hadon walked away and sat down on the stoop of the longhouse. Abeth, frightened at the angry talk, ran to him. He put her on his knee and held her. She wept again. His three friends surrounded him.

Paga, the manling, spoke first.

"Do you really intend to leave Lalila there? To die?"

Hadon looked up. In a low voice, he said, "You are all my friends. I know you won't betray me. No, I do not intend to desert her. But now I must pretend to obey Awineth. If I do not, she will have me killed. When we get to the forest, I will leave at the first chance. But it is a hard thing to do, friends. It brings problems. How can I rejoin you if I have disobeyed Awineth and if I bring Lalila back with me?

51

Awineth is capable of having both of us killed.

"So what do I do then? If Lalila and I do not rejoin you, she will never see Abeth again. She could not endure that; she has had sorrow enough."

Paga said, "First get Lalila. Then think of how to get Abeth away from Awineth. But do not forget that I want to be with Lalila and her daughter. I, too, would grieve if anything were to happen to either of them. But I would make sure that Awineth did not live. She would have little time to enjoy her revenge."

Kebiwabes and Hinokly were shocked. Though they did not love Awineth, they held her in great reverence. It was blasphemy to even think about harming the highest priestess.

Kebiwabes said, "There must be a way. You are too tired to think clearly now, Hadon. Once you have rested, you will find a way. It need not involve the killing of Awineth."

"Paga said that, not I," Hadon said. "Though, come to think of it . . ."

He fell silent. No use upsetting his friends even more.

Paga said, "When you leave, take Abeth and me along. Then you will not have to come back."

"Your legs are too short, Paga. And the child would also hinder me. I must get to Lalila as quickly as possible. She doesn't have much water or food, and there are leopards and hyenas against which she would be helpless."

"Take us with you for some distance then. Leave us where we will be hidden from Minruth's and Awineth's people alike. Then come back with Lalila."

"And where would you go then?" Hinokly asked.

"Far away."

"And spend the rest of your life running and hiding?"

"What else have Lalila, the child and I been doing for years?" Paga said angrily. "What is the great and glorious Queen of the mighty Empire of Khokarsa doing now? She is running and hiding. But I do not plan to live the rest of my days like a hare. No, I know of a place where we could go and be far from Minruth and Awineth and all the other plagues that make this *civilized* nation a pesthole."

Paga glared and looked around him. Hadon studied him. Though the manling stood no higher than Hadon's solar plexus, though he was a savage from the icy lands beyond the Ringing Sea, he was highly intelligent and resourceful. He was perhaps the shrewdest and most perceptive of the group.

He had a large head topped by a tangled mass of brown, gray-threaded hair. His shoulders were as broad as Hadon's; his arms were thickly muscled and long. His torso was thick, long and potbellied. If only his legs were not so short, he would have made an impressive figure of a man. A frightening one, perhaps. One eye was filmed, milky and ringed with thick scar tissue. His wild bushy beard fell almost to his scarred belly button. When he opened his mouth, he exposed extraordinarily thick teeth, beast-like.

His mother had cast him into the wild shortly after he was born. Something about him repelled her, though it may have been that she was sick, or that she had an ominous dream about him. In any event, he was hurled against a stone and he lost one eye when he struck it. His mother walked away and his father, though he searched for him, could not find him.

Paga claimed that he would have died, but a wolf-bitch had found him and brought him to her den. Instead of eating him, she had raised him with her cubs.

Hadon did not know if this was true, though he could see no reason for Paga to lie. There were stories throughout Khokarsa of babies who had been taken in by female beasts: bears, hyenas, wild dogs, lions. He had never met any of these—they were always in the far distant past or in a far off land.

Whatever the truth of the story, Paga had been accepted back into his native tribe. There he had met Wi, who became his only friend. Paga had made an ax for Wi from a fallen star, a massive lump of nickel-iron. Wi had used the ax to kill a giant who had tyrannized over the tribe.

Paga had another friend too, Lalila. She had been found in a cave by Wi, who had taken her into his home, though he had a mate and a child. The women did not like her; they claimed that she was a witch from the sea and so should be put to death. She brought misfortune and evil with her.

Paga had hated all women because of what his mother had done to him. Lalila, however, treated him kindly and so

53

won his love. He was ready to die for her, to die if she went out of his life.

Later, the glacier near the village of Wi had moved in and forced the people to flee. Lalila had been separated from Wi, but she swam through the icy cold waters to the iceberg on which Wi and Paga were stranded. Though this melted as it floated south, the three managed to get to land. From the shore they walked far inland to Lalila's native village. It was deserted; the inhabitants had died of plague or fled enemies.

There Lalila's child by Wi was born. Near there Wi was slain defending his woman and child, swinging his great ax until he had corpses piled up before him. All seemed lost then, but a stranger appeared, armed with a bow and arrow. He killed the savages and took the three under his protection. Lalila had then become with child by him, but she had a miscarriage.

The stranger took them south and, after much wandering, they were south of the Ringing Sea. They met the expedition of which Hinokly was a member. The Khokarsans thought the stranger was Sahhindar, the exiled god of bronze, plants and time, Resu's younger brother. Sahhindar, using his authority as the supposed god, ordered this expedition to take the three back to Khokarsa. He ordered that they be treated well since he would some day come to Khokarsa to make sure of their well-being.

So far the god Sahhindar had not reappeared, but deities often did not show themselves in their true persons, instead manifesting themselves in disguise.

"All right, Paga," Hadon said. "Where is this place?"

"The place you often spoke of when we were roaming the savannas," Paga said. "A place far to the south, at the extreme of the Southern Sea, up in the mountains. Your native city, Hadon. Opar."

8

Kebiwades woke him with rough shakes on his shoulder. He lay for a moment without moving or speaking until the bard whispered fiercely, "Hadon, it's time! Hadon, for the sake of Kho, wake up!"

The sky was black, clouded with the promise of more rain. He turned his head and saw that the campfire had almost died out. A man, wrapped in a blanket, sat by it, his head bent low. Snores issued from him.

The others lay under the pines, blanketed, silent. No, There were some missing. Hinokly, Paga, Abeth.

"They are behind a tree," Kebiwabes said. "We let you sleep until we had everything packed. You need all the rest you can get."

Hadon got up and quickly bundled his blanket around his pack. Making sure that he had his weapons—he was so sleepy he wasn't thinking straight yet—he stumbled after the little bard. The three were waiting for him under the tree, as Kebiwabes had said. Hinokly held the child in his arms, but she was awake. Her eyes were huge holes in a dim whiteness. Before they walked softly and slowly away, he turned for one last look. Awineth was a dark shape under a tree, surrounded by four villagers. The sentinel and two more made seven. All of them were hunters, not fishermen, skilled in providing meat from the forest for the village, familiar with the mountains. They would be good trackers. Hadon, however, was betting that Awineth would not waste time sending them after him. She would rant and rave for a while and talk of what she would do to him when he was caught. But she would know that she was in danger as long as she stayed in this valley.

Though he would be handicapped by them, he had decided to take his friends and the child along. He could not take the chance that Awineth, in her rage, might kill them all. For all he knew, she might be planning on doing just that anyway. Once she had used them to assist her on the perilous way to the stronghold, she could get rid of them. She hated Hadon; Abeth was the child of the woman she hated most, so she would be murdered. And Awineth would take satisfaction in having disposed of Hadon's friends, who had witnessed her humiliation.

They moved along softly in the darkness, bumping into trees or bushes now and then. The trail they had followed up was narrow and winding, felt more than seen. Two hours later, they were partway down the slope. The sun rose and they went more swiftly. At noon they stopped to eat the food in their packs.

Hadon said, "We can't cut straight across the valley. We'll have to go around the edges, up on the slope. From this point, we leave the trail. The underbrush will slow us down even more."

Having eaten, he climbed a tall pine. He was near the top when he saw smoke rising from the lake. He looked around the entire valley carefully, then descended.

"The village is on fire. The soldiers must have taken it."

"And probably slaughtered the fishermen," Kebiwabes said.

"If so, that will mean fewer men will be out hunting for us," Paga said cheerfully. "Those fisherfolk may be peaceful, but they would have fought."

"We are in another Time of Troubles," Hinokly the scribe said. "There will be thousands of such fires before this is over. Minruth will not find it easy to force the people of Kho to admit that She is inferior to Resu. Besides, there are many cities which would like to be independent. They will sieze this opportunity to do so."

"Let us hope that She does not get disgusted with us all and destroy the world," Kebiwabes said. "She did that once, long ago, before the Khoklem came to the Kemu. She was soft-hearted, however, and spared one man and a woman. She may not be so merciful the next time."

"Was it a flood that drowned all but one couple?" Paga asked.

"Yes, how did you know?" the bard said.

"My tribe had a similar story," Paga said. "Only it was not Kho but our god, the Sleeper, who sent the waters to rid the earth of the pernicious race. He too allowed one couple to live. The man built a huge raft and put on it all of the animals of the earth. Some raft, when you consider how many beasts, birds and insects there are! I have seen enough to crowd a raft as big as this mountain if it were flattened out—even if only two of each kind were on it. And I know there must be many more kinds of creatures than I have seen. It would take a raft six times the size of this mountain just to hold them. And a raft twenty times that big to hold the food needed to feed them until the waters subsided.

"And then what? Would not the trees and the grasses be drowned? What would grow for the plant-eaters to eat? And would not the meat-eaters destroy them before they starved?

"For that matter, where did the waters come from? And where did they go?"

Hinokly smiled. Kebiwabes and Hadon were shocked. Then Kebiwabes said, "All things are possible to Kho."

"According to my people it was not Kho but the Sleeper who sent the flood. Does your deity look like an elephant, a hairy elephant, and sleep in a vast block of ice?"

"Kho takes many forms," Kebiwabes said.

"I think the Sleeper was an elephant, bigger and hairier than your southern beast," Paga said. "It fell to its death into the ice and so was kept from decaying. And the ice moved slowly down a valley and out into the sea, carrying this dead beast. And my tribe, the ignorant fools, took it to be a god."*

"You think, then, that the priests and priestesses are lying to us?" Hadon said.

"First they lied to themselves."

Hinokly said, "It would be wise, Paga, not to voice those thoughts. The priestesses are tolerant. They do not mind non-

* The full story is told in H. Rider Haggard's *Allan and the Ice Gods*.

Khokarsans worshiping others than Kho. They say that these really do worship Her because Kho is everywhere and is, in fact, every deity. The minor deities are only Her varying manifestations. But the godless are exiled; if they try to re-enter the land they are killed.

"The priests of Resu maintain that all who do not worship Kho and Resu should be slain. So far their views have not become law, but if Minruth wins he will impose the will of the priests on the people."

There was silence for a long while as they followed a new trail. They went down the slope of the western range, heading for the southwest corner of the valley. Once they stopped as they heard the pig-like grunting of bears somewhere near. Hadon went ahead, spotted a female and her two cubs in a hollow and gestured to the others to follow him. The mother, a large reddish brown fat beast, stood up on her hind legs to sniff the air. She dropped down after a moment and went back to eating berries.

At dusk they were in the oak forest. A fire was too likely to be seen, so they ate a cold meal. Hadon found enough large flat branches among three trees for them to lie on, and they tied themselves to them for a night's sleep. It was broken occasionally by the cough of a leopard, the grunting of a herd of pigs, the scream of an animal caught by a predator, the uproar of a pack of disturbed monkeys. They rose at dawn, ate a hurried breakfast and traveled under the mighty branches. Their progress was swifter now because of the relative scarcity of underbrush. On the other hand, they were more exposed to view.

At the end of half a mile, Hadon stopped, his hand held up. The others halted behind him.

"What is it?" Kebiwabes said in a low voice.

"Men. Coming this way. Get down in that hollow behind that tree."

As they crowded together, Paga said, "Do they have dogs?"

Hadon said, "No, I don't think so. We'd hear them. Abeth, do not say anything no matter what happens. Hinokly, if she opens her mouth, put your hand over it."

"I won't say anything," Abeth said, "I'm not scared." But her pale skin and wide eyes showed that she was just trying to be brave.

"Get down," Hadon said. "Lie absolutely quiet until they have passed."

He pressed into the earth, his ear against the ground. The bard's body, close against him, trembled. Paga, on the other side, was as steady as a rock. Presently the thud of footsteps came faintly through the earth. The men were passing only ten feet from them. They were silent, moving at a swift walk. The odor of long-unwashed bodies drifted to his nose. Someone spit loudly and was shushed. Hadon wondered who they were. The two men he'd seen in the lead were unarmored and carried large packs. They certainly were not soldiers.

Then he remembered the men he'd seen in the valley from the ledge on which he'd left Lalila.

But if they were traders, as he guessed, why were they sneaking through the forest? Why so far from the village? Was it because they had witnessed its destruction? No, they wouldn't be this far off the track. They would either have returned to the lowlands or gone through the next pass to the valley beyond.

Could they be volunteers for the army of Awineth? Had word passed down from the priestesses of Kho to gather in the mountains at the temple two valleys away?

It did not seem likely. Not unless there were long-range plans for just such a situation, calling for the temple to be Awineth's headquarters.

His guess was that these men were outlaws who had taken their loot down to the coast to sell. They had found civil war and, since there were too many soldiers around, they had turned tail.

Or perhaps these were criminals of the city of Khokarsa who had found the lowlands too hot for them and had decided to take refuge in the mountains—after they'd picked up some loot to bring with them.

The last of the band passed by. Hadon warned the others to keep still. He crawled out of the hollow and looked around the trunk. At least ten were still visible; the others had passed around the corner of the trail. The first two were carrying a crude pole stretcher.

On it lay a woman. A shaft of sunlight fell on long golden hair.

"Lalila!"

9

"What did you say?" Paga whispered from below.

Hadon turned a pale face, but he said nothing. Not until the last man had gone around the corner did he speak to them.

"Abeth, don't cry out. Promise?"

She shook her head, Khokarsan for yes. He said, "Maybe you'd better hold her mouth anyway, Hinokly. They have Lalila!"

The scribe was just in time to stop the child from crying out. She struggled against him, then suddenly stopped and began weeping.

The others came out of the hole. Paga growled, "Who are they? What would they want with her?"

"What would any men want with her?" the bard said. "Though I may be doing them an injustice."

"The only thing we can do right now is follow them." Hadon said. "They may be all right. But if I show myself to them, I might find out that they are evil. And then it would be too late. There must be at least thirty-five of them, if they're the same fellows I counted two days ago. Far too many for us to handle if they're hostile."

Abeth got on Hinokly's back and Paga carried the scribe's pack. The five set out with Hadon about fifty yards in the lead. He kept the back of the last man in view, staying far enough behind and off to one side so that if the rearguard should look back, he would not be seen. After a while, he had left his companions way behind. The burdened scribe and the short-legged manling could not match his pace, and Kebi-wabes had been ordered to stay with them.

After an hour, the caravan stopped to rest. Lalila sat up then and accepted a drink of water from a clay jug. She was pale, gaunt and stony-faced. A tall skinny man, heavily bearded, said something to her. She turned her face away while he and his fellows grinned. But they did not laugh. Apparently they had orders to keep the noise down.

Several conferred with the tall man, most likely the leader, then fresh carriers lifted the stretcher and they renewed the march. By then the others had caught up with Hadon.

"I don't think they're friendly," Hadon said. "Lalila doesn't seem to be at ease. They must be outlaws."

The party now cut across the forest to the west, leaving the marked trail. Hadon had no trouble following them, though they were not in sight. After half a mile of increasingly thick undergrowth, he came to another path. This was a hidden trail, starting abruptly from an oak, apparently not used very often. A person not skilled in detecting marks might not have noticed it.

He did not know whether to continue on it or go back to his group. Deciding that Paga was woodsman enough to see the turnoff, he went on.

After a quarter of a mile, the outlaws again stopped to rest. Hadon went back on the trail to make sure that his band had not missed it. Seeing them just coming out from the woods, he gestured for them to follow his tracks.

The oaks thinned out, pines replacing them. The trail zig-zagged back and forth on ever-rougher and steeper ground. He topped a promontory and was looking down into a little bowl-shaped valley. Beyond it, the mountain continued another five hundred feet. Several hundred feet below the apex was an opening in rock, obviously a cave. Several men sat before it, sharpening iron swords. Seeing this, he knew that they were criminals, though he had by then convinced himself they could be nothing else. Some of their swords were those of the *numatenu*, which meant they had stolen them or killed their owners.

Goats browsed in the little valley. Five men sprawled near them, drinking from a goatskin bag under a tree. These jumped up as the caravan filed out from the pines. They ran grinning and shouting toward them.

Hadon lay down to watch. Lalila was carried toward the cave while the men at its mouth entered it. They soon emerged, followed by a dozen more. Lalila was taken into the cave. Her stretcher-bearers came out quickly to join in the drinking and talking. Everybody seemed to be very happy, judging from their laughter.

Paga and the others joined him. Kebiwabes said, "They must not get a chance to have a woman often. Yet they aren't raping her. Why not? The gang that brought her here may have done it already, but those others ... they wouldn't wait."

"Lalila is easily identifiable," Hadon said. "Minruth must have put out the word that he wants her and will give a large reward for her capture—unharmed. What I don't understand is why they didn't take her back to Khokarsa."

Paga hissed with excitement and grabbed Hadon's wrist. He pointed with his other hand. "There's the reason!"

Hadon followed the direction of his finger. A woman had stepped out of the cave into the sunshine. She stood as if reveling in the heat and light. The tall skinny man shouted at her. Two men hurried toward her and she stepped back into the darkness.

"Awineth!" Hadon said.

10

It was not difficult to imagine what had happened. Part of the outlaw band had been returning from the next valley and had intercepted Awineth's party as they came through the pass. Her guides had probably been killed, as they were worthless for ransom purposes. She would have announced her identity, hoping that this might cow them into releasing her. She had probably promised them a big sum if they conducted her to the temple.

Instead they had brought her back here to get their chief's decision on her disposal. He, realizing what a treasure he had, would take her back to the city. There he and his fellows would be pardoned and would become rich citizens. Their cave now held a double prize.

"Who said crime doesn't pay?" Hinokly snarled.

"They'll rest tonight," Hadon said. "Then their leader will send messengers to the capital to notify Minruth that they have the two women. They'll negotiate for all they can get, then they'll arrange to bring the women in. That's why they brought Lalila here. And why they haven't raped her. The King wouldn't want the spoiled meat of filthy outlaws."

"Then we have time to do something," Paga said. "How many men are there?"

"About fifty-five," Hadon said. "But they won't all be around at the same time. A gang that size eats a lot of food. They'll have to send out a number of hunters. We'll just lie low here until nightfall."

Shortly after dusk the men, all drunk, retired into the cave. Two of them piled a great heap of brush over the opening and went through a passageway left in it. They reached out with hooks and dragged in more brush to conceal even that. The covering was thick, but not enough to hide all the light from a fire inside the cave.

"There must be another opening somewhere in there," Hadon said. "Otherwise there'd be no ventilation."

He left after a brief argument with Paga, who wanted to accompany him. He went slowly down the slope and skirted the grove where the goats were kept. They bleated at him. He paid them no attention, knowing that the noise the outlaws were making would drown out the beasts. He made for the side of the cave and climbed up on top of the projection. His nose led him to the smoke issuing from a vent, a natural crack in the rock.

Upwind of it, he placed his ear close to it and was gratified when he was able to distinguish some voices. These were from speakers who stood near the fire. Other voices were mumbles or slurs, though advanced drunkenness could account for the latter. He got the impression that the cave was large, extending deep into the mountain. It had to be to hold so many comfortably.

What seemed hours passed while he tried to eavesdrop. There was so much shouting and singing now that he could not even clearly hear the conversation of those who stood almost directly below the vent. Suddenly all voices but one were stilled. That, he presumed from the words, was the chief's.

"Yes, by Kho, I will have her and only I! I haven't had a woman for three weeks! The last was that stinking fat fisherwoman I caught in the forest and I smelled of fish for a week afterward!"

"You still do!" someone shouted. Laughter bellowed, then died.

"You have heard what the Queen said. The King isn't concerned about her chastity. All he wants is a healthy body he can torture. He isn't going to make her his concubine; he could care less. Ain't that right, Your Majesty?"

"That is right," Awineth's voice came faintly.

"So, if Her Majesty don't care, and His Majesty don't either, why can't I have her?"

"Damn it," a man said, "if you can have her, then why can't we all?"

"You can ... tomorrow! Tonight she's all mine! By the breasts of Adeneth, look at her! Have you ever seen such a beauty? What'll she look like when you horny goats get through with her? She'll be ruined! No, she's mine first ... all night, haw, haw!"

"What're we supposed to do?" the same protester asked. "Play with ourselves while you're thumping her? What the hell, Tenlem, what kind of share-one-share-all is this? You promised..."

"Shut up, Seqo!" Tenlem roared. "Shut up or I'll slit your throat! What I say goes! You all agreed to that! So I say I'm taking this woman out and enjoying myself! I'm entitled! If it wasn't for me, you'd all be hanging upside down in some marketplace bleeding to death from your severed genitals! How many times have I saved you dullwits? How many times have I scouted a fat prospect for you and arranged it so we could take it with only the loss of a few! How many times, I say!"

"Go ahead!" Seqo yelled. "But while you're out there, cheating us out of our rightful enjoyment—share-one-share-all, you said, you liar—maybe we'll be enjoying ourselves with this here woman!"

Silence again. Then a roar, a clash of metal and a scream.

Tenlem, panting a little, spoke loudly. "Any more of you want to die? If so, speak up now!"

Awineth said something, but she was too far away for Hadon to make out her words.

"No, Your Majesty, they won't touch you! They're not going to throw away a hundred thousand *nasuhno* and their pardons! They're drunk as swine, but they won't touch you!"

Awineth's words, now louder, became clear.

"If they should even try, Kho would blast them!"

"Yeah! Kho would hit them with lightning, haw, haw! Your father don't seem to be bothered about Her anger! He ain't been struck with lightning, has he? Come on, violet-eyes! I'm going to show you what a real man is!"

Hadon felt a storm of passion, an almost overwhelming

66

desire to attack Tenlem as he came out of the cave. But he gripped the rock and held on to it and his feelings, trembling. Mingled with his kill-lust was hatred for Awineth. She had urged the chief to assault Lalila, not to save herself, but to get revenge.

Panting, he crawled from the vent to the edge of the rock just above the entrance. He flattened out as a torch flared below him. Two men were carrying Lalila out. Tenlem was holding the torch, walking in front of them. Lalila was not struggling; she lay limp as if she had fainted. He did not think she had; she was too tough for that.

When the party was halfway down the slope, headed for the grove, Hadon slid off the rounded wall of the cave. He walked swiftly through the darkness, lit faintly by the distant torch. It would not do to stumble over something and make a noise.

Instead of following them directly, he curved to the left. The goats were moving back and forth at the ends of their long tethers, bleating. The men would attribute the uneasiness of the animals to their own presence.

He stepped behind a tree. Tenlem had driven the point of the torch into the earth. Now he was sticking the point of his dagger into the ground beside the torch. Evidently, he was making sure that Lalila would be some distance from the weapon. He removed his kilt and loincloth and stood looking down at her.

She lay on her back, naked, unmoving, silent.

The two men stood by the torch and grinned at Tenlem.

Tenlem turned his head and roared, "Get back to the cave you two hyenas!"

"Aw, come on!" one of them said. "At least let us watch!"

"Ain't you guys got any decency?" Tenlem said and he bellowed laughter. "Get back to the cave. And be sure to pile the brush back over the entrance. You want them soldiers to see the light?"

They turned away reluctantly. "Get going!" Tenlem said. He let himself down on Lalila. She erupted, grabbing his nose with one hand and his genitals with the other. He yelled with pain, and the others wheeled back. Tenlem struck her hard on the side of her face with his open hand. Her hands fell away while Tenlem yelled at her, "You want me to soften you up first? Or do you want to make me happy?"

Lalila did not reply. The others walked about forty feet away and hid behind a tree. They giggled and poked each other in the ribs.

Hadon ran out, circling widely, and came up behind them out of the dark. He brought the edge of his sword from the left against the neck of the man on his left, whirled and cut from the right into the other man's neck. Their necks half severed, they fell.

Hadon stepped out from behind the tree. Tenlem, still shouting, was half crouched above Lalila. His hands gripped her shoulders, pinning her to the ground. She writhed soundlessly while he yelled at her to keep struggling since it made him even more excited. Suddenly the yell ascended into a scream. Lalila had brought her knee up hard between his legs.

Tenlem rolled away, doubled up, holding himself again. Lalila got to all fours, her face distorted with the pain from her ankle and with rage. She scuttled toward the dagger standing upright by the torch. Tenlem did not see her; he was too concerned with his own pain. She grabbed both the weapon and the torch and, holding one in each hand, scrambled back to the outlaw.

Hadon moved slowly toward them, his sword held ready.

Tenlem saw her then and somehow got to his knees, facing her. He yelled at her to drop the dagger or he would tear her to pieces. Ignoring him, she continued to crawl until she was several feet from him. She got to her knees and thrust the flaming end of the torch at him as he started to get to his feet. It drove into his mouth and, squalling with agony, holding his face now, he went backward.

Lalila got down on all fours again and went after him. Tenlem called to the two men for help. Lalila got to her knees once more and stopped his cry with the end of the torch in his mouth. He rolled over and over, screaming, toward her. When he rammed into her, he almost knocked her over. She struck him on the head with the torch, then she drove the dagger to the hilt between his ribs.

68

Hadon ran up to her. Tenlem was on his side, jerking, his eyes glazing.

She sat up, staring at him, her mouth working. He knelt down and took her in his arms, and both wept. Finally she said, "How did you...? Never mind. You're here! Where are the others? Where's Abeth?"

"Nearby," he said. "Listen, I'm going to leave you here for a few minutes. I will bring them down here. We can't run; we can't go fast enough because of your ankle."

"It's better now," she said. "But I still can't walk very far."

"I know. So we have to keep them from following us."

"How can you do that? There are so many."

"Never mind. I'll be back."

It took twenty minutes for the round trip. Abeth ran crying to her mother. Paga stroked the top of Lalila's head, Hinokly and Kebiwabes smiled, though tightly. Hadon had told them on the way back what they must do.

Leaving the child and Lalila in the grove, the men climbed the slope to the cave. Hadon carried the torch. At the entrance, he handed it to Kebiwabes. "Don't set the brush on fire until we have blocked this completely."

"But what about Awineth?" the bard said. "She'll die too."

"I can't figure out a way to get her out!" Hadon said, snarling. "Besides, the bitch should die!"

"She is the Queen!" the bard said. "And the highest priestess of Kho! The Goddess will not take this lightly! Also, if she dies, who will be the rallying point for Her against Minruth?"

"If it's at all possible, I'll get her out of there," Hadon said. "But the others die!"

They went to work with Paga's ax and the swords taken from the two Hadon had killed. Though their chopping was loud, the noise would not penetrate into the cave. The brush already piled outside it helped deaden the sound. The walls were thick too, and the mob within was creating a bedlam. In an hour a huge mound of brush was over the opening. Another pile lay by it in reserve. Much of the vegetation was green, but interspersed in it were dry sticks and branches.

The lack of ventilation presently sent the smoke swirling

out from the fire inside the cave. Hadon heard several men approaching down the short corridor which formed the entrance to the large chambers. He snatched the torch from the bard and ignited a number of dry sticks and leaves. There was a shout from within and men started to tear at the barricade.

Hadon waited. If any did burst through, they would be blinded for a moment, helpless against his sword and the weapons of the others.

This did not happen. The dry wood caught quickly; the green, less quickly, but emitting choking fumes.

As the blaze increased, screams and shouts came from inside. Smoke poured out of the vent. Apparently no one had yet thought of stopping it up and so cutting off the draft. Hadon hoped that by the time they did, they would be too overcome to do anything about it.

Men lunged at the brush, trying to bull through. The flames drove them away for a moment. In a few seconds, some of the more hysterical were back, tearing at the barricade with their bare hands, screaming as they were burned, begging for mercy. The fire became a roaring blast and the men retreated. Their coughing mingled with the crackle and whoosh of the flames.

Hadon went up to the vent. He could not look down through it because of the smoke, but he placed his ear close to the edge. He could hear violent racking coughs and a sound as if stones were being thrust up the hole. He rose and drove his spear down it. It hit something solid; someone screamed. He drew the bloodied point out.

Hinokly climbed up to him. The light from the fire at the entrance showed a strained face.

"I understand your hatred of Awineth," he said. "And I would agree with what you are doing—if she were not the Queen. But she is. For the sake of our land, for its people, you should not kill her."

"I have been thinking of that too," Hadon said. "It may be too late now, though. However, we'll see what we can do. I hope we won't regret it."

Paga objected violently. The others told him that he was not native-born; he did not understand how deeply they felt

70

about their Queen, high priestess and chief goddess.

"If you do save her, you'll get no gratitude," Paga said.

"Perhaps not," Hadon said, beginning to knock away the burned and burning branches. It was hot work. By the time they had dragged everything out with the points of their swords and spears, they were blistered, burned and coughing. They stood back for a minute to let the smoke thin out, drinking water from their clay canteens and pouring it over their heads. No sounds came from the cave. They ran in, trying to breathe as little as possible. The torches stuck into the holes in the rock walls were out, their oxygen cut off by the smoke. The fire below the vent was still smoldering. Bodies lay on the floor of the first chamber. The light from Hadon's torch showed him more bodies in the second room. The third was jammed with people who had fled into it because the smoke was less dense here. All were either dead or unconscious. Awineth was leaning against the back wall. She was slumped forward but kept from falling by a man lying across her legs.

Hadon felt the pulse along her neck. "She's still alive." He coughed, then said, "I'll take her outside. Paga, Hinokly, see if anyone else is alive. If they are, kill them."

"Here's one," Paga said. He brought his ax down on the man's skull. "Ah!"

"I found another," the scribe said. He drove his spear into a throat.

Hadon picked up the woman and, coughing, carried her into the open. The three men came out a moment later. The manling said, "One of them sat up. So maybe she is not too near death."

Awineth began coughing. Her eyes opened and she stared at them from a blackened face.

"You'll be all right after a while," Hadon said. He knelt, propped her up and poured water into her mouth. She coughed it out, but he persisted and finally she was able to swallow some. In a hoarse voice, she said, "You came after me?"

"Obviously," he said. "Lie down and rest now."

A long time later, she said, "What happened to your woman?"

"She's all right."

He told her what had happened. A strange expression passed over her. Whether it was disappointment or remorse, he could not tell. He doubted that it was the latter.

Crouching down by her, speaking softly so the others would not hear, he said, "Listen carefully, Awineth. You owe your life to me and me only. If I had gone away, leaving you in the hands of those men, you would have been given to your father. If I had just let the fire keep on burning, you would be dead.

"You owe me the greatest debt possible. You can repay it by giving me your word that you will not harm any of us from this time on."

"My lungs burn," she said. Then, after a silence during which her face twisted with hard thoughts, "And what if I do not give my word?"

"I won't kill you, though I should. We will leave you here. You can make your own way to the temple. But the soldiers are looking for you now and there will be more, many more, joining them. You can bet on that. Perhaps Kebiwabes and Hinokly will stay with you. I don't know; they have little love for you as a person, though much for you as the Queen. Perhaps they might get you through. Neither, however, is a woodsman or a good swordsman."

"You and that woman have hurt me very much," she said.

"Not intentionally. The good I've done far outweighs any involuntary injury to you. Also, you will need every warrior you can get for your struggle with Minruth. I am well-known, since I'm the winner of the Great Games. And I have proved my worth as a warrior. Men will be proud to serve under me, serving you."

She stared at him for a while, chewing her lip.

"Very well. I will give my word."

"You will swear by Kho Herself?"

"I will. I do. But it would please me, if after this is over, you would go to Opar and take that bitch and her cub, and that one-eyed manling, with you. I do not like the sight of any of you. I can, however, endure it until we have won."

"I want your word, not your love," Hadon said.

72

11

The valley at Kloepeth was twenty miles long and fifteen miles wide. Unlike those between it and the Gulf of Gahete, it was heavily populated. It held a large lake and a river and many farms. Its people were relatively more sophisticated too, since it had access at the northwest end to the sea. A pass there led down to the Kemu, and a road had been built to a port there, Notamimkhu. The sea-end of the pass was so strongly fortified, however, that no army could hope to invade through it.

The southern pass was narrow, mountains bulging on both sides of it. Long ago, the priestesses had had a defense system built above the trail.

A month after Hadon and his group entered through it, the pass was closed. An army of two thousand men had attempted to march through it; a thousand got away alive. The avalanches, triggered by the men of Kloepeth, buried the others.

It was a heavy blow to Minruth, who could ill afford the loss. Though his armies had retaken Mineqo and Asema, and Awamuka was on the verge of surrendering, Dythbeth still held out. Qoqada had been bypassed, an army left around it to starve the citizens out. But Kunesa, Oliwa and Saqaba had won a battle against the Sixth Army, its survivors running back to Asema.

Still, Minruth had devasted a hundred villages and lesser cities, burning them out and slaughtering their citizens. Thousands of refugees had crowded into the rebellious cities, straining their facilities and food supplies. Disease had broken out in these areas, sending thousands down to the dark house of dread Sisisken.

Most important at the moment, the King's navy held the sea around the island of Khokarsa. In two pitched battles, it had sunk the fleet of Dythbeth and the combined fleet of the three cities of the southeast.

The people of the capital had moved back in when it seemed that the volcano, Khowot, had subsided. They began the work of rebuilding the houses destroyed by the rock bombs and the lava flow. The shipyards were constructing a fleet of thirty triremes, sixty biremes and several hundred smaller craft. Men were being trained to sail these. The demand for labor was so high that Minruth had stopped the building on the Great Tower. It was said that he had flown into a rage when notified that he would have to do this, and he had cut out the tongue of the officer who gave him the news.

Awineth had established her headquarters in the temple at Kloepeth. She was busy night and day, reading the letters sent her through the secret postal system of the priestesses, interviewing spies from all over. These came to her in a steady stream, though Minruth's ships had set up a blockade of Notamimkhu. The fleet had tried to run the Scylla and Charybdis of the cliffs leading in to the port. After three ships had been burned by giant, oil-soaked flaming missiles shot by catapults high above, the fleet had turned tail.

Word came that Kwasin, Hadon's cousin, had escaped to the city of Dythbeth. And he was now its king!

Awineth had called him and told him the news. Hadon said, "How could he do that?"

"King Roteka was killed while fighting on the walls. His wife Weth married Kwasin the next day."

"Knowing him, I'm not surprised," Hadon said. "Well, his being there will hearten the Dythbethans. Whatever else he is, he is a mighty warrior. Like a hero of old."

"When giants walked the earth," Awineth said sarcastically. She addressed the general of the Ninth Army, located in Kunesu. He had arrived a week before to report to her.

"Keruphe, what do you think of that? Would it be better for me to go to Dythbeth or to your city?"

74

The general, a short, bald-headed, bull-like man of ruddy complexion, frowned with thought. "The southeast area is well entrenched and in no immediate danger. Minruth knows this, so he is concentrating on Dythbeth, which has always been a hotbed of sedition. He is intent on conquering it before he moves on to the next biggest threat. In fact, he has sworn to kill every creature in it, man, woman and child, dog, cat and mouse. My intelligence tells me that for that purpose he has pulled out two armies, one from Minanlu and one from Qoqada.

"Though Dythbeth is in grave danger, it is not a hopeless case. If you were there to hearten the people with Kwasin leading the defense, Dythbeth might hold out. Kwasin is a legend, you know, everybody has heard of his exploits.

"While Minruth is engaged at Dythbeth, our armies could break through the light forces holding Mineqo. From there we could attack Asema. If we could take that, we would control the entrance to the Gulf of Lupoeth. Minruth's navy would still have it blockaded, but that would not prevent us from controlling everything up the Gulf from Asema almost to the capital. That would cut off supplies and food to the capital. It would also threaten it. Minruth might have to draw troops from the siege of Dythbeth to make sure we didn't attack Khokarsa.

"On the other hand, if Dythbeth fell while you were in it, the loss would be grievous. We cannot get along without you, Your Majesty. If you died, the faithful would believe that Resu was stronger than Kho."

"I won't," Awineth said. She looked around the long oblong table. "Is there agreement on this, that I go to Dythbeth?"

The priestesses and officers shook their heads. It was the only thing to do, since she had obviously made up her mind.

She rose. "Very well, I'll leave soon. Just when I won't say now. I know that you are faithful, that you are close-mouthed, but Minruth may have his spies here. I want to leave suddenly, in the dead of night, without fanfare. That way, I will be in Dythbeth before my father's spies can get word to him.

"In the meantime, General, we'll coordinate a detailed campaign. I like what you propose; I think it is the best plan."

The officers rose, bowed and withdrew. The twelve *numatenu* composing Awineth's day-shift bodyguard—among them Hadon—remained. Awineth, still seated, called him to her.

"It will take at least two months to get everything prepared before I go to Dythbeth," she said. "There is no hurry as far as Dythbeth is concerned, since it should be able to hold out for six months or more. My father has tried three times to storm its walls and each time has been repelled with heavy losses." Awineth smiled and said, "That means you have two months to be with your bride."

Hadon kept his face emotionless, though he felt angry.

"Then you are rejecting my petition to take her and the child and Paga along with us?"

"Yes. They will only be burdens. I'll be traveling in a small, fast ship; space is at a premium. Moreover, Dythbeth has enough useless mouths to feed. Besides, why should you want to take them away from here, where they are safe, to a place where they will be in grave danger?"

"My wife says she wants to be with me, wherever I am."

Awineth's smiled showed that she knew he was furious and was enjoying it.

"I think you're both being selfish," she said. "Neither of you are considering the well-being of the Empire. I understand why you don't want to be parted, but this is war and we must all make sacrifices."

"It will be as the Queen wishes," Hadon said stonily.

"We may be gone for a year," she said. "Perhaps two years. Only Kho knows how long it will be before we are victorious. In the meantime, you should be happy knowing that Lalila is safe here. And"—she paused, still smiling—"your baby."

Hadon started. "What?"

"Yes. A messenger told me this morning that your wife is pregnant. Lalila went to the temple to determine if she was conceiving. She was immediately given the necessary ritual and was found to be with child."

Hadon had known about her condition, but he had not been aware that Lalila intended to be tested. This was done through means which only the priestesses knew, though he had heard that it involved the sacrifice of a hare.

"Suguqateth tells me that she had a dream two nights ago about the baby," Awineth said. "That is why she summoned Lalila to the temple this morning. Apparently, if her dream is not false, your child is destined for great things. But it will be necessary for Lalila to visit the oracle before we can learn details of her glorious future."

"Her?"

"Suguqateth dreamed of a female baby. Of course," Awineth continued, "the child may not be yours. My father raped her shortly before you rescued her, though I suppose it is unnecessary to remind you of that. And if she had been a few minutes late in slaying that outlaw chief, there might be even more doubt about the paternity."

Hadon mastered his desire to hit her in the face. He said, "There are not many in this land who can be sure who their father is. It does not matter."

"It is a good thing that Lalila had a child before she married you," Awineth said. "Otherwise she would have followed the ancient custom."

She referred to the holy prostitutes. All women, if they were unpregnant at the time of their first marriage, and had never delivered before, went to a temple to be a holy prostitute for a month. Conception as a result of this attendance was supposed to be of divine origin. Theoretically, a god inhabited the body of the fertilizing male during the intercourse. The god was held to be the father of the child. It was a great honor to the family.

Though the ancients had believed in this literally, it was known now that the male sperm was responsible for conception. But the millennia-old custom held, and the facts were ignored. The ministers of Kho claimed that this made no difference. The god still possessed the body of the man and hence the sperm was metaphysically his, though it was physically that of the human father.

The priests of Resu, the Flaming God, held that this was a false doctrine. If Minruth triumphed this custom was likely to be suppressed, the first step in making women subordinate to men. In fact Minruth had already repealed a number of customs and laws in the capital city regarding the equality—some said the superiority—of women. To do this, it had been necessary to execute a number of resisting women and men as an example.

The main resistance to this new order was in the rural districts. Farmers and fisherfolk were very conservative, stubborn in opposing change. They were especially hardheaded when it came to their religion. The city-dwellers were more flexible, though even they had vigorously opposed the King and the priests until a number of protesters had been publicly hanged.

"The oracle will speak for Kho tomorrow evening," Awineth said. "Suguqateth and I will be there. And so will you. The oracle has asked that you attend, which means that you, of course, will not refuse her invitation."

"I would like to be there," Hadon said.

He was pensive the rest of the day. As a result, he made a bad showing during the exercise with wooden swords in the afternoon. Despite his youth, he was the best swordsman in the Queen's bodyguard, which was composed of veterans of many years of experience. But he could not concentrate properly and so lost on points to men he had always bested before.

Awineth, watching the display, smiled each time he was beaten.

12

The Temple of Kho was on a high hill to the north of the
town. It was surrounded by giant oaks, some of which were
said to be a thousand years old. The building was round and
domed, composed of massive marble blocks transported
through the mountain pass over eight hundred years ago.
Hadon and Lalila passed through a nine-sided entrance
into a chamber whose walls were decorated with murals.
These were painted in cool blues and light reds and depicted
stages in the creation of the world by Kho. A massive bronze
tripod sat in the center; the bell-shaped bronze object on top
of it emitted clouds of burning incense through holes in its
sides.

Hadon glanced through a round doorway to his right and
glimpsed the room of the divine whores. It was separated
into small rooms by light wooden walls, painted scarlet and
blue. In its center was a great round pillar around which the
women waited. Several men were talking to them, among
them Paga and Kebiwabes. The manling, happening to look
his way, grinned and waved. He took the hand of a blonde
who was almost twice as tall as he and led her toward a
room.

The next room had a ceiling twice as high as the first. A
nine-legged altar-stand squatted in its middle. The third held
a twelve-legged stand; its ceiling was three times as high as
the first. Here Awineth and the head priestess of the temple
waited for them. Near them lounged the Queen's nighttime
bodyguard.

Suguqateth beckoned them to follow her. The next chamber

was the holiest, vast, oval-shaped. Its floor was paved with white tiles and a spiral of varicolored mosaics. The spiral began at the centre of the floor and was composed of a line of twelve-sided pieces. On each was painted a tiny scene depicting a great historical event. The spiral went in tight curves, around and around, the outer part almost touching the walls on three sides. It ended just before the base on which stood the statue of Kho. Its termination was a still-unpainted square.

The blank piece bothered many people. Why were there not more pieces to be painted? What did this mean? Surely the history of Khokarsa did not have only one more great event to be portrayed?

Hadon was curious and uneasy about that too, but he asked no questions; the priestesses never divulged such information.

The main object of attention in this chamber was a towering statue of Kho. This had a core of marble over which carved elephant ivory had been fitted. Her crown was of gold, each of its twelve points bearing silver shields inset with many large diamonds. Her eyes were painted solid blue. She was nude and held in her right hand a cornucopia stuffed with sheaves of millet. Her left hand held a sickle, an instrument used for reaping or, as among the original dwellers of this valley, also for war.

Except for the three women and Hadon, the great room was empty. They stood for a moment, making the ancient sign of obeisance, while silence settled around them. The torches placed high above their heads, ringing the room, guttered. Shadows danced along the wall and someone in white peered from around the base of the idol.

The chief priestess said, "We will take off our clothes. When one appears before the voice of Kho, one should be as when one is born."

They shed their garments, leaving them on the floor behind them. Suguqateth led them across the floor. The white-clad figure came from around the base, carrying a three-legged stool of oak. She set it down in front of the statue and removed her robe. She was a very old woman, white-haired and wrinkled. Her pupils were enormously dilated and her breath stank of something acrid.

Hadon noticed then that there was a hole in the floor just in front of the stool. As the old woman climbed onto the tall stool, smoke began to rise from the hole. It was bluish and thin at first, but as the hag, her eyes closed, began to chant, it became denser. It rose toward a hole hidden in the shadows of the domed ceiling, its tentacles swirling out, enveloping all. Hadon coughed as he breathed in a heavy, sweetish odor, one he had never smelled before.

The woman, swaying, chanted in the old ritual tongue. Hadon moved closer to Lalila; the priestess motioned him to return to his original place. She took Lalila's hand and led her to within three paces of the oracle priestess. Then she took three steps backward, stopping by Awineth.

The smoke continued to pour out. The shadows seemed to thicken, to ooze out from the base of the walls. Suddenly Hadon felt cold. The air, though it had been cool when he entered, was now freezing. He shivered and his teeth chattered. Awineth looked back at him with an annoyed expression. He clenched his teeth, but he could not keep from shaking.

Now the shadows were in fact advancing. They crept closer at the same time building up toward the torches. Presently they were halfway toward the ceiling. They covered the torches with roiling veils, never extinguishing them but making them faint and faraway.

Suddenly he gasped and his heart, which had been beating hard before, began racing. The Goddess Kho had moved!

No, it was only his imagination. The statue was as still as stone; it had not stepped toward him.

He could not be sure. Things out of the corners of his eyes were distorted, lengthened. When he turned his head to look directly, they resumed the appearance of normality.

He leaped, uttering a strangled cry, as the sickle swooped over his head. It was a blur, casting a swift shadow, come and gone. But he had heard the hiss as it cut through the air.

Yet Kho had not moved.

Or had She? The blank azure eyes seemed to become liquid, as if alive. Tiny golden flashes swam through them, then lined up into three concentric circles. They began rotating, slowly at first, then more swiftly, whirling and whirling, then expanding into solid golden orbs, burning like stars.

His legs quivered and his belly contracted. His genitals drew up. The floor felt like ice to his feet; a cold wind was blowing down his back.

He fell to his knees, crying, "Great Kho! Spare me!"

The women paid no attention to him; their eyes were locked on the oracle.

She was screaming now, spittle flying from her mouth, her eyes wide, her scrawny arms stretched out to each side of her, then flapping as if she were a vulture.

Abruptly she pitched forward, landing with a thud on the floor.

The smoke thinned out; a moment later it was no longer rising from the floor. The shadows retreated and the cold evaporated. Hadon, shaking, got to his feet. The women had not yet moved, though the hag was obviously in need of attention. Blood was running from her nostrils and mouth.

Presently the chief priestess advanced and knelt down by the old woman. She felt her pulse and looked into an eye. Then she rose, saying loudly, "The oracle is dead! She was unable to bear the presence of the Goddess any longer!"

Awineth, pale beneath her dark pigment, turned wide, dark eyes toward Hadon. "Great Kho has indeed laid a heavy burden on your unborn daughter," she said. "A heavy burden yet one that is glorious!"

Lalila turned then. She was almost blue-white; her eyes had gained dark rings in a few minutes. "What did she say?" she cried.

Suguqateth said, "Your child will become a great priestess! Or else she will have a short and terrible life! She will be the savior of a city and founder of a dynasty that will continue for twelve thousand years! Or she will die when young after the most miserable of existences!"

Awineth said, "It depends upon whether or not she is born in the city of your ancestors, Hadon. If she enters the world there, in Opar, then she is indeed blessed! But if she does not, then she will suffer greatly and go early to the dark house of dread Sisisken!"

Lalila gave a short, sharp cry and collapsed to her knees, weeping.

Hadon was too stunned to say a word. Besides, what use would it be to protest? Kho Herself had spoken.

Lalila raised her head, tears falling on her breasts.

"What else did she prophesy?"

"Much else. But we are forbidden to tell you or anyone else. Kho's secrets will be kept locked in the hearts of myself and the high priestess."

"Then," Hadon said slowly, "Lalila must go to Opar."

"That is up to the Witch-from-the-Sea," Suguqateth said. "No one can force her to go. But if she loves her child . . ."

"Will Hadon be allowed to go with me?" Lalila cried.

"No!" Awineth shouted. "He must stay here or wherever I go! He is my bodyguard, sworn to accompany me wherever I travel, sworn to fight for me until Minruth is dead and I am seated on the throne in the palace of Khokarsa!"

Hadon said nothing. Awineth smiled.

He was in utter despair and would have continued to be so had not a strange thing happened. Suguqateth, the head priestess, had nodded. And she had smiled encouragingly at him. She was secretly saying no to Awineth, though just what that negation implied he did not know.

13

As usual, Paga was skeptical.

"The future cannot be foretold," he said. "If it can be, then it is as fixed as the past, which means that all to come is already here, in effect. It also means that you and I, everybody, all of us, have no choice in what we do. We just think we act freely. But in reality we are helpless to act otherwise than as the deities decree. We are like the puppets in those shows you have described, Hadon. Dolls pulled by strings.

"That is, we are if the future is indeed fixed. But I for one do not believe so. If I did, I would kill myself."

Hinokly said, "But you couldn't commit suicide unless the deities had willed that you should do so."

Paga's good eye flashed and the long graying hair on his face parted to reveal strong blocky teeth.

"A good point, scribe, and an unarguable one. So let us be practical and drop this useless speculation about prophesies and fixed futures. What do we intend to do? Or perhaps I should say, what do we *think* we intend to do? Whatever the truth, we act *as if* we have free will."

They were seated around a large round table of polished oak within a smoky wing of the largest tavern in town. Screens of pine, painted with scenes illustrating stories about Besbesbes, the bee-goddess, were set around the table giving them semi-privacy. The bellowing and laughter and shouting from the tables around made it impossible for anyone to eavesdrop.

Within the circle of the screens were Hadon, Kebiwabes, Hinokly, Paga and Lalila. The child Abeth was home, guarded by a temple retainer sent by the head priestess, Suguqateth.

Lalila sipped at locally brewed sweet mead, then said, "It does not matter whether the prophecy is a true one or one which Awineth arranged. I for one believed that it was indeed the Goddess speaking. If the rest of you had been there, you would believe so too. Even Paga, who believes nothing unless he can see it—and sometimes not then—would have been convinced.

"But whatever the truth, it is evident that Awineth does not want me to stay here. She would like me to make the trip to Opar as soon as possible. Indeed, if I am to get there before the child is born, I should leave at once."

"That is a long enough and dangerous enough trip in the best of times," Hadon said. "Now . . ."

Lalila placed her hand on his. "I would not worry if you were my guide. But that is just it, you're not. Awineth is determined to keep you with her. I don't think it is because she hopes to take you as her lover once I am out of the way. She hates you too much for that. No, she is spiteful and wants to separate us. Her vow keeps her from harming us directly, but it does not stop her from indirect action. She can deny that she is hurting us in any way, is doing the contrary, in fact. Getting me out of the way, sending me to Opar, is for the sake of the unborn child."

"I will be with you and Abeth, wherever you go," the hairy manling said.

"Unless the Queen requires my services," Hinokly the scribe said, "I'll accompany you as far as Rebha, Lalila. I have a brother there who will take me in, and I can get work there. Rebha is probably the safest place in the Empire."

"I'll stay with Hadon," Kebiwabes said. "I must stay with him to the end."

Hadon laughed and said, "Let us hope that the end is not soon."

Kebiwabes smiled but said nothing. During his wanderings over the northern savannas he had decided that Hadon was to be the hero of an epic poem which he would compose. This was titled *Pwamwothadon, The Song of Hadon*. Parts of it had been completed. The bard, accompanying himself with his stringed tortoiseshell harp, had sung these passages in marketplaces, taverns and the chambers of chief priestesses. It covered events from Hadon's departure from Opar for the Great Games in Khokarsa to his stand at the inner pass against the soldiers of Minruth.

Kebiwabes discreetly refrained from singing the latest part. This concerned Hadon's rescue of Awineth and the vow Hadon forced from her. Though the persons of bards were supposed to be sacred, they were not always immune from retaliation. No one, no matter how highly placed, dared exact public revenge, but things could happen to a bard who had insulted someone high. He or she could have an accident or just disappear, never to be seen again. That the Goddess would punish the murderer was no consolation to the murdered.

"There is no need for us to decide who shall go with whom," Paga said, "if Hadon also goes to Opar."

"How can I do that?" Hadon said. "I have sworn to guard the life of Awineth until she is safe on her throne in the palace of Khokarsa."

"But she swore she would not harm us," Lalila said. "Now she is making sure that we are parted and that I have to undertake a very dangerous journey to Opar. She has broken her vow, which means that you cannot be held to yours."

"But you just said that you believed Kho Herself spoke through the oracle. So Awineth is in no way responsible for your going to Opar."

Lalila said, "No, she is not. But she is responsible for your staying here. If the Goddess wants me to get to Opar so that our child may have a long and glorious life, surely She will want the father to be with us. Especially since the father is a hero and so is needed to see us through the dangers. And so Awineth is resisting the orders of the Goddess."

Hadon smiled and said, "I don't know who is better at rationalizing, you or Awineth."

"Rationalization is any woman's other name," Paga said. "Look, you two, Hadon says that Suguqateth indicated that Awineth was not going to get her own way. You don't know why she would go against the Queen, even secretly. But you say she did signify that she intended to do so. If this is true, why haven't you heard from Suguqateth? It's been three days now!"

"I don't know," Hadon said. "But the priestesses seldom do anything prematurely. She will let us know when she feels it is time to act."

Hinokly said, "She had better do so soon. I heard that Awineth leaves this valley within the week and goes to Dythbeth."

"What?" Hadon said. "You heard that? Where? From whom Great Kho's teats! That is supposed to be a staff secret, known only to ... Never mind—I shouldn't even be talking about it. But if you have heard this, who else knows? Who told you?"

"The maid who changes the sheets in my bedchamber," the scribe said. "I talked her into a little extra duty, you might say, and while we were talking afterward, she said that she had overheard a butler tell her supervisor that the royal party would be leaving within ten days."

Hadon slammed his fist on the table, shaking the mugs so hard that some mead slopped onto the wood.

"Don't repeat that to anyone outside this group, Hinokly! The rest of you, keep this to yourself! Do you realize what would happen if Awineth found out how loose-mouthed someone on her staff is? Everybody would be subject to intensive questioning. By intensive, I mean torture! She'd go right through you, Hinokly, the maid, the butler, the supervisor and on to the source of the leak. And none of us here would be safe, since we'd heard about this from you. I would be, I suppose, if I told Awineth about it. But she'd take the opportunity to lock you up, Lalila. She couldn't hurt you, since you obviously aren't involved in disseminating the information. She would, however, keep you incommunicado so you couldn't pass it on. I wouldn't get to see you at all. We'd leave and you'd be released then, sent to Opar."

Lalila had turned pale. The others didn't look too healthy either, not even in the reddish light.

"But if I don't report this I'm disloyal, failing in my duty," Hadon said. "But how can I? You'll all be in grave peril then, and I surely will not see Lalila again!"

He groaned.

"It's not an unsolvable dilemma," Lalila said, stroking his arm. "Send her an anonymous note warning her. But don't tell her the source of your information. That way you fulfill your duty and yet avoid hurting the innocent people."

"Innocent people?" Hadon asked. "Who knows who is or is not guilty? There may be no one guilty on the staff. Awineth herself might have let slip a word to her maids-in-waiting, one of whom might have let slip a few words to her lover. But you can be sure Minruth has his spies here. If they find out that Awineth is leaving the valley, they'll be watching for her. And once she's on the way, accompanied by a relatively small guard, she's open to attack."

"So write anonymously to her that she has to change her plans, that she must not let anyone know about the change until the last moment," Hinokly said.

"Easier said than done," Hadon said. "Just how do I get the note to Awineth? Any messenger will be detained and the identity of the note-sender forced from him, you can bet on that."

"Write the note," Lalila said, "and I will see that it gets into the temple mail system. Suguqateth has asked me to see her tomorrow morning. I do not know why, though I suspect she will tell me what she means to do about you and me, Hadon. In any event, I will drop the note into the offering basket outside the hall of the holy whores."

"It's too bad I have to resort to such indirect ways. It would be nice to be able to go straight to Awineth and tell her she's in danger."

"You're old enough by now to know how the world works," Hinokly said.

"Yes, I am, and I do," Hadon said. "But that doesn't keep me from complaining about it now and then."

"Heroes don't complain," the bard said, but he laughed.

"Heroes exist only in songs and stories," Hadon said. He shoved back his wooden chair and rose. "Heroes are men who happen to deal, more or less adequately, with heroic events. And who are also lucky enough to catch the attention of a singer or a teller of tales. For every sung hero there are a hundred unsung. Anyway, I am tired of this talk of heroes!"

The next day he felt much better. He had written the note and given it to Lalila, who took Abeth with her to the temple while Hadon put on the dress uniform of the Queen's *numatenu* guard. He wore a tall, three-sided scarlet hat, rounded on top, sporting a red fish-eagle's feather. Around his neck was a rosary with one hundred and forty-four blue electrum beads, each nine-sided. Over his shoulders was a short blue shawl of woven papyrus fibers, from the edges of which dangled twenty-four leather tassels, each knotted thrice. These stood for the largest cities in the Khokarsan Empire.

On his shaved chest was painted a stylized head of a red ant, indicating Hadon's totem and incidentally his birthplace, since this totem was found only in Opar.

A broad belt of leopardskin held up his striped kilts of honey badger fur. The belt also supported a rhinoskin sheath for a throwing knife on his right side. On his left was a wooden holder into which was thrust his *numatenu* sword. The slot admitted the blade only to its widest part. This resulted in half of the long, slightly tapering, blunt-edged sword projecting above the holder. Thus Hadon, like all the Queen's uniformed *numatenu*, had to support the upper part by holding the hilt with his left hand. He didn't mind. Only the *numatenu* bore their weapons in this manner; it was an honor.

Hadon had inherited the sword from his father. Kumin had been a *numatenu* who had hired out to the rulers of Opar, though he himself had been born in Dythbeth. Kumin had married Pheneth, daughter of a mining foreman. Pheneth had seven children, but only three reached maturity. Her first child had been by Resu, the Flaming God, conceived in Resu's house during the month when Pheneth dedicated her body to the god's temple. This child had died of a fever.

When Hadon was seven his father lost an arm in a battle with pirates in the vast underground complex beneath the city. His king had also died then and a new king, Gamori, had been chosen and wedded by the widow, Phebha. Kumin had contemplated—and rejected—suicide, the usual course taken by crippled *numatenu*. Instead he accepted a job as a sweeper of floors in the Temple of Golden Kho of Opar.

Hadon's childhood from then on had been penurious. And he had had to endure many humiliations because of the change in his social stature. But his father had taught him to be proud, to endure much for the sake of a worthy goal. His Uncle Phimeth, probably the greatest swordsman in the Empire in his youth, had taught him all he knew about the *tenu*.

Hadon was given his father's sword on winning the Lesser Games in Opar. Though no longer technically a *numatenu*, Kumin had the right to give his weapon to whomever he thought deserved it. Hadon, though he could use the sword by right of inheritance, was not technically a *numatenu*; according to custom, he had a certain time after getting the sword to establish his right to it. If he earned it, then he was to be initiated into the rather loosely organized guild of *numatenu*. He had earned the right at least a dozen times over and so had gone through the rites shortly after entering this valley.

He had expected to be made captain of the guard. After all, if he had not been cheated, he would have been Awineth's husband and thus ruler of all Khokarsa. The least she could have done was make him head of her personal bodyguard. But no, he was given the lieutenancy, immediately under Captain Nowiten, a thirty-five-year-old veteran.

Under other circumstances Hadon would have been grieved and offended. Now he had only two great concerns: to get Lalila to Opar, and make sure that he went with her.

Pondering just how he could accomplish this without breaking his word, he wandered around the town of Akwaphi, first past the Temple of Resu, a large square building of granite topped by phallic minarets at each corner.

Four priests stood talking on the columned porch. Their heads were shaved except for roaches of hair from the forehead to the nape of the neck, brushes kept stiff and upright by eagle grease. They had sported full beards and mustaches in accordance with Minruth's decree, defying ancient tradition, but when the news of Awineth's imprisonment had reached this valley, the priests hurriedly reverted to their shaved state. In addition, they had renounced Minruth's doctrine of the domination of the Flaming God. Whether this step was taken from true orthodoxy or a desire to survive was not known.

Whatever the motive, the priests had saved their lives. If they had stood by Minruth, they would have been torn to pieces by the wrathful worshipers of Kho. The temple might have been taken apart and the idol of Resu shattered or else moved into Kho's temple to be placed at Her feet.

These acts of desecration would have resulted in guilt among the responsible and horror among the nonparticipants. No matter how high passions rose in this matter, Resu was a god. He had been placed on an equal footing with his mother in theological theory, though in practice most worshipers placed Kho first. Yet he was a deity, and to lay violent hands on his vicars, idols and houses of worship was blasphemy. The priestesses said this was permissible, that Resu himself had repudiated those of his worshipers who tried to displace his mother. Those who had committed blasphemy in their wrath still felt uneasy. They expected retribution at any moment.

When divine vengeance did not come after a long period of waiting, the blasphemer had one of two reactions. One was that the priestesses were right: Resu had turned his back on his own people because they had tried to raise him above his mother. But another reaction was the feeling that perhaps Resu was dead—if indeed he had ever lived. And if he had not existed, then what about Kho?

Very few people dared voice such thoughts and they were never uttered publicly, of course.

The priests stood closely together, their flowing robes lifting and falling in the breeze. Their right hands, the ritually pure hands, worked their rosaries while they gestured with their lefts. They stopped talking for a moment as Hadon, passing, saluted. He wondered what they were discussing. Grave matters of theology? The difficulty in getting enough rations in this now overcrowded valley? Or, as many suspected, were they spies transmitting information on Awineth's movements?

If the latter was true, it was not his concern. It was up to Awineth's counterintelligence to determine such matters.

14

Hadon strolled through the marketplace, a broad square formed by various government buildings, the Temple of Takomim, goddess of trade, thieves and the left-handed, the Temple of Besbesbes, goddess of bees and mead, and a gymnasium. In the center of the square was a fountain, a broad shallow bowl of limestone with a statue on a pedestal in its middle. This was of bronze and represented the local river godling, Akwaphi, in the act of making the headwaters of the river. The local belief was that women who had failed to get pregnant as divine prostitutes might become fertile if they drank from the godling's spout. This had also resulted in males shying away from the source of water.

Hadon was thirsty, but instead of drinking from the fountain basin, he purchased a cup of hot hibiscus-steeped water. While sipping it, he looked around at the scene which never failed to interest him. It was noisy and colorful, alive with traders, merchants, townspeople, farmers and hunters. Adding to the clamor were ducks quacking in cages, pigs grunting in pens, domesticated buffalo mooing, obese food-dogs yapping in wickerwork baskets, collared and leashed monkeys chattering on stands, ravens and parrots croaking or screeching, hunting dogs—for sale—barking, a baby leopard in a cage squalling. There were small open booths everywhere, arranged in no pattern, and merchants hawked their wares from these. Fresh and dried fish, dressed carcasses of pigs, sides and legs of beef, unplucked ducks and game fowl hanging by their necks, fresh or hard-boiled duck eggs, loaves of acorn-nut bread, cartloads of millet grain, jugs and barrels of mead, kegs of honey, high-priced hogsheads of wine and beer imported just before the blockade; dried hibiscus leaves and medicines and charms for curing acne, decaying teeth, cataracts, smallpox scars, impotency, piles, glaucoma, obesity, anemia, fevers, worms, amnesia, insomnia, backache, anxiety, bed-wetting, constipation, diarrhea, bad breath, strabismus, stuttering, stammering, shyness, tumors, malaria, colds, the itch, lice, crabs, deafness and the many others in the long, long list of things plaguing humankind even in 10,000 B.C.—giving some people even then a chance to make a profit.

The square was unpaved. Though water was sprinkled on the earth several times a day, it was not enough to prevent the dust from rising. It rose and fell, coating those who hung around all day. Their sweat lined their faces with clean stripes. At the end of the day, the stink of unwashed bodies, human urine, animal dung, bird droppings, spilled and breathed-out mead, wine, beer, decaying meat, fowl and fish, all created a medley of repugnant odors. Nobody knew they were repellent, however. They had been used to them all their lives, just as they were used to the thousands of flies circling, buzzing, crawling on meat, excrement and faces.

Hadon finished the hibiscus-tea and passed on, loitering, idly examining merchandise, eavesdropping, passing the time while waiting for Lalila's interview with the head priestess to end. His attention was finally held by a man who had entered the market a few minutes before. He was about six feet three inches high, a stature which would attract Hadon at any time. Hadon was six foot two, which had made him the tallest man in Opar. On arriving at the capital of Khokarsa, he had been somewhat upset to find that he was not also the tallest man in the Empire. Even so, those who could look down at him were few.

The stranger had walked out from a side street with a bold, long-stepping stride. He held his head high and proudly, resembling an eagle in the manner with which he turned it from side to side. His hair was long, straight and very black. It fell over his forehead in bangs, chopped off several inches above the eyebrows. His large eyes were widely spaced and, when Hadon was near enough, he perceived they were dark gray. They looked strange and unsettling, as if they saw everything before them quite distinctly and analytically, yet also saw things which were not there.

The face was handsome, though not regularly proportioned. The nose was short but straight, the upper lip short, the chin square and deeply cleft. His physique was big-boned and muscular, but suggestive of the leopard rather than the lion.

His only clothing was a loincloth of antelope hide, which made Hadon think that he must be a mountain-dweller, since these folk wore very little during the summer. On the other hand, the hill people wore skins obtained from local animals, and there were no antelopes in this area.

His only weapon was a large long-handled knife in a leather belt.

The soles of his bare feet were calloused at least half an inch thick.

The stranger sauntered around, occasionally meeting Hadon's glance. Hadon did not wish to appear too interested, so he looked away at once. Others were looking at the stranger. His height attracted notice, but the fact that he was a newcomer was enough to cause curious stares and muttered asides. Everybody was spy-conscious, especially since the Queen had offered high rewards for such information.

The stranger moved around, stopping to sip some hibiscus-tea, munching on some nuts, watching a puppet show. Then he chose a shady place under the roof of a hare-seller's booth and squatted. He stayed there so long, motionless except for brushing the flies off his face, that Hadon began to lose interest. The fellow, though striking in appearance, was probably just a hunter. He'd come down to look at the sights and perhaps take in some of the cosmopolitan attractions. He did not seem to have much money; the few coins he'd spent had come from a small flat bag attached to his belt. If he needed women, however, he didn't have to have money. A man of his physique and good looks would be grabbed by the divine whores. His only difficulty might be in getting out of the chamber.

Hadon was chuckling at this thought when he saw five hillmen walk up to the stranger. These wore caps of honey badger fur with the heads still attached, badgerskin vests and loinclothes, and cross-gaitered boots of foxskin. The stylized head of the honey badger was painted on their bare chests and foreheads. They carried leather sacks on their backs and long spears, bronze-tipped, in their hands. Short swords and knives hung in sheaths from their belts.

Hadon drifted closer, drawn more by curiosity than anything. The stranger had not risen; he looked up at his questioners from under heavy lids and smiled faintly. Hadon stopped when he was close enough to hear them. He could also smell the smoke impregnating the badger skins, the long-unwashed armpits and crotches, the rancid badger fat on their hair and the sweetish odor of mead on their breaths.

"We was kinda curious, stranger," one of the men was saying. "We ain't never seen a hunter like you in these parts, if you are a hunter."

"I'm a hunter," the stranger said in a deep slow voice.

"Not from these parts, you ain't," the first speaker said. He swayed and blinked bloodshot eyes. "I know every accent in this valley, all through these here mountains, in fact. No one speaks funny like you do."

"Too bad," the stranger said. "However, my business is not yours."

"Is that so?" another hunter said. "Right now, anybody's business is everybody's business. Minruth's got spies everywhere, and Awineth's people are keeping an eye out for them. Did you report to the commander of the garrison?"

"I didn't know I was supposed to," the stranger said. "I'll do just that. When I feel like it."

He looked at Hadon and said, "*Numatenu*, Son of the Red Ant, citizen of Opar. Perhaps you can tell me if what these badger-men say is true? Am I required to report my visit to the local post?"

"The first time you come here, yes," Hadon said. "Apparently you haven't been here before."

The first speaker, a tall, heavily built man with brown, gray-flecked hair, hunkered down. He leaned forward to look at the knife at the stranger's side. "Say! That ain't bronze! That's iron! By Renamam'a, it's iron but not like any iron I ever saw!"

Hadon saw that about half an inch of shiny gray blade stuck up from the sheath.

"Would that be steel, stranger?" he asked. "My own sword is made of carbonized iron, but I have seen a sword made of carbonized iron mixed with nickel and tempered to a great hardness, holding an edge such as no metal ever had before. Kwasin, my cousin—you may have heard of him—has an ax which is made of the hardest iron I've ever seen. It came from a falling star, though, and so must be the metal used by the deities."

"That would be the ax of Wi, fashioned by a one-eyed hairy manling named Pag," the stranger said. "How did it fall into the hands of this Kwasin?"

Hadon was too amazed to answer. This stranger was no hunter from the hills, ignorant of affairs outside this valley. Moreover, he was no native speaker of Khokarsan, forced by the phonetic structure of the language to add -a to Pag. But how would this fellow know that Pag was the true name of the manling?

Hadon, speechless for the moment, stared at the stranger. Meanwhile, the big hillman rose to his feet swiftly, almost losing his balance, and reached out to grab the stranger by the wrist. But he missed as the gray-eyed man stepped back.

"Listen," the hillman said. "How'd you ever get a knife like that? You ain't no rich man or *numatenu*. You musta stole it!"

"The knife was my father's," the gray-eyed man said. "However, I don't have to account to you or any man."

He stared around him. The hillmen had gathered in front of him in a semicircle. His retreat was cut off by the booth.

Hadon stepped away, saying, "He's right. His only duty is to report to the post-commander. He doesn't have to answer any questions from you."

"Yeah?" the big hunter asked. "And if we let him go how do we know he's going to report? What's to keep him from just walking out of town, back to his spy-post in the hills?"

"You've accused me of being a thief and a spy," the stranger said quietly.

"Yeah? Well, so what?"

Another hillman, lean, one-eyed, snaggle-toothed, broken-nosed, said, "Better give us your knife, totemless. You do that and we'll forget your insults."

The gray eyes widened but he did not reply. Hadon saw now what they meant to do. They were not concerned about his being a spy; they coveted the knife. And they intended to get it if they had to kill for it. After all, he was unknown, hence a suspect. He wore no totem mark to bring his fellows to his defense.

Hadon said, "This man is under no obligation to give you his knife. You have no authority here. So back off. I'll take him to the post myself."

"He's a spy and a thief!" the big hunter bellowed. "Surrender that there knife, bootless! Or by the Great Badger herself, we'll take it from you!"

Two of the men turned toward Hadon, gripping their spears in ready position. "Now you just go on and mind your own business, *numatenu*," one said. "We'll take care of this here dirty spy."

"Thank you for trying to protect me," the stranger said to Hadon. "But you can avoid trouble and bloodshed if you'll just allow me to handle this."

The man certainly spoke a strange Khokarsan, his manner and language belying his savage appearance. He sounded very much like a well-educated upper-class person.

"I don't allow mangy acorn-knockers to order me around," Hadon said. He still did not draw his sword, since he hoped to scare the hillmen away. Once he had removed the blade from its sheath, he was committed to use it.

"Acorn-knockers!" the nearest man bellowed, his eyes wide, his face red. "Why, you big-city popinjay, I'll show you who's an acorn-knocker!"

He lunged with his spear. Hadon whipped out his blade just as the man finished his sentence. It sheared off the bronze spear's leaf-shaped point, came around and severed the man's left hand. Hadon whirled then, bringing up the blade at the end of the cycle, repeating the first stroke, removing the head from the shaft of the spear of another back woodsman. This man dropped the shaft and hightailed it through the market, screaming for help.

All this had taken perhaps six seconds. Now three of the hillmen lay on the dirt, dead. The throats of two were slashed; the third had a bloody wound in his solar plexus.

The stranger wiped his knife on the vest of the biggest man and stuck it into its sheath. He straightened up then and brushed his bangs away in an angry gesture. Hadon glimpsed a thin scar which started just above the left eye, ran across the top of the head and ended above the right ear.

"This whole affair was stupid," he said. "I tried to avoid it, but they insisted."

"There shouldn't be much trouble," Hadon said. "They were the aggressors; I'll testify to that. Some of their totem might decide to get blood revenge, though. These hill people are old-fashioned, you know. There is no doubt they were trying to rob you, however, so their kin might take that into consideration."

"The knife was just an excuse," the stranger said. "They knew that I saw them commit a crime two days ago, in the mountains north of here. I was coming down the trail when I heard some cries. I took to the bush and crept up unobserved on these men. They had cut the throat of a farmer and his two children and were raping the wife. Or trying to. They were all so drunk that none could manage it. So they cut her throat too, and staggered away with their pitiful loot.

"They came out of the woods to check the dead and one of the killers happened to turn around and see me. I walked away, but they did not try to trail me. I came here and we met again. You saw what happened."

Hadon looked across the marketplace at the northwest corner. Officers, led by the surviving hunter, were swarming out of the constabulary building. The man was shouting and pointing at Hadon and the stranger. After a brief conference, the constables walked swiftly toward them, the hillman trotting ahead of them, turning his head now and then to shout back at them.

Hadon thought that the hillman either had an excess of confidence or else he was too drunk to care for the consequences. He knew that the stranger had witnessed the murders, so why was he bringing in the police? Did he think that his accusations of espionage would cloud the issue, discredit anything the stranger might say?

He might have been correct but, in his intoxication, he had forgotten that Hadon could testify against him. And if he

98

thought the constables would also arrest Hadon, he was very mistaken.

Hadon started to tell the stranger this, but the man smiled and said, "I am no spy. But I can't afford to be questioned."

He was gone. Hadon stared at him in astonishment. He had never seen a man run so swiftly yet so easily. He looked like he was loafing, saving energy for an emergency.

"He went that way!" the hillman shouted. The constables started to follow him but were called back by Hadon. He explained what had happened; as a result, the hillman was arrested and taken off to jail.

The chief constable was deferential but firm.

"We can't hold the man unless you charge him with unprovoked assault," he said. "After all, we have only the stranger's report of the murder, if it was a murder. It may have just been a feud killing, in which case the respective totems will take care of the matter. Unless the stranger appears as a witness, we can do nothing. And you must admit it's suspicious that he fled."

"Not necessarily," Hadon said. "There is so much hysteria about spies that he may have felt he wouldn't be safe no matter how innocent he was. As for the hillman, I do charge him with unprovoked assault with intention to kill."

"It's his word against yours," the constable said. "So the trial'll be a mere formality. Do you want him executed, beaten or sold into slavery?"

"I surrender my prerogative to the judge," Hadon said. "I suggest, however, that if he's enslaved he not be sold to an individual. He's too dangerous for that. He should go into a government chain gang."

"I'll give your recommendation to the judge," the constable said. He saluted and then gave instructions for the disposal of the corpses.

Hadon left the marketplace, arriving at the Temple of Kho a few minutes before Lalila walked out from it. She looked haggard, as if she had been through an ordeal. On seeing Hadon she smiled, then she looked wide-eyed. Hadon looked down and saw dried blood on his legs, almost hidden under the cluster of flies.

"I overlooked that," he said. As they walked to their apartment he told her about the incident in the marketplace.

She stopped, her hand on her breast. "Sahhindar!" she said.

"What?" he said, shock running through him, followed by a feeling of unreality. "You can't mean ...?"

"Who else is six feet three and has black hair cut in bangs, hiding such a scar, and has gray eyes and speaks archaic Khokarsan? Who else has such a knife, a knife of such hard keen metal?

"But what is he doing here? Is he checking up on us, Abeth, Paga and myself? He said he would."

"I have seen a god," Hadon half whispered. "A god in the flesh."

"He said that he was no god, that he was as vulnerable to death by accident or homicide as any of us," Lalila said. "It is just that he ages very slowly. I didn't understand most of what he told me; he comes from a different world."

"Whatever the truth," Hadon said, "he doesn't concern us unless he makes us his business. And it's up to him to let us know that. What did Suguqateth tell you?"

Lalila looked around her and lowered her voice, though no one seemed to be interested in them.

"She said first that we must not tell anyone else what I am going to tell you. Kho would not like it. Second, when we were with the old oracle, Awineth did not tell us all that the old woman said. Suguqateth heard everything, of course, but she had been ordered by Awineth to keep silent. Suguqateth feels that Awineth is wrong, however; she has no right to suppress Kho's words when they were addressed to us. Awineth, she feels, is putting her personal feelings above the dictates of the Goddess. And so Suguqateth feels she is justified in revealing all of Kho's words."

"Which were?" Hadon said.

"I must leave for Opar as soon as possible. And you must accompany me there. Only thus will our unborn child achieve long life and greatness."

15

At one hour to midnight, the party left the Inn of the Red Parrot. The sky was clouded; the only lights were a few distant torches carried by the night patrols. All were cloaked and hooded and carried weapons and bags of provisions—all except Abeth, who rode sleeping on Hinokly's back. Their guide was a priestess, muffled in a black cloak.

By dawn they were in the mountains northwest of the town. They continued up, reaching the narrow precipitous pass at noon. This led them down into a little valley and up another steep and even higher mountain.

Near dusk of the next day, they climbed onto a plateau. By the setting sun they saw the Kemu, the Great Water.

"We need rest, but we cannot stop," the priestess said. "Awineth will have an army out looking for you. Doubtless she has sent troops through the pass at Notamimkhu. They'll be searching along the shores east and west of the pass. The port at Notamimkhu is blockaded, but that doesn't stop us from using small ships elsewhere."

She led them to the edge of the plateau and gestured at something below. About four hundred feet down, at the foot of the cliff, the sea rose and fell sullenly in the moonlit darkness. Something gleamed whitely in it, a ship riding at anchor about a quarter mile out.

The priestess blew on a bone whistle shaped like a parrot-headed fish. From a cave nearby came six men carrying ropes, blocks and heavy wooden tripods. They set up the equipment, and in a short time Hadon was being lowered in a sling at the end of a rope.

A ledge jutted from the cliff several feet above the surface of the sea. Hadon landed on this, got out of the sling, yanked twice on the rope and watched the sling climb back up. Within fifteen minutes all of the party, including the priestess, were on the ledge. She lit a storm-lantern and waved it back and forth. Presently the dim bulk of a rowboat could be distinguished putting out from the white sailship.

Hadon, Abeth, Lalila, Paga, Hinokly and Kebiwabes were on the ship in two trips. They were hustled belowdecks at once, and the anchor was pulled up. The ship began moving out toward the sea, slowly at first, then heeling suddenly under a breeze.

Morning found them crowded and cramped together, with the ship rolling more than at first. The hatch was opened and daylight flooded in. At the top of the ladder was a young fellow, freckled, blue-eyed, red-haired. He wore a vest of brown sea otter, a rosary of wooden beads, each carved with the face of Piqabes, goddess of the sea, and a codpiece formed from the head of a fish-eagle. His chest bore the blue outline of the deep-sea gruntfish.

"Captain Ruseth at your service!" he said merrily. "Come on out! Breakfast, such as it is, will be served soon!"

Ruseth did not look old enough to be a captain, though Hadon reminded himself that the title was not necessarily a grand one. A commander of a two-man ship would be the captain. His mission was an important one, however, even if he was young, so he had to be very competent. Suguqateth would not have trusted him otherwise.

They came out yawning, scratching, farting and blinking. The sun was up in a cloudless sky. The sea was heavier, coming in great broad rolls. To the south, just visible, were the tops of the mountains along the northwest coast of the island of Khokarsa. There were no other ships in sight. No other living creatures, indeed, except some of the omnipresent *datoekem*, large white birds with hooked black beaks.

There was a good breeze, coming from the northwest. The ship was sailing almost straight east. The swinging yardarm was let out to the right by ropes so the wind struck it at an angle, causing the ship to heel over at an angle uncomfortable for the landlubbers. Ruseth and his four sailors seemed at ease.

One of the seamen brought buckets filled with hard biscuits made from emmer wheat, hard-boiled duck eggs, beef jerky, olives and wine. Hadon took his over the sloping deck to Ruseth, who had taken over the rudder. "I am no sailor," he said, "but we seem to be moving along more swiftly than any ship I've ever seen."

"Isn't she a beauty!" Ruseth cried. "I designed and built her myself. And I invented that triangular sail; I call it the fore-and-aft, as contrasted with the old square sail."

"It looks weird, I must admit," Hadon said. "Just how is it superior to the square sail?"

"It enables us to sail against the wind!" Ruseth said, grinning proudly.

"Against?"

Hadon stepped back from the redhead. "That smacks of——"

"Magic? Evil magic? Nonsense, my friend! Do you think for one moment that the vicars of great Kho would be my patrons if I were using evil forces? No way!" And he proceeded to explain tacking into the wind with a rotatable yardarm.

Hadon listened, then said, "Amazing. It seems so simple when you describe it. I wonder why no one ever thought of it before?"

Ruseth looked angry, then he laughed. "That was probably said to the man who first thought of making fire. Or to the man who first made mead.

"I conceived this when I was sixteen, living in a little fishing village off the northwest corner of the island. The idea came to me one night in a dream, so I can't take credit for it. Piqabes herself undoubtedly sent it, though I had been thinking about sails and sailing for a long time. Anyway, I dreamed of the fore-and-aft sail and worked on some small models in my spare time. No much of that, you know, for a fisherlad. Then I made a small ship of my own—took me a year to do that. And months to learn how to sail the craft.

"The villagers were interested; they admitted I could sail faster than they could, but they said the old ways were good

103

enough for them. I thought I had a fortune in this, so I went to the capital to get a hearing from the Naval Department. It took me three months to get it—I had to work nights at an inn as a waiter. Daytimes I sat in an outer office cooling my heels until an admiral deigned to see me.

"I showed him how my invention worked, with models and sketches. I invited him to come for a trial run in my little ship.

"Here was something revolutionary. It would change the whole history of ships, make sailing much faster and easier. So guess what?"

"I think I can guess," Hadon said. "I've had some experience with the military mind."

"I was thrown out! And told not to come back! That admiral, a heavy-drinking old duck, said I was crazy. In the first place the rig wouldn't work the way I said it would. And in the second place, its principle was against nature, it was blasphemous.

"I was angry, scared too, because I didn't want the admiral siccing the priests of Resu on me. I thought about going home and maybe forgetting the whole thing. Instead I went to the Temple of Piqabes on a little island near the mouth of the Gulf of Gahete. I showed the head priestess there what I had shown the naval bureaucrat. I told her how much more swiftly my ship could carry the temple mail. She liked the idea and, to make a long story short, here I am, sailing a ship built by the Temple of Kho, in the service of Awineth, taking you to a far-off city of the Southern Sea, the Kemu-wopar. Think of it! I've never even been to the mainland north of here!"

Hinokly had been standing nearby. He said, "Then this ship can outrun and outsail anything on the seas?"

"No doubt about it!" Ruseth said. "The *Wind-Spirit* can show her heels to any craft on the two seas!"

"And if the wind fails how will she get away from a galley?"

"She won't," Ruseth said. "The only thing to do then is pray to Piqabes to raise a wind."

Hadon talked for a long time with the little redhead. Ruseth said they would proceed east along the north coast of the island but stay about ten to fifteen miles out to sea. Most of the patrolling by Minruth's navy was done very close to shore. Once the island of Khokarsa was behind them, they would sail southwesterly along the coast of the mainland toward the city of Qethruth.

"Under ordinary conditions, I would head directly southwest toward the pile-city of Rebha," Ruseth said. "But the ship is overloaded now. We don't have enough food to last us until Rebha, so we'll stop off at a village about four hundred miles upcoast from Oethruth. I've never been there, of course, but the priestess gave me directions and also a letter of introduction to the priestess at Karkkoom. We'll reprovision and then cut south for Rebha."

Hadon asked what they would do if the village was blockaded. Ruseth laughed and said, "You don't know much about naval realities, do you, my tall friend? Minruth's forces are spread thin enough as they are. He doesn't have ships to blockade every little village along the coast or even on Khokarsa itself. I doubt that he even has a bireme at Qethruth."

"What about Rebha?"

"You were on Awineth's staff," Ruseth said. "What did you hear about Rebha?"

"Nothing," Hadon said. "No courier ships arrived from Rebha. It's a long way, and ships are always disappearing."

"Yes," Ruseth said. "I would guess that the navy does have some big ships stationed at Rebha. It's a very important reprovisioning and refitting port, if it can be called a port. It also controls the southern part of the Kemu and, in a sense, the Strait of Keth."

Days and nights passed without incident. The weather was generally good, though there were rains and an occasional squall. They saw ships now and then, but always at a distance. Most of them seemed to be merchant galleys or fishing ships hauling their dried cargo from the waters off the mainland to the islands.

"There are rumors that piracy is flourishing again in these parts," Ruseth said. "It's only to be expected, of course. Minruth's navy is too occupied with the war to go chasing pirates. We don't need to worry. No pirate could catch us."

"Unless there's a calm," Hinokly said.

Ruseth laughed, but he did look worried afterward.

Conditions were crowded. The cabin became too hot and odorous when they all slept in it. Whenever the weather and the seas permitted, Hadon, the scribe and the bard slept on deck. After a week, Hadon became impatient and irritable. It was impossible to lie with Lalila because of the lack of privacy; they were not Gokako, the apish slaves of Opar who coupled publicly and often en masse. Besides, there was not much to do on board a small vessel. Hadon did dissipate some of the boredom by learning all he could about sailing. Before a week was up, he was relieving the sailors in their duties.

Hadon took the rudder every day for two hours. He was nervous at first and made some bad mistakes in tacking or beating. Ruseth was at hand to take over if anything went wrong, and nothing disastrous happened.

"You're a good fair-weather sailor now," Ruseth said. "We'll find out what you are when we get a bad storm, though I pray Piqabes spares us that."

Hadon insisted that the others also learn as much as possible about the ship. For one thing, it kept them from being bored. For another, it ensured that they would not be handicapped or helpless if anything should happen to the sailors. "Also," Hadon said, "in the future we might have to handle a ship like this by ourselves. We might even have to steal a ship and take it into the deep seas."

Because of this, Hadon also had Ruseth teach him all he could about navigation.

"The sun by day and the stars at night," Ruseth said. "Unfortunately, the Kemu is often clouded and there is much rain, though I've been told that the climate is drier and hotter than it used to be. Either way, you can't depend very often on the stars to guide you. But the lodestone compass is fairly dependable. My grandfather says that it's not so dependable in the Kemuwopar, the Sea of Opar. He claims there are too many mountains with too much iron ore along the shores."

"I doubt that," Hinokly said. And the two were off into another argument.

To make the time pass more pleasantly, Kebiwabes sang. While plucking on his tortoiseshell lyre, he recited love songs, sea chanties, ballads, mourning songs, prayers and the epics: *The Song of Gahete*, *The Song of Rimasweth*, *The Song of Kethna*. He also tried out on them passages and sections from his work in progress: *The Song of the Wanderings of Hadon of Opar*.

The subject of this enjoyed hearing his adventures recast into poetry. Much of it was exaggerated or distorted or sometimes it was even a downright lie. But he did not object. Poetry was about the spirit, not the surface, of reality. Nor did he mind at all hearing himself described in glowing terms as a hero. Modesty was not a virtue in Khokarsa.

After two weeks, they began seeing more ships. Most were fishing vessels from the coastal towns and villages, but the number of merchant galleys rose in proportion. Though the rebellion had cut down maritime trade considerably, there were still many men who would brave pirates and blockaders to make a profit.

Karkoom was a village of about five hundred in population, a cluster of huts and longhouses on stilts behind a stockade. It was at the end of a rather narrow harbor formed by two rocky peninsulas. Ruseth took the ship in cautiously, ready to run if any naval vessels were at anchor there. There was just enough room in the passage for him to wheel tightly about, though not much space for tacking or beating against the wind.

They breathed relief when they saw that the four large vessels were merchantmen. Two were from Qethruth, one from Miklemres, one from Siwudawa.

Ruseth took the ship in and tied up at a dock. Leaving two of the crew to guard the ship, Ruseth and the rest visited the local Temple of Kho. They were well received after Ruseth had handed in his letter of introduction. The head priestess, Siha, gave orders that the vessel be provisioned. She then held a small private feast for them where she heard the news from Khokarsa and passed on the news and rumors she had received in the last few months.

For the first time in a long time, Hadon and Lalila slept together—and on a bed that did not rise and fall, roll and yaw. The next day they left at noon, after, of course, a ritual blessing by the priestess.

Several priests from the Temple of Resu were also there; they seemed friendly enough. The villagers, like the citizens of Qethruth, had declared neutrality, but Hadon did not trust them. For all he knew, the priests could have sent a ship out with the news that the refugees were here. On the other hand, to whom would they take the information?

By the time the news got to Khokarsa, it would be too late for Minruth to do anything about it. There might be a naval vessel stationed somewhere near the coast, but that wouldn't make any difference. No ship was going to catch up with the *Wind-Spirit*.

It was possible, however, that a message would be sent to Rebha. The priests could guess, or could find out through espionage, that Hadon was taking Lalila there.

If this was so, there was nothing he could do about it. He shrugged. He would consider the possibility when they got to their destination.

16

Rebha rose slowly out of the southern horizon. Ruseth was delighted because he'd had to spend only two days circling the area before he found the city. During this time they passed many ships, which meant that Rebha had to be in the neighborhood. Ruseth hailed a number of them, but they were in the same situation. Some of them, convinced that the captain of this strange-looking vessel might be a magician who would know the way, had attempted to follow them. But large heavy ships depending on oars could not even keep the *Wind-Spirit* in sight.

"Many ships must miss Rebha," Hadon said to Ruseth.

"No," the redhead said. "Their captains have been on this route so often that they have developed an extra sense. They feel something tingle when they are in the area; they know almost to the minute when it's time to slow down and start casting about. Besides, a captain who keeps a close watch on his knottage and his compass, on the sun and the stars when they're visible, isn't going to be off course much."

An hour later, he shouted. The others came running to the tiller, which he was still handling. "See that smoke to the northwest?" he asked. "That's from the top of the tower in the center of the pile. Unless, of course," he added, "it's a ship on fire."

It was not. Late the next day they saw the upper part of the structure, called the Tower of Diheteth. This was of cedar and had been built a hundred years ago by the admiral who was its regent. Its top, five hundred feet high, was floored with stone. A large fire was kept burning there so that ships could observe its smoke or light. On a clear day the top of the smoke cloud could be seen from over a hundred and twenty miles away, provided the wind was not so strong it dissipated the smoke too quickly. On a clear night, the fire on top of the tower was visible for over twenty-six miles.

The traffic at this point was increasing: uniremes, biremes, triremes and sailing craft were on every side, though separated by hundreds of yards. Hadon was amazed at their number. Rebha had to be large to handle all these craft.

Indeed it was large, Ruseth assured him. It stood on top of a submerged island into which thousands of wooden and stone piles had been driven or built. The sea-bottom was twenty-five to fifty feet below the surface of the island, and the city rose on piles thirty to fifty feet above the island—not counting the signal tower. The piles had been sunk into the ooze overlaying the limestone surface of the broad plateau. The city was roughly circular with a diameter of two miles. The estimated population, permanent and transient, was about forty thousand.

Hadon was eager to see this fabled city on stilts. He had heard much about it on the voyage from Opar to the Great Games, but the galley taking him had bypassed it, going directly from the Strait of Kethna to the island of Khokarsa.

Ruseth refused to enter it during the day, circling it instead, waiting for nightfall. When dusk came, Ruseth headed the *Wind-Spirit* for the setting sun, a red coal in the dark smoke. Presently the stars came out and with them the small bright flare on top of the Tower of Diheteth. It increased in size and brilliance, rising like a star as they neared.

When they were within a mile of the vast dark pile, shot with tiny lights here and there, he hauled the mainsail down. By this time the stink from the city, carried by the wind, was powerful.

Hinokly, who had been to Rebha once to visit his brother, explained the reason for the odor.

"All garbage, refuse and excrement is dumped into the sea beneath. Most of it is slowly carried out by the current, but much is caught by the piles and the floating docks. You saw the garbage floating in the sea when we were passing southeast of Rebha. We were miles away, yet it was thick."

"Yes," Hadon said, as he helped Hinokly with one edge of the sail. "I also saw the sea crocodiles, the gruntfish, the birds and the sea otters. There must be thousands around here, living off the garbage and the excrement."

Hinokly added, "There are so many birds that Rebha is half white with their droppings. Under the city, the crocodiles and the otters make life very dangerous for anyone who happens to fall into the water or ventures too close to the edge of the docks. Every now and then, according to my brother, a massive hunt is organized to clear the predators out. They kill a lot of crocodiles and gruntfish, though not so many otters. These are too smart; they swim out and away as soon as they get wind of the hunt. No ships can catch up with them.

"So Rebha has a big crocodile feast—they're good eating—and for a while it's comparatively safe to walk on the under docks. That is, the sea crocodiles are scarce then, though the two-legged crocodiles are not. Rebha has a serious crime problem, but what city doesn't?"

The wind died suddenly and the sea subsided into long flat rollers. As the ship slid forward on its own momentum, the crew stepped down the mast. Then they hauled out long heavy paddles and began the work of getting the vessel under the bottom of the city. It moved slowly under the bulk overhead, passing between two massive pylons bearing huge white numbers. Though it was dark, there was enough light from distant torches and large fires in braziers to see a hundred feet ahead. They steered by docks at which lay huge merchant galleys, small private galleys, fishing boats and even rowboats. Some two hundred yards in, torches flared around a building by a long dock. They were too far away to distinguish the words painted above the structure, but Hinokly said that the building housed customs inspectors and marines.

They headed away from it, passing behind a series of great monoliths and vessels in docks. Several times they bumped against a ship or grated along a dock, but their slow passage prevented any loud noise or damage. Occasionally they heard a deep grunting, like that of swine, or a slurping noise. These were made by the monstrous deep-sea fish that fed here. Hadon dimly saw one by the distant light of a cluster of torches. Its flat oily back was wide enough for three men to stand abreast; its length would have taxed him to long-jump across it. Tendrils of thick knobby flesh sprouted from above its eyes. Its mouth was shaped like two shovels, one above the other.

A few minutes later Ruseth stopped paddling. In a low voice he said, "*Kwa-kemu-kawuru-wu.*"

Something moved a few feet away in the water to Hadon's right. Foam shone dirty white in the dimness as an object as long as their ship slid by. Hadon had an impression of knobbed eyes and a ridged back and a long tail, but that could be his imagination, since he knew it was a great sea crocodile. Then it was gone.

They resumed their paddling, feeling that at any moment rows of teeth set in iron-strong jaws might clamp on the blades of their paddles and tear them out of their hands. It had happened before, if Hinokly's stories were true.

They were forced to veer from their desired path by a brightly lit galley. Armed men moved over its decks, and from it depths came grunting and squealing and the stench of pigs.

"Livestock has to be guarded until it can be hauled up to the first level," Hinokly said. "There are human thieves, though these are not the greatest threat. The sea otters will get into a ship and suck the blood from cattle and pigs, then eat them. They won't attack a man unless cornered, but then they are as dangerous as a leopard. Maybe more so, since they are bigger than leopards. I saw a sea otter fight a leopard once—this was at a party given by my employer in Khokarsa—and the otter killed the leopard. It died two days later, though, of its wounds."

Something creaked above them. Hadon looked up and saw a faint oblong appear in the darkness about fifty feet above. Something splashed into the water, just missing the vessel, throwing a spray against his side. The oblong disappeared.

Hinokly said, "Somebody dumped their garbage."

"Paddle faster," Ruseth said. "The noise and the odor will bring the beasts."

They hastened to obey. Hadon thought it time to ask a question: "How do you know where you're going in this dark maze?"

"The head priestess gave me a map and also verbal in-structions," Ruseth said. "I was to take the ship in through the fortieth and forty-first piles from the southwest corner along the south side. We were then to shift one row of piles to the west every twelve piles. After reaching the tenth row, we were to proceed past tweny piles to a dock on which are three burning torches," he continued. "That one ahead. We couldn't take a straight path in because we had to avoid certain well-patrolled docks and water lanes."

The ship bumped slightly on its starboard against the edge of a slip and then bumped harder against the end. A face appeared in the window of a shack. A moment later three robed and hooded figures came out. One quickly doused the torches in the water. Another said, "What word, strangers?"

Ruseth said, "That Word spoken in the Beginning..."

"By great Kho Herself," the priestess answered. "Come into the shack."

They crowded in. The woman closed the wooden shutters, putting them all in darkness. A moment later a spark flew from flint against iron, fell into a basin full of oil, and the oil burned. By its dim, bluely flickering flame, the woman ignited a candle, then three more. She placed a metal cover over the basin, extinguishing the fire, but not before the smoke had set them to coughing.

Her hood was thrown back, revealing the face of a woman in middle-age. "You have papers?"

Ruseth took a roll of papyrus paper from a leather bag slung over his shoulder. She broke the seal and spread it out on a table to read it by the candle's light. Her eyes widened, and she looked up now and then to stare at the newcomers. Finally she took a bronze-tipped bone pen, dipped it into a bottle of ink and wrote a note at the bottom of the last page. She signed it with a flourish, sanded the ink, pressed it, rolled the paper up and affixed a seal to it. She handed it to Ruseth.

"So you are Hadon," she said. "The man who should have been Emperor, consort of our high priestess, if the Voice of Kho had not decreed otherwise. And you," she said, staring at Lalila, "are the Witch-from-the-Sea. Sugaqateth tells me that you carry one in your belly who is destined for great things—if she is born in the treasure city of Opar. We will see what we can do to get you there."

Hadon had read her signature. He said, "Karsuh, you seem to have been waiting for us. Apparently the news about us has raced ahead of us, though we were in the swiftest ship on the two seas."

"No, Hadon," she said, "we were not waiting for anyone in particular. A watch is always kept here; this is a station in the secret message-transient system. It is true, however, that we have heard something about you. Four days ago a swift naval galley docked here. Admiral Poedy received a message from Minruth. It warned the admiral that Awineth, Hadon and others could possibly be on the way to Rebha. There was no positive data to this effect. It was just that the authorities at Rebha should be on the lookout for you. Minruth thought you might try to flee Khokarsa if Awineth's forces suffered defeat. There was no description of your ship, Ruseth, which is fortunate. But that does not mean there won't be."

"If we could get provisioned tonight, we could leave before dawn," Hadon said.

"That won't be possible," Karsuh said. "We can get a certain amount of food into the ship tonight. But there is so much patrol activity now that a large amount being moved at one time would be certain to attract attention. It will take several days. You see, Admiral Poedy fears—and rightly—that there are many people loyal to Awineth in Rebha. These don't include most of the great merchants who live on Rebha, and Poedy is certain that the majority of his officers are faithful to Minruth. It is the lower classes, the fisherfolk, the sailors, the laborers, the smugglers of Rebha whom he mistrusts. So he keeps patrols busy at all hours, especially at night. That is why we have to move slowly and circumspectly.

"In fact, if he should discover that the Temple of Piqabes is aiding Hadon and Lalila, he would arrest every priestess in the city. He is looking for an excuse, though he realizes the dangers. Perhaps he even hopes for an uprising, since that would give him a chance to clean out the slums. We know through our spies that he has marked at least three thousand men and women for death, people whom he suspects of criminal activity or subversion. Rightly, I might add."

"How long will the restocking take?" Ruseth said.

"From what you've told me of your lack of supplies, about three nights," Karsuh said. "In the meantime, we must hide your ship. Even with the mast stepped down, its lines are obviously unfamiliar. An inspector would know at once that it had entered illegally. If such a vessel had come in through proper channels, he would have heard about it, you may be sure of that."

"I must know where you're taking the ship," Hadon said, "in case we have to leave suddenly; we'd be in a bad situation if we didn't even know where the ship was."

"It'll be in an enclosed dock ten piles west and thirty north of this pile," the priestess said. "My men will take it there. Come, let's get out of here."

The woman leading, holding a fish-oil lantern, they walked along the dock until they came to the bottom of a wooden staircase which wound upward into the darkness. They climbed swiftly, pausing on three landings to catch their breaths. At the top, they found themselves in a narrow street. Here, above the city, the sky was cloudless except for a half-veiled moon. On both sides rose unpainted wooden houses three stories high. The windows on the street level were shuttered; the doors looked solid and were fitted with massive bronze locks. The windows on the upper stories were open. The far corner of the street was dimly lit and, when they arrived there, they saw two giant torches burning on stanchions before the door of a large building. As they passed it they heard sounds of revelry from within. Over the doorway was a large board on which was painted the head of a beach baboon. This marked the hall where sailors of this totem could stay and where Rebha citizens of the same totem gathered for social events.

The priestess led them on, up a flight of steps alongside a ramp to a higher level. Hadon tried to memorize the route, but the darkness and the many turnings and climbings and descents confused him. He wondered at the absence of people at this early hour. Karsuh told him that there was a curfew.

"Poedy imposed it two months ago, ostensibly to prevent

any more rioting. It also makes it easier to control criminal activities. Anyone caught out after dusk is automatically convicted, except for provable emergencies, of course."

She stopped. "Oh, oh!"

A light had suddenly illuminated the corner of the street about a hundred yards down. It swiftly became stronger.

"The patrol!"

17

She turned and ran by them, and they hastened after her.
Kebiwabes, who was carrying the sleeping Abeth, began to
fall behind. Hadon took the child from him. The party fled
back up the steps until it came to the previous junction.
There they turned to the north and walked swiftly until
Karsuh halted.

"This is the Street of the Overturned Hives," she said.

She rapped on the door of a run-down structure, giving
three quick beats with her fist, then six, then nine. She waited
and presently somebody on the other side of the door rapped
twelve times. Karsuh struck the door three times.

Just then lights flared strongly at the junction. Several
men, their bronze helmets, cuirasses and spearpoints gleaming in torchlight, stepped into the open. A few seconds later
lights appeared at the other end of the street, and a second
patrol appeared in the junction there. The party was caught
between the two.

Chains rattled behind the door. Karsuh said, "For our
sakes, lovers of Kho, open quickly."

A chain banged; a bolt was withdrawn; wood squealed
against wood as if a bar had been fitted into too tight arms. A
patrolman shouted, his cry echoed by the group at the other
junction. At the same time both patrols began running toward
the group in front of the door.

It swung open suddenly. The priestess' lamp showed a man
clad only in a kilt, clutching a short sword, blinking. Behind
him was a narrow hall with walls of peeling paint and a
stairway halfway down it.

"Karsuh!" the man said. He stepped back, and the refugees poured in.

"The patrol!" Karsuh said. "They're after us! Lock the door!"

The man quickly obeyed, though he had just shot the bronze bolt when men hammered on the other side.

"Open in the name of the Emperor Minruth and his vicar, Admiral Poedy!"

"There's little time for explanation!" Karsuh said to the man. "These people are important! This is Hadon of Opar; you know of him. This woman and her child are under the protection of Kho Herself."

The door shook under hard buffetings. Suddenly a spear-point rammed an inch through the wood. Lights appeared in the hallway and at the top of the stairway. Men, women and children looked out from the doors and the steps.

"Gahoruphi," the priestess continued, "you'll have to move everybody out of here. The soldiers will call in help and seize everyone. Poedy is looking for a chance to make an example of those who resist him. It'll be the crocodiles for all of you, even the children!"

"I know," Gahoruphi said. He turned and shouted at the people who were now filling the hall. Hadon wondered where they had all come from; they must have been stacked in their rooms.

A fat naked woman nursing an infant gestured at the priestess, who told the others to follow her. They single-filed down the hall between armed men and up the creaking stairway. The blows on the door were getting louder and more frequent. Hadon looked back down the steps. The head of an ax crashed through the wood. It was withdrawn, and Gahoruphi stabbed his spear through the hole. A man cried out. Gahoruphi withdrew his spear and shouted, "First blood!"

Lalila said to the priestess, "Won't they be massacred?"

"Some will be killed," Karsuh said. "But the rest will follow us through secret ways to the temple."

Abeth, who had been silent with terror since being so savagely awakened, now began to cry. Lalila took her and comforted her.

On the hallway of the second story, others poured out of

the rooms. The reek of unwashed bodies filled the air, and shouts and questions dinned around them. The priestess stopped to tell them to follow her. Hadon, however, grabbed her by the arm.

"Why should we run?" he said. "There are still only a few soldiers outside. Why can't we kill them before they call more and then dump their bodies into the sea?"

There was a crash from below as the door fell in. The clang of blades and the cries of injured men arose.

"I will take the woman and the child to the temple!" Karsuh said. She called to the fat woman, whose baby was bawling loudly. "Hinqa! You stay here until Hadon is forced to run, then lead him to the temple."

Lalila gave a despairing look at Hadon, as if she did not expect to see him again. Then she hurried away down the hall and up another flight of steps. Presumably she would go to the roof and across it to wherever the priestess led her.

The manling Paga hesitated for a moment. He was evidently torn between his desire to fight by Hadon's side and his desire to make sure that Lalila was safe. Hadon pointed his sword at Lalila, saying, "She will need a man to guard her, Paga, if I should fall."

The scribe and the bard looked longingly after Lalila. They wanted to get away from the bloodshed to come, but they were not cowards and so would do their duty.

Hadon rammed his way down the stairs through the crowd. Kebiwabes and Hinokly followed him. The hall was jammed with men trying to get at the soldiers, who had advanced only a few feet into the house. Hadon, seeing that the situation made it impossible for him to help, retreated. He fought his way back through the screaming women and children to the second floor. There he went to the window overlooking the street and opened its wooden shutters. Below were about two dozen soldiers. Two were blowing bronze whistles to call in more patrols.

By now the windows all along the streets, as far as he could see, were lit. Heads protruded from them, and there were even citizens out on the street, some with lamps, some with torches. All carried swords, axes or knives.

Hadon went into the nearest apartment, two rooms with

119

blankets on the floor for beds, and rushed through them to stop at the window and look down. The street just below him was unoccupied. The soldiers were all crowding around the door or hammering at the shutters on the windows with spears and axes.

Kebiwabes, Hinokly, Ruseth and his four sailors entered a moment later. Hadon said, "Follow me!" and he let himself out of the window. After dangling for a moment at arm's length, he dropped. He brushed against the side of the house, shoved with his hands, propelled himself a little away. His long legs, bent, took the impact easily. And then he had his *tenu*, Karken, Tree of Death, out of its scabbard. Its edge cut into the back of a soldier, then into another and another. The head of a fourth fell on the planks; the arm of a fifth thumped into it.

A spearman turned then, his mouth opening to cry alarm, his weapon turning toward Hadon. Karken severed the head of the weapon from the shaft and the head of the man from the trunk. Ruseth joined him then, picking up a spear from a fallen man and driving it into the throat of a man just turning around.

Men came running from doorways up and down the streets, emboldened by this attack on the patrol. Within two minutes it was all over for the two dozen soldiers.

But their whistles had called in more patrolmen. From a distance came shouts and shrill replying whistles, and the light of many torches lit the tops of houses some streets away. It was at this moment, as the mob that had spilled out of the houses into the street suddenly became quiet, that the wind struck the city of Rebha.

One moment all was stillness as if a sack had been jammed down over everyone. The noise of the approaching patrolmen was still distant. The next moment the wind whistled over the houses and down the streets, and the flames of the torches leaned away from the wind. The sweat on their bodies cooled them, evaporating suddenly.

To the north, lightning still flickered. Dark, angry-looking shapes, evil faces, were revealed in the twisting blazes. These hastened toward the city.

The fat woman, Hinqa, holding the baby with one arm,

120

snatched a torch from the hand of a man near her. Screaming, causing the baby to start screaming again, she whipped the torch over her head. All turned to look at her.

"Kho has sent us a wind!" she cried. "Let's use it as She intends!"

Hadon stared at her, wondering what she meant, what she intended to do. He was not the only one. Those near her shrank from her, scared of her wild-eyed look, her obvious possession. The Goddess seemed to have taken her over; her eyes seemed to blaze like the distant lightning.

"Burn down the city!" she cried. "Burn! Burn! Burn! Destroy the worshipers of Resu and the subjects of Minruth the Tyrant! Let the faithful of the Flaming God burn in flames!"

Her torch soared in an arc which ended inside a second-story window. That it had found sustenance was evident a moment later. Flames broke the darkness of the window and quickly spread through the room.

"Yes! Let it burn!" a man shouted. He threw his torch through the window of a house across the street.

"Burn! Burn! For Kho's sake, burn!"

Hadon was appalled. They seemed to have all gone crazy at once, as if the wind had indeed blown divine madness on them. If they burned the city down, where would they run to? They would either have to flee in ships, of which there were not nearly enough, or jump into the sea. And there they would drown or be devoured by the crocodiles, the otters, the gruntfish.

"Stop it! Stop it!" he yelled. No one heard him except the bard, the scribe and Ruseth. They looked as pale as he felt, gathered together as if they were the only islet of sanity in a sea of craziness.

Now everybody was throwing torches through the windows. The wind whipped the flames as if they were galley slaves, urging them to work faster.

Now the patrolmen were running, drawn by the flames and the mob. The mob threw itself on the patrolmen, overwhelming them, tearing them to pieces with their nails or hacking them to bits.

In the distance, upwind, the shrilling of many whistles

floated down. Drums beat somewhere, and then a great bell began to clang. This was soon followed by the clamor of many bells. It seemed that the city was vibrating in wood and air, shivering everywhere from strokes of bronze.

Hinokly shouted in Hadon's ear, "They're mad, mad! They *will* burn the city down, the fools! Unless the authorities can put the fire out! But these people aren't going to let the firemen get close enough to do that! What's the matter with them?"

"I don't know!" Hadon said. "We have to find Lalila! We have to get back to the ship as soon as possible!"

He motioned to the others to follow him. With some difficulty he got through the ever-increasing crowd to the house. It was empty inside, but flames and clouds of smoke filled the second-story hallway. The whole house would be on fire within a few minutes.

With the others behind him, he ascended the stairs to the third story and up a ladder to the roof. This was flat enough to allow them to walk along its sloping surface. The roof of the neighbouring house was accessible; a long step and they were on it. A trapdoor lay open there—was it the one Lalila and the priestess had gone through?

Smoke began curling from the trapdoor. Several seconds later, flame tongued from it.

"The roof behind it," Hadon shouted, and he led them across the roof, which was hot on their bare feet, to the next roof. This belonged to a house along the next street over. At that moment he wondered what had happened to Ruseth's four crewmen. Never mind. They would have to save themselves.

He looked over the edge of the roof. This street was also filled with a maniacal mob, and torches were being applied to houses and furniture. The wind was driving these fires southward; some sparks and small burning pieces of wood were being carried across the street to the houses on the other side. These were already burning, but this transmission of flame indicated how quickly the whole city would soon be on fire.

There were many lights out at sea. Hadon supposed these were naval vessels sent out to stand by. From the rapid rise and fall of the torches and lamps, the sea was very choppy.

"We have to get down before we're cut off!" Kebiwabes shouted. Hadon nodded, and they raised a trapdoor and went quickly to the ground floor. They made it just in time, emerging into the street with scorched clothing and singed hair.

Much of the mob had left by this time, apparently having gone to join a battle several streets away. From the clash of blades and the screams of wounded and dying, Hadon supposed that several hundred must be engaged there.

Seeing the entrance to a public stairway, he ran to it. There were some people on it with the same idea. He followed them down the turnings until he was on a dock. The wind blew the flames of the torches set in brackets on a shack wall; if it got much stronger, the torches would be extinguished. By their guttering light men, women and children were climbing into boats or ships or already pulling away. The sea was heavy here, long and rolling, broken somewhat by the massive piles. Several of the vessels were carried, despite their crews' efforts, against the sides of the piles. The side of one was smashed and it began to sink.

"Not everybody is a maniac," Hinokly said. "Soon everyone, crazed or not, will be down here, striving to get away from the inferno."

Hadon did not reply. He pulled a woman from the water onto the dock and while she sat gasping, he asked, "Where is the Temple of Kho?"

"My husband was killed," she said, moaning.

Hadon shook her by a shoulder. "Where is the Temple of Kho?"

"I don't care."

"If you don't tell me, I'll let you stay here and die!"

"I don't care," she said, and she began keening.

Kebiwabes said, "The street above us is on fire. It'll be coming down the stairway next. This dry wood."

Screams came down from above, from those trapped by the flames. The fires they had originated were turning on them.

"We'll swim to that dock over there," Hadon said. "There are ships there, and nobody is on the dock."

"There they come," Ruseth said, pointing at the steps where a dozen people were scrambling down.

Hadon put his sword in its sheath and dived into the water. He came up in a large swell with stinking garbage and turds. A huge round-sided, flat-backed form rose before him, grunted and then sank. He swam over it, feeling panic for a second as his foot struck something soft and greasy.

It was twenty yards to the next dock. Hadon climbed up and then helped Ruseth and the others up to it. By then six craft had been seized, three rowboats and three small fishing boats. A longboat with a single mast was the only one left, and a dozen people were running toward it. Hadon roared and dashed up to them, grabbing them from behind and hurling them into the water. Six went in before the others realized what was happening. They turned with knives and swords in hand. Ruseth joined him, and the two advanced against the six men and women. They did not try to close with him; the fact that he wielded a *tenu* discouraged them. Suddenly Hadon halted and said, "There is no need for bloodshed. I want this boat just long enough to get to the Temple of Kho. You can come with us and, after we get there, you can go on with the boat. In fact, it'll be better that way for all. We need you to help us paddle the boat there, and you need us."

Kebiwabes and Hinokly ranged themselves by Hadon's side. This additional force, as much as the logic of Hadon's argument, convinced the six that cooperation was best. They all got in and pushed the boat away from the dock as more people ran screaming out onto it. Some leaped into the water in a vain attempt to get aboard. All but one made it back to the dock; this man screamed and threw his hands up in the air and disappeared as if something had pulled him under— which no doubt was what had happened.

With ten paddlers, the boat moved along swiftly enough. There were several tense moments when a swell lifted it against a pillar, but they were able to avoid collision by shoving their paddles against it. A section of the street floor above fell in once, the flaming wood hissing and splashing water into the boat. Sparks and hot fragments fell on the paddlers, causing them to cry out in pain or fright, but none was seriously burned.

Their guide, paddling in the lead on the right, turned now and then to order a change of direction. Within ten minutes they seemed to be past the area of fire. At least the light cast by the flames lessened, and there was no odor of smoke. But there was much activity overhead everywhere, people shouting, bells ringing, occasionally a heavy thudding as of many men running. The number of people running in panic down the stairways and seizing vessels steadily increased. Evidently they were taking no chances. If the city did go up in flames, they would not be there to be burned.

At last the man gestured to his right and made a peculiar sign with his hand. Hadon said, "What's that mean?"

Ruseth said, "It means we dock there," pointing to a series of parallel platforms, rising and falling with the swells.

The longboat came in on the crest of a swell between two platforms; the people on the right grabbed the free ends of ropes tied to posts. With some difficulty, Hadon and his group got out onto the dock and clung to the rope railing. Those in the longboat shoved against the dock or dug in their paddles, and the boat moved out from between the platforms.

The ends of the center platform extended outside and past the stairway, sliding up and down as the swells rose and fell. An ingenious mechanism of bronze worked back and forth, up and down, to permit the platform dock to move vertically without being disconnected or bumping into the stairway. The metal arms and joints squeaked however, as if they needed oil.

Hadon leading, they got to the stairway. There was light furnished by torches on the platforms, but it diminished as they climbed up. By the time they were at street level, they could see only dimly. They came out of the staircase into a dark room. Hadon told the others to stand still while he groped around for a doorway. Presently he found one. Its latch moved easily upward, and he stepped through into another dark room. He immediately felt something light across his face, chest and legs. Whatever the things were, they moved easily at first, then began to resist. Little bells tinkled in the room. Suddenly a door at the opposite end was thrown open. Light streamed in. Men armed with swords poured in. More light fell, this time from a trapdoor in the ceiling. Men looked down at him from behind their spears.

18

The bells had given their warning when Hadon pulled the strings attached to them. He stood still but he cried, "I am Hadon, husband of Lalila, the woman who came here only a short time ago! Karsuh brought her here with the child!"

An officer said "I know." He gave an order and the strings fell to the floor. After checking out the rest of the party—evidently Karsuh had described them—he led them into the next room. They climbed another high spiraling staircase to emerge into a large chamber. This was made of marble and was decorated with murals and statuettes of ivory and gold set in niches. They followed the officer through a series of splendid rooms and ascended another staircase to the third story. They walked down a hallway and then went up another staircase for seven stories inside a tower, as they saw when they got to the top. Lalila, Abeth, Karsuh and a number of others were in the open-sided chamber. They were looking down at a city rapidly being consumed. The flames had spread to new areas, and fires had started in many places remote from the main blaze. These had evidently been ignited by people infected with the same hysteria and self-destructive mania which had seized those in the Street of the Overturned Hives.

Much could be seen from this height. The flames lit up firemen and volunteers pulling buckets of water up through openings in the streets, soldiers battling rioters and looters, people cramming avenues, running into soldiers intent on getting to the flames to extinguish them, refugees piling up on top of each other, screaming and clawing outside the entrances to the stairways.

Here and there, buildings folded into themselves and into the flames, sometimes collapsing through the bottom level and leaving empty smoking spaces.

Hadon took a quick look, then put his arm around Lalila's waist and kissed her. She gave a startled cry—she had not seen him arrive—and then buried her face against his chest.

"Wherever I go," she said, "wherever I go, death, misery, hate, destruction."

"That's only because there is death, misery, hate and destruction everywhere," Hadon said. "You are not under a curse. No more than anybody else."

She started to say something, but the outcry of those around them drowned her words. They looked out to see the cause of the uproar. Fire had broken out in the buildings around the base of the great tower in the center of the city. Whether it had been deliberately started by someone or if the wind had carried sparks and burning pieces to the houses, no one knew. Nor did it matter. The flames were raging now, lighting up the houses and the streets, which were jammed. At the rate the fire was traveling—flames were licking at the first story—the tower would soon be past saving.

Karsuh turned away from the scene. The lights from the fires and the torches set along the railing made her face glisten. It was a copper mask of grief.

"Rebha will soon be aflame from one end to the other," she said. "Kho must have sent this wind; Kho has driven the people out of their minds. Together, wind and madness will burn ancient Rebha to the sea. Nothing, not even the piles, will be left."

"Then we must get away," Hadon said. "Will you lead us to our ship, *Wind-Spirit?* You can go with us, of course."

Karsuh shouted at her guards, who surrounded the entire party. They went down the stairway quickly enough; the temple seemed to be empty except for those who had gathered at the top of the watch tower. Hadon carried Abeth this time. The child clung to him, her face pressed into his neck. She did not cry out or even whisper; she was too frightened.

Whatever her internal feelings, outwardly she was as still as if dead.

When they reached the staircase below the street level, Karsuh cried out. "The boats are all gone!"

The men ahead of Hadon roared and began running down the steps. He turned and thrust Abeth at Hinokly and raced after the guards. Their quarry was a rowboat just leaving the dock. Six persons were in it, three men, two women and a boy of about twelve. They were all bent to their task, which was to get the boat away before it was boarded by others. On the dock, rolling back and forth, were the bodies of a dozen people, some temple guards, some thieves. The latter must have swum over from docks under nearby streets after every craft on those docks was seized. Some must have drowned in the attempt; others had been killed fighting for the boats. And now the last boat was being rowed away.

The guards were brave. They leaped without hesitation out after the boat. One landed on the stern and sprawled forward. Before he could rise, he was struck on the neck with the edge of a paddle. Another guard fell into the sea and grabbed the edge of the stern. He started to pull himself up but was hit on the top of the helmet by an oar. He still managed to cling on, then lost his grip as the oar broke the bones of his fingers.

The boat lost some headway, however, when its rowers stopped to beat off the guards. Three of them, though they had fallen short of the craft were now swimming toward it. Though their bronze helmets and cuirasses weighed them down, they managed to keep their noses above water. What they intended to do when they reached the boat was something they probably had not considered. They were obeying the orders of the priestess, and that was all they had to think about for the moment.

Hadon stopped at the foot of the steps, then stepped to one side to allow the others to pass by. Three of the rowers were still using their oars; the others were standing up, or attempting to, holding their oars to bring down on the swimming guards. One of the rowers was the young boy and he was not very effective.

There was a distance of about thirty feet now from the

dock. Too far for him to jump even if he had been able to make a good run.

He reached out and grabbed Ruseth. "We have to get that boat," he said. "Otherwise we'll burn to death—or drown ourselves to keep from burning. How good a swimmer are you?"

"You're asking a fisherlad from Bhabhobes?" Ruseth replied.

"We'll swim out and then dive under and come out ahead of them," Hadon said. "I'll climb up on the left side of the bow—"

"The port," Ruseth said.

"To hell with that," Hadon said. "The left side. You take the right—"

"The starboard," Ruseth said, grinning. Hadon did not know whether to hit him or pat him. The little redhead certainly had guts. To jest at a time like this!

"We have to come up, out and on very swiftly," Hadon said. "Let's go!"

Shouting, he rammed his way through the crowd, knocking people down and some into the water. He poised at the edge as Ruseth arranged himself by his side. As the dock rose to the top of a swell, he leaped out. He stayed under the surface of the water, striking out with all his strength, letting his heavy sword drag him down a little. The current tended to sweep him to the right, but then it was doing the same to the rowboat.

When he could not hold his breath any longer, and his arms and legs seemed filled with lead pellets, he came up, ahead of the boat by ten feet. He could see the rowers frantically working against the torchlight from the docks. He hoped they would not be able to see him in the darkness ahead.

A head emerged a few feet from his—Ruseth. The sailor turned and his teeth gleamed. Hadon gestured at the boat, which was approaching rapidly. He dived again and came up as the boat started to slide down a swell. He reached up and grabbed the wood of the prow just ahead of the nose. With a heave that cracked the muscles in his back—or was it the timbers of the boat?—he was up on the edge, his belly pressing down on it. A moment later, Ruseth's head appeared on the other side, rising, then falling forward as Ruseth also fell on his belly. He held his knife between his teeth.

The two closest rowers were the boy and a woman. The boy was on the left, only a few feet from Hadon. He and the woman must have heard them or felt their weight on the prow. Yelling, they rose to their feet and turned, using their oars as weapons. Hadon, scraping his belly raw, pulled himself over the edge. Ruseth did the same; they collided. The boat pitched, and the woman and the boy lurched back down again on the bench, their oars still up in the air. The boy was not strong enough to keep his up; it went back over his shoulder. The woman raised hers and got halfway up from the bench, intending to bring the oar down on Ruseth.

By then the two men had scrambled up, hampering each other, but still working effectively enough. Hadon kicked the boy in the face; Ruseth stabbed the woman in the neck. Behind them the other four quit rowing and rose to bring their oars into play. The boat swung sideways and then slid down a swell. For a moment the four were diverted by the need to keep their footing. Hadon ignored this, though he could have been hurled out by any too violent a pitch, and advanced. By then he had his sword out. Within twenty seconds, he had cleared the boat.

Ruseth threw the woman, who was wounded in the neck, and the unconscious boy into the sea. The boy, apparently shocked into consciousness, began swimming toward the dock. Hadon did not think he would make it, but he wished him luck. He had nothing against him. In fact, if there had been room, he would have let him stay aboard. But his own came first, Lalila and the child, then Paga, because he loved Lalila and she loved him, then his friends.

Getting the boat back was not difficult, since it had not progressed far. It came in so fast, sliding down a swell and then up it, that its side ground against the dock. Some people on the edge of the dock had been too hasty in trying to get to the boat. They were crushed between the hull and the platform. Fortunately, Lalila and the others had not been on the edge. They had been pushed back by those who were now drowning or screaming with pain and horror.

While Ruseth grabbed a rope to keep the boat from drifting away, Hadon whirled the sword above his head. Those on the edge of the dock shrank back. The priestess Karsuh, shouting commands and threats, aided by her surviving guards, got the others away from the dock. Lalila, Abeth and Paga, the scribe and the bard clambered in. Hadon told the priestess to get in too. There was room for her.

She said, "No. I stay here. It is my duty to pray for salvation for my poor people."

Hadon saluted her, admiring her devotion but doubting her good sense. He gave the order and the others shoved off. As they pulled away, they saw more people descending, their press so great that some were spilled over the sides of the stairway. Smoke belched down after them, and then trickles of fire ran along the tar in the joinings of the planks.

Karsuh tried to get through the crowd to the stairway. She was swept to one side and into the water. If she had been on the near side, Hadon would have made an effort to get her into the boat. But she was quickly lost from view on the other side of the dock.

Hadon took an oar and began rowing with the others. They headed at an angle for the outer waters, beyond the area covered by the pile-city. Because of the heavy seas, it was impossible to cut straight west, the shortest route to safety, or at least a lessening of the present danger. The only practical route was to go straight between the piles in the direction of the current. That way they would avoid being carried sideways into piles. Even so, they had to go around a number of floating docks, which caused them to come perilously close to the massive columns from time to time.

When near the docks they were also threatened by hundreds of refugees who leaped into the sea and swam after the boat. Hadon had to keep urging his crew to row and pay no attention to the people trying to grab the oars and the sides of the craft. Though desperate, the swimmers were not strong enough to retain their holds on the oars. Their hands slipped away and they fell back. A few did manage to seize the edge of the stern. Only then would Hadon allow Hunokly and Paga, the rearmost, to stop rowing for a moment and stab the hands of the would-be boarders.

Finally they pulled out from under the cover of Rebha. Here the sea was even heavier, unbroken by the great piles. They needed rest, but Hadon made them press on.

"They're still swimming out," he said. "We can slow down after a while, when we're beyond the range of even the strongest swimmers."

By then the entire city seemed to be on fire. The flames rose high everywhere, outlining the crazy staggered levels of the buildings, the tower of the Temple of Kho and the Tower of Diheteth. The light showed hundreds of tiny dark figures along the edges of the outermost streets, milling around, then leaping, sometimes singly, sometimes by the dozens. The wind carried the screams even above the roar of the flames and the crash of falling walls and sections of foundation. Then the great Tower of Diheteth, wrapped in a red and orange winding sheet, toppled. Its collapse drowned out all other sounds. It struck the buildings below, sending a spray of flaming fragments high into the air, broke through the foundation and, carrying with it many of the surrounding structures, smashed into the sea. Though much of it was extinguished, a huge part was still burning. This bumped into pillars and docks, setting several aflame, and was lost in the general holocaust. By then wide areas of the city were falling into the sea. The smaller Tower of Kho slid gracefully through the foundation, retaining its vertical position until its base plunged hissing into the waters.

The rowers continued working, though they were numbed with awe. Within two hours, a mighty city of forty thousand people, an old city, the work of many hands and minds, through many generations, a unique place, erected in the desert of the sea, had been destroyed.

Hadon had had doubts about the rationality of human beings before this. From now on, he would never believe that people acted according to the dictates of reason. Perhaps they did most of the time. But behind, or below, that mask of logic was anarchy, unreason, emotion.

He exempted himself from this indictment, of course.

19

The storm struck a few minutes after the Tower of Kho fell.
The survivors would connect the two later in cause and
effect, the story would spread throughout the two seas that it
was Kho Herself who had started the fires and then sent the
storm to uproot even the piles and scatter the debris of Rebha
across the Kemu. Where once it had risen fifty feet above the
waters, where its tower could be seen for twenty-six miles
away, where the smoke from the tower could be seen a
hundred and twenty miles away, now there was nothing to
show that anything but the sea had ever rolled over this
place.

At this moment, those in the rowboat were concerned only
for themselves. The first blow of the storm front almost overturned them. They recovered and, while Lalila and Abeth
bailed with crocodile-leather buckets, the men bent their backs
to keep the boat in a straight line with the waves. If it was
allowed to slide at an angle down the mighty waves, it
might—undoubtedly would—go under or roll over and not
come up again. At least not with its occupants still in it.

A trireme came up then, and somehow they managed to
transfer to it, climbing up rope ladders, hanging on to other
ropes thrown down to them. Abeth clung tightly to Hadon's
neck, her legs wrapped around his torso, while he was half
lifted to the deck. An especially heavy sea buried the deck a
moment later. He heard a cry and, when he had shaken the
water from his eyes, looked around. A moment ago Hinokly
had been beside Hadon. Now he was gone. There was no time
to reflect on his fate or feel sorrow for him. He had come

through many adventures, survived much while others had died. And then, after all that, he too had gone down to dread Sisisken's house.

Clinging to ropes stretched along the decks, they followed an officer. Twice, heavy seas almost tore them loose. They half fell down a ladder into a hold jammed with refugees picked up before the storm burst. The hatch was closed and the people were left in darkness and terror, where the stench of vomit fought with that of fear. The child Abeth whimpered now and then; Lalila soothed her, but her voice betrayed her own suppressed panic. Hadon sat by them, holding one arm around Lalila. Paga and Kebiwabes pressed close to his back; Ruseth huddled in front of him. After what seemed hours, and might have been, Hadon spoke to Ruseth.

"How long can such a ship stand up to a storm like this?"

"There is no way of predicting," Ruseth said. "We can only hope that Piqabes has no plans for taking us to her bosom."

A minute later everyone in the hold was hurled forward, forming a heap six feet high against the bulkhead. A rending of timbers sounded even above their cries. Something struck the hatch cover, splintering it, and water poured in. Hadon fought to his feet and pulled Lalila, who was clinging to Abeth, out of the writhing, kicking, yelling mass. He held her up as he dragged her and the child to the foot of the ladder. Just as they reached it, the deck canted far to one side, pitching them backward against the far bulkhead. Fortunately for them, their impact was softened by the bodies of others.

They scrambled up to try for the ladder again. Once more the deck tilted, this time precipitating them forward against the ladder. Again they were spared immediate contact with hard wood. Those who had been trying to get up the ladder involuntarily acted as shields. Nevertheless, even the reduced effect of collision was enough to hurt Hadon and Lalila. Abeth was lucky; she suffered very little injury.

Those who were able to got up the ladder by pushing or pulling others out of the way. Presently all except the badly injured and Hadon's party were out of the hold. Hadon had restrained his comrades from joining the panic-stricken flight. He had yelled at them to wait, even punching the bard in the belly to keep him from the ladder. Then, with the way cleared, he said, "We can go now."

Hadon leading, they climbed up the steep steps. By then they could see things better; dawn had just come. The sky was still blackish gray, but the wind had died down as if Piqabes had issued a fiat. The waves were rollers again, no longer the high sharp cliffs which had sent the ship bucking and plunging.

In fact the ship, though leaning to one side now, did not seem to be moving much. Its rise and fall were very slight, and its forward progress seemed to be nil.

Hadon gave a cry. The others, crowding up after him, exclaimed also. They were on the forward section of the vessel, a fortunate circumstance for them. The aft part was gone. It had broken off and disappeared into the sea.

Hadon went down the leaning deck to the railing. He looked over the side at the shattered stumps of oars projecting from the three tiers below. Bodies hung out of the ports, but others, injured or whole men, were climbing out of the ports down to a surface under the wreck.

Hadon felt a sense of unreality. What had the ship struck? What was holding it up?

"It looks like logs, hundreds of tree trunks, thousands perhaps," he murmured.

"That's what they are," Ruseth said. "We have struck one of the colossal rafts of the K'ud"em'o, people of the Sea Otter totem who dwell on the coast below the city of Bawaku."

Bawaku, Hadon knew, was an important port city on the western coast of the Kemu. It too was in revolt against Minruth.

There was more life abord the ship now. The sailors had recovered from the shock of the collision and were untying themselves from the ropes on the decks or coming up out of the hatches. An officer was shouting at some seamen to cut the rigging loose from the mast, which had snapped off and fallen across the foredeck. Several bodies lay beneath it.

"What does he think he's doing?" Ruseth said. "This ship isn't ever going to sail again."

Hadon looked around, then said, "The officer is a *datoe-*

poegu, a lieutenant. He's the only officer I see. The others must have been on the aft section or injured belowdecks."

"There are many hurt men," Lalila said, referring to the cries and calls for help from below.

Hadon pointed across the logs. "Here come some people. These must be the K'ud"em'o."

About fifty men and women with some children and dogs were advancing across the surface of the immense raft, their dark features indicating basic Khoklem stock: snub noses, thick lips, straight dark hair. Their chests were painted with red stylized heads of sea otters. Their long hair was gathered into seven pigtails, caught around the roots in bright blue beaded bands. The teeth of the men were filed to sharp points. They wore otterskin codpieces secured by narrow strips of skin around the hips and thighs. Aside from these and metal bracelets, anklets and rosaries, they were naked.

The women wore little triangular aprons of skin held by strings around the hips. Their cheeks were heavily rouged; their lips were painted with some bluish substance; large rings of bronze or gold dangled from their noses. All carried tridents or short stabbing swords. They did not, however, act belligerent or defensive; they just seemed curious.

By this time the lieutenant had realized he was the only officer aboard. He called the men away from the useless task of freeing the mast and set them to attending to the wounded, as he should have done at first.

Hadon threw a rope over the side of the vessel and let himself down. The ship had broken through the waist-high wall of small logs along the edge of the raft and thus admitted the sea. Water was ankle-deep here, mainly because the weight of the ship was causing this part of the raft to sink a little below the surface.

Hadon advanced through the water past the ship for twenty yards, then halted where the logs were just surface-wet. The raft people slowed down, talking among themselves. Their dogs, large skinny, mangy brutes, ran barking toward him. He waited, his right hand held up in the universal sign of peace. The beasts stopped only a few inches from him, and one nosed his calf from behind. He did not flinch; he waited, as still as a tree. A man wearing the only hat in the crowd, a high wide-brimmed cylinder with three long white feathers projecting from the top, came up to him. He was very broad, huge-paunched, slit-eyed, and stank of fish. Hadon supposed his grin was friendly, though the filed teeth made it look sinister.

Introductions were made. The man was Qasin, the chief of the Red Sea Otter clan. His name meant Black Heart, though this did not necessarily imply anything derogatory about his character. He certainly seemed generous enough. He offered to take the injured off and have them carried to a "sick persons' area." At least this was the interpretation Hadon made of the man's pronunciation. Qasin spoke Trade Khokarsan, the lingo understood in most large seaports and used by the polyglot crews of merchant and naval ships. His pronunciation of certain consonants and vowels made it difficult to understand him.

Hadon was able to make him understand that he had no authority over the ship or its crew. He and his friends were just passengers, picked up after the destruction of Rebha.

At this Qasin's eyes widened, and he asked Hadon to explain. The chief gave a shout then, and the others ran up to him. He jabbered away at them in a language which did not sound in the least like any Khokarsan Hadon had ever heard. In fact it resembled the language of the Klemqaba, the primitive peoples who lived far south of Bawaku.

Partway through the speech, the crowd began to rejoice, singing, dancing, whirling around and around, hugging and kissing. When the chief was finished speaking to his people, he turned to Hadon.

"We do not exult because all those people have been killed," he said. "Though doubtless they must have done something to deserve it, otherwise Piqabes would not have sent such a death among them. But we are happy because this means that Rebha is no longer a peril to us. Too many times our rafts have drifted into it, and the commander of Rebha has fined us heavily for the damage and the deaths our rafts caused. Yet we cannot be blamed for that, since Piqabes sends the currents which take our rafts sometimes into the piles of Rebha.

"Other times, though we do not come within dangerous

proximity of Rebha, yet we come too close to it according to the laws of Rebha. Then the commander sends his marines to our rafts, and we are fined for breaking the laws. And the profits made from our hard voyage are taken away from us. These marines also take our women aside, presumably for questioning, and then rape them. If we dare complain, we are fined for making trouble, for lying!

"We have no love for Rebha and especially none for its navy. But Piqabes has revenged us. All honor to the Goddess of the Two Seas!"

Qasin uttered what sounded like a string of orders to his people. Meanwhile others had joined them, coming from up and down the raft. At least three hundred were finally gathered there. When their chief had finished, they swarmed up the ropes of the canted vessel. The *datoepoegu* tried to stop them, but they ignored him. When he drew his sword and threatened them, he was struck from behind with the flat of an ax. His unconscious body was dragged along the deck and thrown into the sea from the broken end of the galley. Hadon thought he was surely dead, but the officer broke surface a minute later, sputtering and choking. He managed to swim to the raft, where Hadon gave him a helping hand aboard.

After he had recovered enough to sit up and speak, the officer said, "I must have your name! I want you to be a witness when the time comes to put these savages on trial! You saw how they made an unauthorized boarding of one of His Majesty's ships and how they attacked *me*, one of his commissioned officers!"

"If I were you, I'd keep silent about my intentions," Hadon said. He turned and waded away.

He helped Lalila and Abeth down off the ship. By then most of the living sailors and refugees were off. Those who could walk were pressed into service to carry their more injured companions. Litters were taken from the ship's stores or quickly made from planks torn from the vessel. As soon as the sailors were marched away, under guard, the dismantling of the galley started. Hammers, saws and crowbars of bronze ripped up planks; ropes were coiled and carried off; the stores were emptied. In an astonishingly short time, the ship had disappeared. Its wood and metal fittings were transported inland—if such a term could be used for what was after all only a huge raft. The stores and ropes were carried toward a small village at the western end.

The dead from the ship had been laid out, side by side. Their clothes and rings and weapons were removed and taken away somewhere. The lieutenant was by then up on his feet and protesting vigorously. No one paid him any attention, which was a kindness, relatively speaking. The officer kept demanding that Hadon help him get the ship back. Hadon told him to leave them alone. Couldn't he see that he was completely at the mercy of the raft people? If the K'ud"em'o wished, they could kill him and throw his body into the sea. If he persisted, Hadon said, he would be endangering his whole crew. Should the Red Sea Otters find it necessary to slay him, then they would have to kill all the witnesses—which also meant that Hadon and his group could be in grave danger, even though they were not naval personnel.

In fact, Hadon said, glaring at the officer, if he did not cease his useless, indeed dangerous, meddling, Hadon himself might shove him back into the sea. He wasn't particularly concerned about the possibility of the lieutenant's sudden demise, but he did not want to get involved in repercussions.

"You are a traitor!"

"I am no follower of the blasphemer and traitor, King Minruth," Hadon said, sneering. He put his hand on the hilt of his sword. Should he behead this stupid fellow and avoid trouble in the future? Not to mention earning the gratitude of the raft people?

"You are a rebel, a denier of the primacy of Resu!" the officer said.

"Since I am in my right mind, of course I am," Hadon said. "As for who is the rebel and who is not, there is no question. You are the rebel and the traitor, and no doubt loathsome Sisisken, great Kho's eldest daughter, has marked you as an early guest in her house."

The officer turned pale. Hadon walked away, going toward a priestess who was administering final rites to the dead. She chanted the song of the dead while daubing the forehead of each corpse with black, blue and red clay, arranging the spots to form the corners of a triangle. Her nubile attendant, whose face and breasts were painted in alternating circles of black and white, swung a censer of burning pine needles over the face of each corpse after the priestess daubed it. Nine times the censer swung while the attendant shouted the name of the victim. Where she had not been able to learn the name from the survivors because of too mutilated features, she gave the name of the first man created by Kho, Qawi.

The chief, Qasin, stood for a while watching his wife and Queen, the head priestess, work among the dead. Then he nodded, and six muscular men began to throw the bodies into the sea. After the eighth corpse sank, the greasy back of a gruntfish appeared, and the ninth corpse was swallowed by cavernous jaws.

"Piqabes wastes nothing," Qasin said, making the ancient sign used now only among old people and primitives. "The fish eat our dead, and we eat the fish."

20

While they followed the chief to the central village, Hadon told the story of his group. He had hesitated at first about revealing their identities, but the attitude of the K'ud"em'o seemed to make it safe. Besides, Hadon felt this would assure the K'ud"em'o that they were not with the sailors.

The chief was astonished. He had had no news since the raft had been launched from the homeland coast five months ago, and news from Khokarsa reached there three months late.

Qasin listened carefully, though interrupting frequently with exclamations of horror or rage. It was not, however, the political changes which upset him, since his tribe's loyalty to the concept of empire was rather tenuous; it was the religious upheaval which drove him into a frenzy.

They came to the central part of the raft which, Hadon learned, was a mile and a half long and half a mile wide at its broadest. Here stood fifty beehive-shaped huts made of bamboo poles and mahogany shingles. They stood on stilts, the ends of which were driven into holes drilled into the logs. Each housed about ten people and several dogs. In bad weather, they also held goats and the pet monkeys and parrots.

The center hut was the largest. This was the shrine of green-eyed Piqabes, goddess of the sea. Standing before its entrance was a great block of mahogany wood with a stairway of twelve steps cut on each side. On top of this was set an immense upright oblong of granite. A hole had been cut through its upper part, and its interior had been chiseled into a spiral arrangement.

"The stone of C'ak'oguq"o," the chief said, seeing Hadon's questioning expression. "She is our goddess of healing, though you may call her Qawo if you wish. The stone sits before her temple in our chief village," Qasin continued. "That is, until we have put together our raft and placed our supplies and trading goods on it. Then it is carried with much ceremony to the raft and placed here, before the Temple of Piqabes."

Hadon was amazed at the chief's story. Every two years an enormous number of valuable trees were cut in the highlands of the K'ud"em'o country. These were floated down the main river, through a number of rapids and over many cataracts. Eventually they were brought to the mouth of the river and into a bay protected by a great breakwater of earth built by the tribe. The mouth of the river was at a shallow level at this time, since the tribe had diverted the main flow through an ancient channel.

The logs were arranged in the quiet area behind the breakwater into a raft three times as long as wide. Great vines held two-thirds of the logs together. The rest were secured by bridges of wood, fitted with underpins driven into holes bored in the logs. After the raft was completed, houses erected on it and the supplies, animals and people moved onto it, the breakwater was destroyed. This was comparatively easy, since the action of the sea had been slowly tearing it down anyway. The river was rediverted into the main channel, which moved the raft seaward and helped crumble the earthen breakwater.

The river's pressure slowly pushed the raft out into the Kenu. Here the sea current caught it and ponderously shoved the giant assemblage of logs toward the southeast.

The raft people lived on their floating wooden island for six months while it moved toward Wethna. Their main food was the fish they caught, but they drank goat milk and ate goat meat; their storehouses provided nuts and berries, okra for soup and emmer wheat and millet flour to bake bread. They also drank wine and the harsh peaty liquor, *s"okoko*, purchased from the Klemqaba to the south. They kept enough to sell at Wethna after watering it down five to one. The K'ud"em'o were not cheating the Wethnans by this dilution; only the Klemqaba could drink the fiery liquid straight and live to brag of it.

In addition, the raft tribe sold its logs for a great profit, since mahogany and the other valuable trees did not grow on the Wethnan side of the coast. They also sold or bartered artifacts, carved good-luck godlets, whistles of eagle bone, phallic jadeite statues of their aboriginal deities, fascinating to the Wethnans because of their unfamiliarity. And aphrodisiac and contraceptive powders, fertility charms, bracelets to ward off the evil eye and diseases, ceremonial dildos fringed with the feathers of a kingfisher found only in the K'ud"em'o country.

"Surely you don't end your voyage at the harbor of Wethna?" Hadon said. "The current could not bring you right to its doorstep every time."

"It doesn't," Qasin said. "The rafts usually end up about fifty to seventy miles either way from Wethna. Then arrangements are made with the merchants of the city to transport the logs and goods on the coastal road. We pay for that, of course."

Once everything was sold, the tribe built a number of small ships and rowed back to their mainland. The largest carried the stone of their goddess of healing.

"Have you ever lost it in a storm or an accident?" Hadon asked.

"Never. We have been doing this for three hundred years and, though we have been in some terrible storms, always the raft with the stone gets through safely. There is a prophecy among my people, however, that if the stone should be lost, then the two seas will dry up."

Having arrived home after a two-month return trip, going against the current and the wind, the voyagers summoned those left behind. From the coast and the hills the tribesmen came down to rejoice with the rafters. The festival ran until all the money was spent, sometimes taking two months or more. During this occasion, all feasted and drank for free. Burials were conducted in drunken hilarity. Marriage ceremonies were held and infants, some of whom had waited for three years, were given their public names.

"Nothing of any real importance is done except during the

festival of the homecoming," Qasin said. "Until then, the dead are placed in the open on top of a hill. When the festival is to start, their bones are collected, washed and wrapped in palm leaves and brought down to the coast for burial. No one can be married until this time, though of course couples live together and have children. Nor can one be divorced until the festival, though people do separate meanwhile. Nor can property change hands or accused law-breakers be judged until then."

"If, as you say, the judge, the prosecutor, the defendant and his protector are all drunk, then you must have some grave miscarriages of justice," Hadon commented.

"No more than when all are sober," the chief said.

"But isn't it unjust to jail a man for two years while he waits trial?"

"We don't jail the accused until time for the festival," Qasin said, "unless he is an obvious public menace, in which case we kill him. If he has fled to the hills, then he is auto-matically assumed to be guilty."

Qasin mounted a platform and ordered a large bronze bell rung. This summoned people from the little settlements at the four corners of the raft. When all were assembled, the chief gave them the news of the terrible schism which had plunged the Empire into a bloody time. There was an uproar which lasted for half an hour. The chief then restored order by having the bell clanged again.

The injured seamen and refugees, bandaged and smeared with healing salves, limped or were carried in. The priestess chanted over them, and then, one by one, they went through the hole in the stone. If they could not crawl through by themselves, they were dragged through. After each had been slid like the end of a thread through the eye of a needle, he was examined by two doctors, a priestess and priest, who felt the bodies and heads of the injured. They then made signs to twenty young men who stood nearby. The men took some off to a nearby group of huts to convalesce. Others they removed on litters to a hut set some distance westward of the central village.

Hadon asked the reason for the segregation.

"You see the spirals on the inside of the hole in the

144

stone?" Qasin asked. "These are magical markings which collect the currents that pass through the body of the earth and the sea. They focus them, amplify them, build them up. The field of force is healing, and anybody who passes through it is healed of whatever ails them. Or, if healthy, then one becomes supercharged with the currents of goodness."

"Goodness?" Hadon asked.

"Yes," the chief answered. "To be good is to be healthy and vice versa. A man may be evil and yet seem to have perfect health, but he is not really healthy."

"What happens to those who were put in that hut to the west?"

"They are too far gone to benefit from the healing field in the hole," Qasin said. "They will be knocked on the head with specially blessed clubs—we don't want their ghosts haunting this raft—and then thrown into the sea."

"But—but—they may survive!" Hadon said.

"No, they won't," Qasin said. "The vicars of C'ak'oguq"o are sensitive to the aura which her stone lips radiate. They can feel the lack of the vital force; they shudder at the cold of dread Sisisken's hand on the flesh of the unfortunate. It is true that the sick might live for some time. But why drag out their pain and misery? Besides, we don't have a surplus of food aboard; we really can't afford to feed all these sailors. So..."

A few moments later the injured men were dragged out and their skulls shattered with stone axes. The lieutenant ran up to the slaughter and protested loudly. The chief made a sign with one hand and a young man swung his ax down on the head of the officer.

"We don't like people who interfere with our traditions," the chief said.

"I personally have always believed that a stranger should honor the customs of the people he finds himself among," Hadon said. But he felt sick when he turned away. Later he told himself that the killing of the officer was the best thing that could have happened. Now he could never report that the long-sought Hadon of Opar and the Witch-from-the-Sea were in Wethna.

This thought made him wonder about the fate of the sailors who had been spared. He asked Qasin about them.

"They will be questioned," Qasin said. "Those who are loyal to Kho, but who had to conceal their true feelings because they were in Minruth's service, will be allowed to step off the raft when we get to the coast. Those who would lift the Flaming God above his natural rank, who would degrade the White Goddess, Mother of All, will not be with us when we sight the shores of Wethna."

Further questioning disclosed that the raft carried no small ships which Hadon and his party could take for a faster voyage to the coast.

"You will have to remain here for the next two months," Qasin said. "Unless some ship comes near enough for us to hail and so put you aboard. That is not very likely to happen."

"Lalila is two months pregnant now," Hadon said. "She will be four months along when we get to Wethna. And it is a long and dangerous way to Opar from there. Ordinarily I would not worry about the time, since a galley or a swift sailing ship could get us there in two months. But there are pirates abroad now, and there is no Empire to maintain law. Every city is setting itself up to be independent, and many of the small towns and villages are eager to break away from the rule of the cities. We won't know what to expect whenever we put in to a port. Besides, from what I have heard, Minruth did leave enough ships and men to shut off the Strait of Keth, which means we'll have to go overland to Kethna. The peninsula is a wild, rough, dangerous area, mountainous, full of four- and two-legged predators. Five months is really not much time to get from Wethna to Opar under these conditions."

"True," Qasin said. "But why worry? You can do nothing until you get to Wethna. Meanwhile, enjoy yourself. Come to my hut. I will open a jug of s''okoko for us, and you will soon forget your troubles. Let us drift with the raft and enjoy life."

He grinned at Hadon with triangular teeth. He doubtless meant to show friendliness, but the smile still looked sinister.

21

Seventy days later, all of Hadon's party except for Ruseth left Wethna on a merchant sailing ship. Ruseth stayed behind, intending to embark the next day as deckhand on a merchant galley. Since his ship was lost, he considered that he was no longer under orders to take Lalila to Opar. He would return to Khokarsa and try to interest Awineth in building a fleet of fore-and aft sailing ships. He would say nothing to her, of course, about his part in getting Hadon and Lalila off the island.

"I'll go to Dythbeth," Ruseth had said. "Or I'll try to get into the city. By now it may have fallen. If Awineth is alive and uncaptured, I'll find her and talk her into building a new navy. If she is in a position to do so ... well, never mind. I'll see what I can do when I get there. If I get there. The Wethnans say there are many pirates now that the navy can no longer keep order on the high seas."

Hadon wished him luck, but he did not think Ruseth had much likelihood of success.

For that matter, his own chances were none too good. Neither of the two routes open was easy or free from perils. The regular way into the Sea of Opar was through the Strait of Keth. But this, according to Wethnan reports, was blockaded at its northern end. There were six triremes, four biremes and a number of smaller naval ships at anchor there. In addition, at least two hundred marines were stationed on the top of the cliffs forming the entrance to the strait. Minruth had ordered his fleet to remain on guard there, even though he needed them very much at Khokarsa.

Minruth knew well how ambitious the ruler of Kethna was. The kings of this city had always been overly independent, often arrogant, because they held the southern end of the strait. No ship could leave the Kemuwopar to carry its trade goods from Opar into the Kemu unless the Kethnan fleet permitted it to do so. And in times of troubles, the Kethnan fleets had ventured out into the Kemu and ravaged Khokarsan shipping and navies. A Kethnan expedition had in fact once raided the shores of Khokarsa itself and come very close to capturing the Emperor.

There was no communication from Kethna at the moment, but the authorities in Wethna expected the Kethnan fleet to come through the strait some day and attack the Khokarsan fleet. After all, the Kethnans had a much larger fleet available, and they could send an overland expedition against the marines holding the cliff exit.

Indeed, the main subject of conversation in the marketplace and on the docks was why Kethna had not already attacked. Some people speculated that Kethna had more immediate projects, such as defending itself against the pirates of Mikawuru. No one knew what the true situation was, since all communication had been cut off; of course this did not keep people from reporting all sorts of wild tales as the truth. It never had and never would.

Hadon considered going along the coast westward until they reached a small village about thirty miles east of the strait. Here they could disembark and proceed over the mountains of the peninsula to the Sea of Opar. They could make their way along the precipitous shore to the city of Kethna. And there, hopefully, they could buy passage on a merchant ship to Opar. Or else they could purchase a small sailing ship. Or, if they had no money, steal a vessel.

The main trouble with this plan was that the journey through the mountains, though relatively short, was known to be very dangerous. Of the two trails available, both were difficult to traverse and beset with wild beasts and outlaws. It was even said that a mountain-loving type of Nukaar, the hairy ape-men of the trees, dwelt in that area. Much was said about this land, none of it good.

Another route would be directly south of Wethna. This too

would be over mountains, and the passage through these would take about five times longer than the former route. Having crossed, however, the party would be much closer to Opar. They would, theoretically, come out close to the city of Wentisuh. From there they could take a ship or even a coastal boat to the port which served the inland city of Opar. After much asking about it in the bazaar and on the docks, however, Hadon decided against the second route. It was so dangerous that nobody knew of anyone who had ever used it successfully.

Paga suggested a third alternative.

"Why not take a small vessel into the strait under cover of night? If there is no moon, and the ship is little enough, we could slip by the big vessels. They won't be anchoring against the cliffs or across the mouth of the strait, you may be sure of that."

"No," Hadon said. "But the strait is very narrow; its only about eighty feet wide at the mouth. The cliffs on both sides reach a height of two hundred feet there, though the mountains immediately beyond them tower several thousand feet. If there are marines stationed on both sides, they can observe anything that passes through on the waters below. They will most assuredly have torches or lamps floating on buoys in the mouth of the strait, and these will enable the marines to see at night too. They will undoubtedly also have large rocks ready to be cast down on a ship, and flaming oil and Kho only knows what else. They will be able to summon the blockading ships by bell or signal fire or some means, who knows?

"Besides, there is nothing to prevent them from stretching a net across the mouth."

"Could we slip past the guards on either side above?" Lalila said. "Then walk along the top of the cliffs to the other end of the strait?"

"No," Hadon said. "The cliffs become sheer mountains. There are some plateaus further along, but I wouldn't know how to get to them. Besides, the wild Klemqaba roam those parts."

While he was deciding what to do, Hadon took a job as bodyguard for a rich Wethnan merchant. Kebiwabes picked up some money by singing in the streets and in the taverns. Paga apprenticed himself to a blacksmith. Though he did not earn much, he did learn a lot about the skill of working iron. This went on for thirty-five days, at the end of which there was enough money to buy passage to the village of Phetapoeth. There was not nearly enough, however, to buy a small ship for their purposes.

"It will take three more months just to save enough to buy a very small fishing skiff," Hadon said. "Lalila has about four months left before the baby comes. I doubt that we could get to Opar in a month's time—not with the troubled situation. But if we took passage on a ship to Phetapoeth now, we couldn't leave the village after we got there. There are no jobs there. So . . ."

"So we steal a ship!" Lalila said. "Or we go to Phetapoeth and then go over the mountains!"

"I think," Hadon said slowly, "that we will try to go through the strait after all. It is dangerous, but the least dangerous way."

"And if we can't get through, then we can try the mountain passes above Phetapoeth?" Lalila asked.

She looked anxious, and rightly so, since such a trip would make strong men look forward to it with anything but joy. For a pregnant woman and a little child to venture there with only a bard, a manling and Hadon—swordsman though he was—was madness, or not far from it.

Hadon felt angry. Somehow he had failed her, yet what else could he do? He was not one of the heroes of ancient times, Nakadeth, for instance, who could steal a pair of magical shoes from an evil spider and walk across the skies upside down, thus going over instead of around those very mountains.

Lalila, looking intently at him, said, "Do not be angry, Hadon. You cannot help it that you are only human."

He was astonished, not for the first time, at her ability to read his thoughts. Sometimes he wondered if she was indeed a witch from the sea. The idea made him proud that such a woman would love him, yet, at the same time, it made him feel uneasy too, thinking of certain undesirable thoughts he'd had. For instance, if Lalila could read his thoughts when he saw the beautiful wife of the merchant for whom he was working, what would she do?

Come to think of it, she always had a rather peculiar smile at these times.

"What's the matter now, Hadon?" Lalila said.

"Oh!" he said, staring. "Nothing. I was just trying to envision the strait as I saw it some years ago."

She had that same peculiar smile.

He went to the docks that night after his shift. He inquired around, found a dockmaster and asked him about passage to Phetapoeth.

"Why would you want to take your woman and child to that Kho-forsaken place?" the dockmaster asked. "There's no work for a *numatenu* there. Besides, too many ships have disappeared on their way there. There are pirates along that route, honored swordsman. They lurk in every little bay and cove, ready to dash out and intercept any ship that looks like easy prey."

Hadon hesitated. His first impulse had been to tell the man that he was sticking his nose up the ape's ass.* He checked himself, however, because he did not want to anger the fellow. If he became suspicious of Hadon, he could notify the authorities and they could—no, would—arrest him for questioning. As in all countries, the spy-hunting fever was raging. Wethna was theoretically neutral, having declared for neither Awineth nor Minruth. This placed Wethna in a delicate situation, since whoever triumphed might decide to punish Wethna for not having taken a definite stand. In fact, Hadon thought, this would inevitably occur. The city fathers and mothers should have gone one way or the other, even if they had had to resort to tossing a coin.

The reasoning for Wethna's neutrality was the hope that the winner would be grateful to them for not fighting on the side of the enemy. Hadon considered this very unrealistic. Kings and queens always regarded the person who was not for

* A literal translation of a widespread Khokarsan phrase. This is based on an old folk tale which is too repulsive even for the standards of modern American publishing. However, like most old jokes, it originated in the Old Stone Age and is found, in one form or another, in all countries.

them as against them. And history had verified that retaliation for less than wholehearted backing was a terrible thing. Entire cities had been leveled and their population, man, woman and beast, had been slaughtered because of lukewarm loyalty.

This was not, however, Hadon's concern. Even if it was he would have forgotten it because of a sudden and much more immediate worry. Five days before the group was to leave on a merchant galley, plague struck Wethna.

No one knew who brought the disease into Wethna, but most supposed that some sailors were responsible. It did not matter. What did was that this particular plague, called the sweating sickness, spread with frightening swiftness. And it killed with even more terrifying speed.

Kebiwabes was the first of the group to hear of it. He hurried home from a tavern at which he had been singing. He was bursting to tell the news, which was that several dozen people on the docks had been laid low with the disease. He found Hadon in its grip.

It ran its course in the usual three days. First Hadon was seized with an unaccountable sense of dread, a sense of overpowering but nameless doom. About fifteen minutes later he began shivering violently. He felt as if he had suddenly been plunged into the icy waters of a mountain lake. Then he became dizzy, suffered an agonizing headache and great pain in his neck, shoulders, arms and legs. He was unable to lift even his head.

Three hours later he felt like he was on fire and began the profuse sweating which lasted for a day and a night. The perspiring stopped suddenly, but it was followed by more headache, intense thirst, a rapid beating of the heart and then delirium.

At the end of its course, Hadon was free of the plague's symptoms but was forced to stay in bed for four days because of extreme weakness. He was unattended by any doctor during this whole time. Though the bard and Lalila took turns looking for a physician while Hadon was nursed by one or the other, they could not get one. The doctors were either too busy to come or were themselves sick or dead. His friends could only nurse him and hope for the best. Lalila and Paga took turns squeezing water from a rag over his feverish body and lifting his head so he could drink great quantities of water.

The noise of the streets outside, the chatter and yelling of nearby pedestrians and the not too distant sounds of the marketplace, had died. Except for the tramping of feet and muffled booming of a drum as patrols passed, or the cry of the corpse-collectors to bring out the dead, all was quiet. Now and then a man or a woman screamed or a child cried.

A day after Hadon's sickness passed, Kebiwabes was seized with the irresistible sensation of impending death. Lalila and Paga now had two patients to take care of, though Hadon was no longer a constant concern.

The bard did not die during the first day, which meant he would probably survive.

Lalila and Paga had to take turns going out after water and food. The bazaar was closed, the sellers having fled to their homes or out into the country. But there was food to be had if one had enough money. A few merchants had set up a market on the docks, guarded by soldiers who would admit only those who could show their money. Once Lalila was robbed on her way home by a hungry trio. She was knocked down and her basket was grabbed and run off with. She made two trips that day, taking Paga with her the second time. She did not like to leave the convalescent and the sick one without any care, but if they did not get food, they would die anyway.

Sometimes, when the wind shifted, they could smell the odor of bodies burning in the great charnel pit outside the west wall. Then the giant bronze bells in the temples of Kho and Resu would toll sadly.

Lalila and Paga waited to be struck, thinking it inevitable. But neither was felled, and the child also escaped the malady. Abeth did become ill four weeks later, though with a sickness which resembled typhus.

The sweating disease raged through the city, slaying ten thousand out of a population of fifty thousand. At least a third of the city fled into the country as soon as the disease gained momentum. They took it with them, of course, and it spread through the rural areas. Eighty thousand farmers, fishermen, woodcutters and artisans died. The whole land of Wethna lay under a pall of stinking smoke from corpse-fires.

Among the victims was the beautiful wife of the rich merchant. He had stayed in the city, gathering the profits from his food supplies. She went to their villa up in the hills and was killed, not by the sweating sickness, but from snakebite. She encountered a cobra while strolling in her garden one evening.

In seven weeks the sickness had passed through the land and was gone. The survivors came out of hiding and began to put the nation together again.

Abeth's sickness passed, leaving her thin and listless. Not until almost two months after they had arrived at Wethna was the child fit for travel.

Hadon had gone back to work for the merchant since they needed money desperately. His position as bodyguard enabled him to overhear many of the details of his employer's business. He learned about a small fishing boat which the merchant had purchased at a low sum from the widow of a man who'd died of the plague. After looking it over, Hadon decided it was just the size he needed. He bought it at a fair price and still had money saved to rerig the boat. The men he hired to do the work evidently thought he was crazy. What was the yard attached to near the bottom of the mast and running lengthwise? What was the purpose of this? And why was he cutting a perfectly good sail diagonally, so that he now had two useless triangular sails?

Hadon smiled and said he was trying an experiment. He did not tell the truth because of what Ruseth had said about people's reactions to his own ship. He did not want to be suspected of sorcery and subjected to a court of inquiry.

One morning, an hour after midnight, he and the others took the boat out of the harbor. By dawn they were out of sight of the city. Hadon did not worry about being pursued. Who could care that he left? His employer would just shrug his shoulders and count himself lucky that he did not have to pay him for the last week—until he found that Hadon had charged his account for the provisions. The two sums balanced each other, so Hadon figured he had not done anything dishonest.

They reached the strait in five days. Before then, though, they knew something had happened there. They saw the wreck of a beached trireme, and two miles further on they came across a number of corpses floating over a wide area. Hadon took the vessel up boldly in daylight to the very mouth. There was no sign of a fleet until he got close to the entrance of the strait. The stern of a bireme jutted up from the water, almost blocking off the passage of Hadon's craft. He could not understand what was keeping the ship from sinking, since the depth here was about four hundred feet.

He had the sails dropped, and they rowed slowly past the wreck and the western wall. The sun was directly overhead at this time, enabling them to see for some distance down into the water. Hadon whistled and Kebiwabes swore. The galley was held up by a score of other ships, piled one on top of each other.

"There must have been a hell of a battle here," Hadon said. "But who tried to get out? The Kethnans?"

"More than likely," the bard said. "They have tried to run the gauntlet of the marines on the cliffs. And some must have made it, otherwise Minruth's fleet would still be here. They must have closed with the blockaders then, and in the battle everybody was sunk."

That seemed the only logical explanation, though it could be pirates who came through the strait, not Kethnans. Who it was did not matter; the way was clear. The marines stationed above had either deserted their posts or been killed by the invading fleet. Maybe a Khokarsan ship or two had survived the battle and taken the marines home, since one ship could not maintain the blockade.

The strait was still going to be closed to any vessel larger than a small fishing boat for some time. Eventually the current would move the wrecks on out into the deeper waters, or else the Kethnans would clear the top wrecks. Meanwhile, Hadon and his crew, not even excepting Lalila, who was far gone in pregnancy, rowed the boat through the fifty dark, silent miles of the winding strait. Because of their short-handedness they made slow progress, having to sleep at night. It took them over a week to get their vessel through, during which they worried about pirates or Kethnans. They were done for if they encountered another craft of any size. It would be impossible to flee.

But no one else was in the strait and, on the tenth day, they came out against the current from the darkness and the silence. Like Keth, the ancient hero who first entered the Southern Sea, they were dazzled by the brightness of the equatorial sun.

Hadon said, "Lalila! I was afraid our child would not be born in Opar. But now we have a good chance to make it on time. If Kho is with us, we shall be in my native city a week before your term is up."

Lalila smiled, though she looked tired, wan and anxious. Paga, forever the pessimist, growled, "Babies do not always come on schedule, Hadon."

22

Kebiwabes said that their journey from Khokarsa to Wethna had enough material for two epics. The voyage from Wethna to Opar had enough adventures to make three epics, and it wasn't even finished. Hadon, in a typical statement, replied that all bards exaggerated enormously, though their experiences since the flight from the capital of Khokarsa could easily make one epic, if the bard was long-winded enough.

"And I suppose," Kebiwabes said, "that you would compress all of the adventures into a lyric, into nine or twenty-seven lines?"

"That would be the ultimate in poetry," Hadon said. Then, seeing that the bard looked hurt, he added, "Don't pay any attention to what I say now, Kebiwabes. I am tired and hungry and anxious, since Lalila is so swelled that she seems about to burst like an overloaded wine sack. And I am taking my frustration and fear out on you."

"Not to mention that you have no taste," Kebiwabes said. He walked to the other end of the boat, which wasn't very far, and looked out ahead. His back expressed his anger.

What the bard had said was not really too exaggerated. There had been many times when Hadon thought they would all be dead within a minute. But somehow, with mighty Kho giving them invisible yet evident help, they had come through.

There had been other times when no danger pressed close, yet they felt imperiled. Just three days before, at dusk, their boat was passing close to a desolate marshy region, swamps which stretched inland for miles, then abruptly ended at

157

sheer mountains. The only protuberance between the sea and the mountains was a hilly mass about a mile inward. Hadon was telling them that this was supposed to be the site of an ancient city.

"It was founded by Bessem, the exiled son of Keth. He quarreled with his father and then killed his brother in a rage, so he was forced to flee. Keth did not go after him—he was an old man then, almost sixty—but he proclaimed that if Bessem came back, he was to be slain instantly, without trial. So Bessem traveled south along this coast and stopped when he got here. This was not a marsh at that time, but a lowland which sloped gently to the mountains. And here Bessem built a city of red stone quarried from the mountains. It was called, of course, Mibessem, the city of Bessem.

"All went well. Many people came from Kethna and Sakawuru and from the Northern Sea, the Kemu, to live in the city of giant stone blocks. This was when the Sea of Opar was almost unknown and Mikethna was itself only a small colony. In fact it was about the same time that the priestess Lupoeth led an expedition into the hinterland and found the place which would later become Opar, city of treasures.

"Though the city of Mibessem prospered, however, there were at the same time unsettling stories told of something which lived in the mountains beyond the city. It was said to play a reed flute, its music driving men mad and enchanting women so they followed the player into the mountain forests and were never seen again. Misshapen creatures would be seen at dusk, near the limits of the farmlands around the city, and these, though they seemed bestial, resembled some of the women who had wandered away.

"It was said that Bessem, in an ill-advised moment, had chosen to build his city in the land of a demon. And it was said that this demon was in fact the chief of demons, the leader of those nameless creatures whom mighty Kho scourged from the Kemu so that Her people might settle there. The demons who were not killed or buried so deeply underground that they would not be able to dig their way back until the crack of doom—these demons fled into the land along the Southern Sea.

"And so now the nameless demon was angry because his

refuge had been invaded. Yet he was under the ancient restraint imposed by great Kho on his kind. He could not lay a hand or a paw or a tentacle on a human being in anger. What the Mother of All had failed to do, however, was to prohibit the nameless ones from using other methods. Moreover, a demon could touch, or even embrace, a human if it did not do it in anger or with intent to harm. And so the flutist of the shadows, the distorted one, the nameless one who breathes at night outside windows, this thing played his reed flute. And men went crazy and women followed him into the burrow near the mountains. And there they laid strangely with it and conceived and bore hideous children.

"Now Bessem was a hero of old, you understand, a mighty man whose like the two seas have not seen for centuries. So he armed himself with a spear that two strong men today could not pick up, and he strode into the wilderness to find the nameless thing and destroy it. But he did not come back, and the flute played again in the fields outside the city. Sailors told about this in Kethna and the ports of the Kemu.

"And so one day the Empress of Khokarsa sent a ship to Mibessem to determine if the stories she had heard were indeed true. If they were, a priestess was to rid the land of the demon. The ship took a year to get to Kethna because of storms and troubles with pirates. There the captain was told that he was too late. A Kethnan merchantman putting into the port of Mibessem at dusk had heard weird blood-chilling music from a reed flute. It was heard miles over the still sea, long before the lookout could see the red city. In fact he never did see it, since he had mistaken the dark hill where it once stood. Or perhaps he saw its outer shell, the earth piled up over it by the nameless demon. No one knows, because no one has ever dared enter the swamp and dig into the hill.

"And so the ship neared the shore, which was no longer a fine sand beach but a swamp. The gentle slope had subsided into a perfect flatness, and crocodiles and hippopotamuses swam among the palm trees and the other trees growing on little islets.

"Where were the people? No one knew, but it was feared they had met some terrible fate and were lying under the waters of the swamp. Or perhaps under the earth that something evil and irresistible had thrown over the once-proud towers and massive walls of Mibessem.

"In any event, the crew of the ship did not stay long. The fluting became louder and louder, and they heard a splash as of mighty feet in the swamp. The trees bent as though something gigantic was brushing against them. Even the priestess became frightened, and the captain shouted at his rowers to get the galley out of there. They did escape whatever was walking in the swamp, but they did not outrun the noise of the flute until they had put many miles between them and the former land of Mibessem."

Hadon stopped. The only sound was the wind whistling through the rigging and the splash of water against the bow. And then, sending utter terror into them, there came from the shore the music of a flute.

Abeth screamed. Kebiwabes swore and turned pale beneath his sunbronze. Lalila's large violet eyes became even larger. Paga grabbed some shrouds and clung to them while he stared inland, his eyes huge and the nostrils of his flat nose distended. Hadon gripped the tiller as if it were the only real thing in the world. All else seemed wavy, slightly distorted, impalpable. Until that moment he had been enjoying the story, scaring himself and the others. Paga, of course, had looked skeptical and he had several times snorted disbelief. But evidently he had been more impressed than he had let on.

The sun disappeared below the horizon of the sea. Darkness fell swiftly. The shrilling notes became louder.

Hadon came out of his freeze and gave orders, quietly, so that the player in the swamps, whatever it was, would not hear him. He moved the tiller until the boat swung southwest. The boom traveled around, restrained by ropes in the hands of Paga and Kebiwabes. Hadon kept her steady, not coming around to beat back until the music had disappeared for an hour.

After a while Paga asked, "What do you suppose it was? Some fisherboy playing his flute?"

Hadon replied, "There are no fisherfolk, no villages, in this area. No one would dare live here."

"Maybe some fishing boat was driven into the swamp by a

160

storm," Paga said. "Maybe it was wrecked. One of the survivors, perhaps the only one, used his flute to attract our attention."

"He could have done that better by shouting," Hadon said. "Do you want us to go back there to look for him?"

Paga did not reply. The others said nothing, but they would not have kept silent, it was evident, if Hadon had put the boat about. He had no intention of doing that.

The subject was not brought up again. It seemed best to everyone that they talk no more about the unknown flutist.

23

The pillar of smoke they saw all day was not from the port of Opar, Nangukar. That place had already been burned down and the ashes cooled by the rain. This smoke was from a pyre of pirate corpses. Eighty Mikawuru had been slain during the pirate raid. The attackers had been beaten off but had managed to rescue twenty of their dead. They had sailed off, leaving sixty of their fellows and a town in flames. The pirate corpses were being consumed by flames now, which meant their souls would flit through the clouds until Kho decided they had suffered enough as phantom nomads, driven by the winds. Then their ghosts would be sent down into the earth to awful Sisisken's dark house.

As Hadon swung his boat to the beach—all the quays were destroyed—he was stunned. All the buildings around the fort were burned. The huts and houses, the long halls, the warehouses, the stores and taverns, everything was in ashes. The two great wooden gates of the fort had been torn off, and some of the wooden buildings inside the walls had been leveled by fire.

Rebuilding had already started. The place was a buzz and yell of labor, with wagons full of newly cut lumber or bamboo, drawn by oxen, everywhere. Hammers and saws pounded and screeched.

Hadon anchored the boat about a hundred yards offshore. A longboat paddled by four men put out from the beach toward the newly arrived craft. Hadon bargained with the owner and presently all were being ferried to shore. Here a customs officer started to question them, then stopped as he recognized Hadon.

"How did you get here all the way from Khokarsa!" he cried.

"Kho Herself, through Her Voice, ordered me to return to my native city," Hadon said. "It was to fulfill a prophecy and so, though the way was long and dangerous, we are here."

The officer did not ask him what the prophecy was. He would have been indiscreet to probe into matters involving the Goddess.

"If things had gone a little differently," the officer said, "you might have arrived just in time to fall into the hands of the pirates. They were having their own way, storming the fort and breaking into the central keep. Fortunately about three hundred men had been ordered from Opar to reinforce the port just in case something like this happened. We caught the Mikawuru from the rear, and the garrison sallied out and attacked them from the front. They fought their way out and got to their ships, but their casualties were very heavy. We captured forty, most of whom were wounded."

Hadon did not ask what would happen to the captives. He knew that their chiefs would be tortured to get information about plans for future attacks. Torture of pirate leaders was a custom, based on the principle that it exacted vengeance. After all possible information was obtained, the chiefs would be beheaded and the able rank and file sent off as slaves to the mines in the hills above Opar. The badly wounded, the crippled, would be beheaded.

"You are the latest to get here from Khokarsa," the officer said. "We are hungry for news."

Hadon tried to tell him that he knew very little outside of rumors. He had been too isolated and so could not say truthfully what had happened. This made no difference. The people wanted to hear everything, fact, surmise, rumor, obvious untruth. The party was hustled in through the gateway and to the temple, where Hadon saw the head priestess, Klyhy, for the first time in years. She was still as beautiful as the night he and she had lain together, the night before Hadon was to embark for the Great Games at the city of Khokarsa. She had put on some weight, and her large shapely breasts had sagged a little, but the great gray eyes, the thick dark eyebrows, the long narrow nose, the full lips, the rounded chin, these formed one of the most beautiful and sensual faces Hadon had ever seen.

She smiled at Hadon and rose from her diamond-encrusted chair. See wore a tall thin crown of gold set with nine emeralds on the scalloped edges, a rosary of emeralds and rubies and an ankle-length skirt of white cloth. Her belt was of gold links adorned with tiny rubies. Her bare breasts were painted in concentric circles, red, white and blue, the nipples forming the red centers. She held in her right hand a long staff of oak wood, imported from Khokarsa. Its upper end held the carved representation of Kho as a steatopygic hippopotamus-headed woman.

"Thrice welcome, Hadon of Opar!" she cried. "He who should be Emperor by all rights but whom Kho decreed should not hold that rank! And thrice welcome, Lalila from beyond the Ringing Sea, the Witch-from-the-Sea! Welcome also to your daughter, of whom we have heard much, and to the unborn child, of whom much will be heard. Welcome also to the little man, though he claims to be an enemy of our sex, and to Kebiwabes, the bard who would be great!"

Hadon was not surprised at this greeting. The intelligence system of the priestesses was exceedingly good, and thus it was to be expected that Klyhy would have learned much about his party and his mission. There was probably very little he could tell her that was new, except for their adventures at Rebha and afterward.

Chairs were brought in by initiate priestesses and the party sat down. Abeth was taken off with the children of the temple. Food, mead and wine were offered and eagerly accepted. Klyhy questioned Hadon until, by the time he had eaten and drunk his fill, his tale was told. Silence fell for a while, broken only by belches from the guests, politely indicating that they found the food excellent.

Finally Klyhy said, "I have already sent a messenger to Opar to inform the Queen that you and Lalila are here. The messenger will reserve the news for the ear of the Queen alone. And I have also ordered Kaheli"—the customs officer who had talked to Hadon—"to tell no one that you are here."

Hadon, alarmed, said, "Why is that?"

"King Gamori has found out that you are—were—on the way here. He has many spies, not all of whom are priests of Resu. You see, Hadon, the schism which has rent the Empire in the Kemus is also working here. Gamori is a very ambitous man, like Minruth, and he too would like to elevate the Flaming God above the Great Mother—not for religious reasons but for ambition's sake. But we also have our spies and we know some of what passes between Gamori and the lesser priests of Resu. We know that Gamori loathes being subordinate to his wife. At the moment, indeed, Gamori and our high priestess, Queen Phebha, are no longer living together. They have parted after years of an unhappy marriage, quarreling on policy and the relative status of king and queen, of man and woman. Gamori is now living in the Temple of Resu, and he has not bedded Phebha for a year. He only appears with her at state functions.

"Also, as you are well aware, Gamori has never liked your father, Kumin. This stems from that fight in the tunnels against the outlaws when the old king, Phebha's first husband, was killed. Before your father lost an arm in that battle, he had, according to Gamori, tried to kill him. Your father claims that it was an accident, that the poor light and the heat of combat caused him to mistake Gamori for an outlaw. This is reasonable. Why should Kumin try to kill one of his comrades? Gamori claimed that he and your father had quarreled bitterly about something—what doesn't matter now—and that Kumin was trying to slay him because of this.

"Whatever the truth, Gamori then married Phebha and became King and high priest, in a position to persecute your father. It was only Phebha's protection which kept your father from being charged with attempted murder."

"I know that too well," Hadon said. "My father had to take a job inside the Temple of Kho, from which he seldom ventured because of fear that Gamori's men would murder him. My father, once one of the greatest *numatenu* of the Empire, was reduced to sweeping the temple floors for a living. Not that he was not grateful to Phebha for the work. If it hadn't been for her, we all would have starved to death.

Gamori was very upset that I was one of the three youths to win the honor of representing Opar in the Great Games. He hates my whole family because of his old grudge against my father."

"Which is why Gamori must not know you are here," Klyhy said. "You see, there is another reason why Gamori would not want you to get to Opar alive or, once there, to take sanctuary in the Temple of Kho. Through his spies he has heard of Lalila, this Witch-from-the-Sea. He knows that great things are expected of her child. Rumors—unfounded of course, but still potent—rumors are that the child will be the sole ruler of Opar, that there will be no more kings here. This is ridiculous, but Gamori is frightened. Unreasoning beast that he is, he does not see that the child could be no possible danger to him; he will be dead before she attains her majority.

"On the other hand, the rumors may be correct in a sense. If Gamori attempts to harm her, he is liable to precipitate the very danger he fears. He will cause a confrontation which might have been avoided."

"What are we supposed to do?" Hadon said.

"You will stay here until nightfall. Then all of you will be escorted out of here, as inconspicuously as possible. You will be smuggled into Opar and thence to the Temple of Kho. Once inside the temple, you will be safe. Not even Gamori would dare violate its holiness."

"At one time I would have said that was a safe thing to bet on," Hadon said. "But Minruth has violated many of the temples, not to mention the priestesses. Nothing is safe from blasphemy or profanement nowadays."

"You may be right," Klyhy said. "But you can't stay here. According to the Voice of Kho, Lalila must bear her child in the temple. From her appearance, I would say that she has very little time to get there."

She picked up a little bronze gong from a recess in the arm of the chair and struck it with a tiny bronze hammer, the head of which was fashioned like a leopard's. At the third stroke a curtain at the far entrance parted. A boy of about four years of age was ushered into the chamber by a middle-aged priestess. He ran toward Klyhy crying, "Mommy! Mommy!"

She picked him up and kissed him, then turned smiling to Hadon.

"This is the fruit of our love, Hadon," she said. "He is our son, Kohr."

24

It took three days to travel up the river from the sea to the cataract. Hadon's party was in a longboat paddled by ten strong soldiers. Klyhy rode in the lead boat with the little boy. Sometimes she asked Abeth to get into her boat so the two children could play together. And sometimes she had Hadon sit by her side in the prow so they could talk. Several times Lalila sat with her.

Lalila had been as surprised at the presentation of Kohr as Hadon. She had not, however, been jealous, knowing there was no reason for her to be. Klyhy had no designs on Hadon, nor any desire to take him away from Lalila. She had merely taken Hadon as a lover for several nights, not using sterility herbs during that time. She had wanted a child by a man who might win the Great Games. Klyhy had had many lovers before Hadon and many since and would have many more still.

"A dream convinced me that Hadon should be the father," she told Lalila. "Bhukla, the ancient goddess of war before Resu usurped her functions, appeared to me. She said I should lie with Hadon and conceive by him. I didn't need any orders for the first act, though I was happy to have divine sanction. As for the second, I felt that it was time I had a child anyway."

"And now," Lalila said, "what about Kohr? Does he stay with you or go with Hadon?"

Klyhy looked astonished. Then she said, "Oh, yes, I forgot! You would not be familiar with all our customs. If I should decide to get married soon, Kohr would stay with me and my husband. I don't plan to do that so, at the age of five, he will go to live with his father half of the year. You will be his mother-substitute during that period. If I should die, then Kohr becomes Hadon's full-time child. And yours."

The evening of the fourth day, they camped at the foot of the great falls. Here were a number of other people, members of trading caravans from Opar on their way to the port. At the advice of Klyhy, Hadon stayed in his tent as much as possible. If he was recognized, one of the priests of Resu might turn around and hasten back to Opar with the news.

Hadon, sitting in the tent, saw at least ten people he had known well in Opar. Others he remembered as being citizens of that city. Since he had lived all his life in Opar until a few years ago, he was a familiar figure there. After all, Opar had a permanent population of only thirty thousand. Since he had won the Lesser Games, he was familiar to all.

His tent was not struck until after the caravans had left downriver, then the party proceeded up the road cut along the face of the cliff. At noon they had reached the top and from there walked over the jungle path until they reached a docking area. Here were longboats left by the travelers they had met below the falls. They took two of the smallest and the soldiers bent their backs again. It was hard work because they rowed against the current all the way. They took three days, passing along bush-covered banks, occasionally coming to muddy flats where crocodiles gaped and bellowed or slid oozily into the brown river. At night they camped at walled places, sitting by large fires, hearing the coughs of leopards. They all stank abominably, having smeared themselves with hog fat to deter the multitudes of mosquitoes.

Four times they passed fleets of longboats laden with goods, heading for the port. Hadon ducked down when this happened, hoping the wide-brimmed hat he wore would keep his face hidden.

"Now that the Strait of Keth is closed, where are the goods going?" Hadon asked Klyhy.

"There are still Kethna, Wentisuh and Sakawuru," she said. "Though the pirates of Mikawuru are on the rampage, commerce still goes on. Moreover, a new settlement has been founded south of the Kemuwopar. Kartenkloe. It's purely a mining community so far; there is much copper and some gold down there. But it is the gateway to the savannas beyond the mountains, where great herds of elephants roam. The ivory trade is expected to become enormous, and Kartenkloe will handle everything passing through. It is ruled by Opar, and so Opar will get most of the profits. Some of those goods you saw are headed for Kartenkloe."

Hadon looked at the boy. Kohr was certainly his son: he had the same curly red-bronze hair, the same high and narrow forehead, slightly swelling at the corners. His ears were small and close to his head and somewhat pointed at the tips. His eyebrows were thick, almost joined. His nose was straight and not overlong, though he was too young for development of a long nose. His upper lip was short, his lips were full but not thick, and his chin was clefted.

His legs were long in relation to his torso and his arms seemed very long. He would have his father's stride and reach.

His eyes, however, were his mother's, large and dark gray.

"A beautiful child," Klyhy said, catching Hadon's look. "I love him very much. But I fear I will not be his mother very long."

"What do you mean?" Hadon said. She was an exceptionally merry person, always smiling and laughing. But now she looked grave.

"Shortly before you came to the port, I had a dream. I was in a dark place deep under the ground, wandering through a tunnel of some sort. And something terrible was chasing me. It caught me. Then I woke up, trembling, crying."

"But you were not slain in the dream?"

"No. But I had a feeling of unavoidable doom."

She smiled and said, "Now that you are here to take care of him, I am not worried. As for what may happen to me, well, no one lives forever. And I am getting fat, my breasts are starting to sag; I look in the mirror and see a face that can still attract lovers but in another ten years will turn them away. I have lived a good life, much better than most people have. And if I should die at this moment, I would be unhappy only because my son would grieve for me."

"If everybody had your attitude," Hadon said, "this world might not be such a miserable place."

"There wouldn't be any wars," she said. "Or so many going mad."

When Hadon had made his trip downriver, it had taken four days to reach the cataracts and three to get to the port from the falls. Going against the current, it took four to get to the falls and five and a half to Opar. An hour after high noon, the longboats rounded a curve of the river. The stream, which had been a quarter of a mile wide, suddenly widened out to a lake a mile and a half across. To their right was a narrow strip of flatland beyond which the cliffs rose abruptly. Past the cliffs were towering peaks. On the left, a mile away, was Opar. Opar, city of fabulous treasures, gold and jewels, gold-sheeted towers, minarets and domes, high massive walls of granite. Opar, his native city.

Tears filled his eyes. He felt a hurt in his breast; a sob burst loose from him. Lalila, seeing him so moved, put her arm around his waist and pulled his face down to kiss his cheek.

The longboats remained in the center of the stream until they had put half a mile behind them. Then they headed at an angle to their former course toward the city. There was much traffic here, fishing boats, skiffs and longboats carrying the produce of farms along the western shore north of Opar. This valley was long and relatively narrow, extending for fifteen miles until it terminated in a great falls to the north.

The western shore was flatter and broader than the eastern, but then the foothills began and after them the mighty peaks, tall as those to the east.

A mile directly due east of the city was an islet, the only one in the lake. Trees ringed its circumference; its inner part was dominated by a white domed temple. The islet was tenanted by only three people, priestesses who served the shrine of Lupoeth. The islet was the first place the explorer-priestess Lupoeth had stepped in the valley. It was there that she had met the first inhabitants of the valley, the primitive Gokako. And it was there that she had asked one what the name of the place was. And he, replying in his own language, had said "*Opar*," meaning, "I don't understand you." Lupoeth had named this valley Opar, mistakenly thinking that was its native name. Later, the settlement had also been named Opar.

The islet was also where the priestess had died at the advanced age of seventy. She had been deified, a temple erected to her. The Isle of Lupoeth, like that of the goddess Karneth, was taboo to males.

The boats glided through the paths of others and passed the wooden shacks and longhouses built outside the city walls. These extended for half a mile westward and a quarter of a mile inland. They were the homes of the Gokako slaves and freemen, and the human supervisors, foremen and soldiers who kept them in order. There were also large warehouses fronting on the wooden quays. Above the northern walls was a similar wooden city, but this housed the poorer classes, all freemen and human.

Hadon tied the strings of his hat under his jaw. The wind was blowing strongly today, and it would not do to have the hat sail off and reveal his hair and face. To further the concealment, he had tied a black patch over his left eye. His *numatenu* sword was wrapped in a blanket. He carried it over his shoulder along with a flat box of some trade goods. He was to trail behind Klyhy as if he were her servant.

The longboats tied up at a wooden quay belonging to the Temple of Kho. The priestess waited until they were ready to leave and then strode boldly along the street outside the wall. A soldier opened a parasol of bamboo and ran up to hold it over her; another beat a small drum; a third played a reed flute. Klyhy would have preferred to go quietly but, since many would recognize her, she thought it best to go in accustomed style. Otherwise people might have wondered why she was trying to be so unnoticeable.

The outer wall was fifty feet in height and composed of cyclopean granite blocks veined with pink quartz. Midway in the eastern wall was a gateway, wide enough for twenty men shoulder to shoulder to march through. The two gates were of massive bronze, ten feet thick, bearing scenes from Oparian history in high-relief. The gates had only been closed three times since being put up eight hundred years ago. They had been dashed to the ground three times, however, each time by an earthquake. The city itself had been rebuilt thrice and

172

doubtless would be built many times again.

The travelers passed through the marketplace, which stretched along the riverfront for half a mile. This was much like any other market-bazaar in the Empire except for the presence of so many Gokako. These hairy people—short, squat, thick-necked, massively chested, slant-browed—were once numerous, but were now found only in this valley, though it was said that wild ones were to be found elsewhere in the Southern Sea.

On both sides of the gateway were spearmen. Each contingent numbered thirty: those on the left were the King's; the other, the Queen's.

Klyhy did not check her pace but proceeded as if she were on open and honest business. Which, indeed, Hadon thought, she would be if Gamori would be trusted. The officers of the guards saluted her; she blessed them and went on. The party went past the outer wall, twenty feet thick, and came to the inner wall. This was equally high but was topped with alternating small round towers and pointed granite monoliths. The towers held sentries; the monoliths memorialized the heroes and heroines of Opar. There should be two set up in his honor, Hadon thought, since he had won both the Lesser and the Great Games. They would be further down the line, however, out of view.

The inner gateway was also open, its ponderous bronze gates swung aside. They walked out onto the broad Avenue of the Deities-as-Birds. This was one hundred and fifty feet wide, much of it occupied by another market. Here many of the animals and birds on sale were to be sacrificed in the Temple of Kho across the street.

Klyhy led them through the stalls, pens and sheds past the noisy beasts, birds and noisier merchants and customers. Her goal was the gigantic nonagonal doorway in the temple, a massive granite-blocked pile capped with a gargantuan onion-shaped dome, covered with sheets of gold. On both sides of the doorway were three rows of granite monoliths, twelve in a row. Each was twice as tall as Hadon, and each was carved at the upper end into the shape of a bird. The attributes of the birds, all modeled on real ones, had been exaggerated and distorted. The heads were larger or smaller than normal, the beaks more curved or even twisted, the eyes numbered from one to nine, the feathers were too long or too broad, the claws enormous or sometimes nonexistent.

Though they seemed to have been carved by a demented person, they became intelligible after a close look. All represented birds turning into human beings, stages of various metamorphoses.

Hadon had been nervous and sweating ever since they had left the boat. Now, only twenty feet away from the doorway to the temple, he began to breathe easier. His mouth was still dry, but he could drink from the fountain that jetted just within the entrance.

And then he heard a call: "Hadon! Hadon!"

He turned and saw an old friend, Sembes, a childhood playmate and competitor at the Lesser Games. He had been eliminated during the wrestling matches by Hadon, but he had not been angry. When Hadon left for Khokarsa, in fact, Sembes had given him a gift and his good wishes.

But things might have changed now. Or Sembes might be under orders; he would be a good officer and do his duty, even if he was reluctant to obey.

Hadon was forewarned by Sembes' uniform, which was that of a lieutenant of the guard of the Temple of Resu, the Flaming God.

Sembes should have been smiling on seeing a friend who had been absent for years, but perhaps he was in a slight case of shock. Certainly his voice had been tight, as if he was under a great strain.

Behind him was a squad, twelve spearmen.

He strode toward Hadon, holding out his hand. His face seemed to break, then reform, then break again. His eyes looked narrow and bright and they shifted from Hadon to Klyhy to the rest of the party and back to Hadon.

"Listen, Hadon! I just happened to be patrolling this area and behold! I see you! I thought you were in Khokarsa!"

Behind Hadon, Lalila murmured, "Beware, Hadon! He is lying! He stinks of fear!"

Klyhy had stopped. Now she hissed like a snake and said, "Lalila is right! Someone saw you at the dock, Hadon, and sped to the King! His spies are everywhere!"

"Greetings, my old friend!" Hadon said. He eased the burden from his shoulder and put his hand within the blanket on its top. His fingers closed round the hilt of Karken, a piece of elephant ivory carved with ridges for better gripping.

Sembes stopped and said, "What happened to your eye, Hadon?"

Hadon said, "I have been resting it," and he ripped off the patch. To Klyhy, he said softly, "Get the others into the temple."

Sembes put his hand on the hilt of his sword, a heavy weapon of expensive carbonized iron formed from welded strips. It had the same leaf shape as the enlisted men's but was about a foot longer.

"So you know!" Sembes said, his eyebrows going up. "Well, I am indeed sorry, Hadon, but I have orders. You are under arrest for suspicion of treason!"

Hadon waited a moment before replying. Lalila, holding Abeth's and Kohr's hands, hurried behind him toward the doorway. Sembes' eyes shifted to her for a minute, but evidently he had no instructions concerning her. Paga was rolling after her, scowling, his hand on the hilt of his short sword. Kebiwabes hesitated, then said, "Officer, I am a bard and so my person is sacred." He added, "Inviolate in the eyes of great Kho and of all humankind."

"Stand aside then," Sembes said. Sweat rolled from him. He wiped it from his eyes with the back of his arm and then yanked his sword from its sheath. This was a signal for the soldiers to spread out into a semicircle, their spears leveled toward Hadon.

Kebiwabes, behind Hadon now, whispered, "I just said that to gain time, Hadon. I will fight by your side."

"Thanks," Hadon said in a low voice. "But get into the temple as quickly as you can. I don't want you in the way."

The bard gasped, then muttered something insulting. Hadon had no time to explain. He pulled his *tenu* from the pack and stepped forward.

At the same time Klyhy also advanced. She held up her staff and cried, "Hold! This man is under the protection of Phebha and hence mighty Kho Herself! He is the husband of a woman who has been smiled upon by Kho and who has been spoken for by Her Voice! Touch either and you will suffer the wrath of the Goddess!"

Sembes sweated even more heavily. The spearmen were all pale.

Hadon looked around. The screech and shout and chatter of the marketplace had died down. Most of the sellers and buyers were staring silently at them; the only noise was from the animals.

Sembes said, "I have my orders, Priestess, and they come from the King, the highest priest of Resu himself. Unless they are countermanded by an agent of the King, or by the Queen in person, I must do my duty. You understand that, of course."

"I understand that you are ignoring all I have told you!" she shouted. "Must I repeat it?"

Hadon looked to his left again. Lalila and the children were now inside the temple. Paga was standing in the entrance, glaring at them. He seemed uncertain, as if he could not make up his mind to stay and protect Lalila or come back out to help Hadon.

Hadon said, "Run as if Kopoethken herself were after your manhood, Kebiwabes! I can't hold them off any longer! Now go!"

With a shout, he stepped forward once more, holding Karken's hilt with both hands, the right palm cupping its end, the left gripping it above the ball of the right hand. Sembes yelled and advanced, his right foot forward, his torso leaning out to form a straight line with his left leg. Hadon's blade knocked his to one side and the keen edge slid along Sembes' jugular vein. Hadon stepped back while Sembes, his neck spouting blood, fell. Sembes was not the swordsman Hadon was, but he was the victim of the system. Only *numatenu* used the long blunt-ended, slightly curved weapon. Though this was obviously superior to the shorter stabbing blade in individual combat, its use was forbidden to military and naval personnel all over the Empire—except in Mikawuru, but the pirates had no sense of decency. It was true that Sembes, even if he had been armed with a *tenu*, would have lost anyway, but it would not have been in such a short time, and his spearmen might have moved in to drive Hadon off.

Now, before the spearmen could change their stance, lift their shafts to throw them, Hadon was off and away. The doorway was twenty paces away, and he was the swiftest runner in the Empire. Even so, he could not take the chance that spears might be flying before he reached the sanctuary. Within the last six feet he launched himself out, holding the *tenu* up with one hand, and slid on the pavement facedown. He burned his chest and knees and toes, but he shot inside the shadows of the chamber.

Paga had thrown himself to one side just in time to keep from being knocked down. Three spears came close, one hitting the side of the doorway, one flying over Hadon and transfixing a porter, one bouncing off the cement and sliding along to come to rest beside Hadon.

He was up and on his feet, bounding to one side. Though he was theoretically safe from further attack, he did not trust the spearmen to be cool enough to remember that.

Hadon got to his feet again. Paga, who seemed to be nothing but a beard with feet tumbled in a corner, struggled up. The unlucky porter lay on his back, the shaft projecting from his chest; he coughed blood and kicked a few times before dying.

Lalila and the two children were gone, supposedly into the next chamber.

Klyhy entered then. It was evident that she was shocked.

"You certainly did not try to talk your way out of that," she said. "I really expected to cow them, to get you in without bloodshed."

"I have a feeling for such situations," he said. "Talk was only going to delay the inevitable. Besides, I know Sembes—knew him. He was a fine fellow, a stickler for proper procedure, for legality—and he was in the service of the King. He would have been put off only so long. The first step I took toward the temple would have been my last; I would have gotten his sword in my back. I had to surprise him and his men. Too bad too—I liked Sembes. But there's no time to grieve for him now. That will come later."

If ever, he added mentally. Events had been going too fast lately for such things as sorrow or regret. And he felt the tempo would become even more demanding and swift in the near future.

The chamber he was in had not changed any since he had last seen it—not surprising, since it had not changed a whit in five hundred years. Its floor was of concrete—not the original, of course—and its walls were of granite covered with a thick plaster. This had been painted with murals of scenes from the religion and history of Opar. Most of them were set in the jungle, depicted in poisonous greens and bloody reds. Here and there, between the murals, were the carved figures of men and beasts. Oblong tablets of gold were fixed to the walls between the murals. These bore hieroglyphs, relics of the days before the hero Awines' syllabary had been adopted. It was an ancient place, like all the chambers and holy places of the temple. Time seemed to brood somberly over it, radiating a thick gray aura through the chatter of the crowds that filled it night and day. Time sat heavily here, soaking the granite walls and the artifacts, and seemed to have paid rent for eternity. It was said that the temple would abide for ten thousand years, that mighty Kho Herself had promised this to the builder, the priestess Lupoeth. It was indeed the only building in Opar which had not fallen during the three great earthquakes, though extensive repair had been necessary.

Hadon's reverie was brief. An uproar outside brought him back to the doorway. For a moment he could not determine what was happening. A mob was swirling just outside the entrance, screeching, yelling, crying. Then an opening in the wall of bodies revealed a spearman being beaten to death by the outraged crowd.

It was all over in a few minutes as whistles shrilled up and down the street. The mob came to its senses, realized the King's men were coming and scattered. They left behind them twelve purplish and bloody corpses.

25

Presently the street was emptied of civilians. Its only occupants were the beasts and birds abandoned by their frightened owners and about fifty soldiers. Hadon was glad to see an equal number of the Queen's soldiers arrive several minutes later. Otherwise, he would have felt compelled to retreat deep within the temple. Theoretically at least, he was safe a foot within the doorway, but he felt that in practice the over-excited King's men might violate the sanctuary. Now, faced by the Queen's men, they would not dare.

Klyhy had sent a novitiate after the Queen. She had then administered the last rites over the unfortunate porter. That finished, she went outside. She was saluted by the commanders of both forces, whom she took aside to discuss the situation.

While they were talking heatedly, Phebha appeared. She was a tall gaunt woman of about fifty. She had been beautiful as a young woman, her breasts full and upright, softly rounded in body, long-legged, her features striking despite a rather long nose. Now, wasting for some years with a fever of mysterious origin despite the prayers of her subjects, she was a hag. But she was still impressive and she could be frightening when she wished.

She wore a leopardess-skin kilt secured to her waist by a short girdle of interlocked gold rings embossed with diamonds. Her long black hair was tied in a Psyche knot and confined with a cap made of many oval and circular gold pieces. From each side of it strings of oval gold coins dangled to her waist. Her arms and legs were covered with many massive, jewel-encrusted gold bands. A long jeweled dagger was stuck through a gold ring attached to her girdle, and in her right hand she held a long thin wand of oak in the end of which was set an enormous diamond.

As she strode through the chamber, followed by a horde of priestesses, counselors and attendants, male and female, she greeted Hadon. Then she was in the street and loudly demanding to know what was happening.

Hadon was about to follow her when he heard his name. He turned at the sound of the familiar voice and hastened to embrace his father. Kumin put his one good arm around the shoulders of his son and wept. When he had mastered himself, he said, "I am weeping not only because you have returned after a long absence, my son, I weep because your mother is dead!"

"When?"

"Three days ago, son. She went to bed complaining of pain in her lower abdomen. She woke me sometime before dawn saying she was in intense pain, though I could tell that by looking at her in candlelight. She should have wakened me long before, though I doubt it would have done much good. I went for a doctor, but before she could come your mother gave a great scream and a few minutes later she died in great agony.

"The doctors performed an autopsy, since it was necessary to determine if she had died from poison or witchcraft or because great Kho had willed it. The doctors reported that some organ in her had been diseased for some time and had burst, loosing its poisons into her body.

"Your brother and his family were called down from the hills—he began working as a mining engineer there after you left—and she was buried at noon of the next day."

Hadon nodded. "I will sacrifice a fine cow over her grave," Hadon said, "when I get a chance." Then he wept with his father. Soon Lalila shook his shoulder and he looked up.

"The pains have started," she said.

Hadon rose, wiping his eyes. From outside came Phebha's strident voice. She was denouncing the King's men for having violated sanctuary, even though it was an accident. They had slain a temple porter, and Kho would not easily forgive that.

The colonel of the King's men shouted that the soldiers who had done the deed were dead, that they had paid. Anyway, it was an accident, as she admitted, and therefore was no profanation. She replied that she was not used to being argued with, but sacrilege was done, accidental or intended. The colonel started to say something, but she cried that he should keep silent. Then brass trumpets blared and drums beat and people cried out. "The King! The King!"

Hadon called to a middle-aged priestess at the back of the crowd inside the doorway. "Darbha!"

She turned and said "Yes?" and then, recognizing him, smiled and cried, "Hadon!"

"My wife Lalila is having labor pains," he said. "She should be taken to the Chamber of the Moon."

Darbha had a difficult time tearing herself away from the events in the street. Hadon said loudly, "She is Lalila! Do you know of the prophecy about her child?"

Darbha replied, "Yes, we know. We heard yesterday."

She forced her way through the crowd and spoke to Klyhy, who was standing just outside the door. Klyhy reluctantly left her post but, when she observed Lalila, she went into action very quickly. She called three priestesses to her side and issued orders that they should take Lalila to the chamber prepared for her.

Hadon kissed Lalila and said, "It will be all right."

"I wish it would be!" she cried. "But I fear that something terrible is going to happen here, Hadon! Very soon!"

"There is nothing you can do about it if it is so," he said. Coldness passed over his skin and dug into the back of his neck, but he acted as if her words were of no moment. "You must go with Klyhy. All will be well. We are in the temple now and, according to the oracle, our child will have a long and glorious life if she is born within these walls."

Klyhy spoke to a fourth priestess. "At the first chance you get, speak to Phebha. Tell her that Lalila is here and will soon be giving birth."

Klyhy and the others formed around Lalila and, while one began a slow chant, they hurried her off. Hadon turned back to the doorway. He would not be admitted into the Chamber of the Moon, so he could do nothing to comfort her.

His father looked puzzled. Evidently the priestesses had not told him anything about the prophecy. Hadon started to explain, but a flourish of trumpets and drums interrupted him. He said, "Later, Father, when there is time," and made his way through the crowd to the doorway.

The King had appeared with about a hundred more soldiers. He and his wife faced each other in the space between their two forces. They were almost nose to nose, in fact, shouting at each other. Gamori was a thickly built man, hawk-nosed, blue-jawed, hairy and dark, but with much gray in his black hair. His tresses fell below his shoulders, concealing the fact that he had long ago lost his right ear. It had been severed during the fight in which Kumin had lost his arm.

Phebha, as if tired of arguing and aware that she was in danger of completely losing her dignity, abruptly stopped speaking. She turned and walked toward the doorway while Gamori yelled after her. He ordered her to come back, but she, Queen and high priestess—therefore of higher rank—paid him no attention.

His face almost purple, Gamori whirled, seized a spear and yanked it from the hands of the nearest soldier. A cry of horror went up from the crowd, including many of his own men. Hadon yelled at her to beware and darted out toward her, his sword unsheathed. At the same time, the officer of the Queen's forces ran forward to defend her. Gamori snarled at him—Hadon could see his expression but could not hear his words—and thrust the spear into the officer's face. The blade drove into his mouth; the man dropped his sword and clutched the shaft, then fell backward. At this a roar went up from the Queen's men and they charged. Hadon grabbed Phebha around the waist and half carried her to the doorway, keeping his right side between her and the soldiers of the King. Gamori could have stabbed him in the back then but, his own back turned, he was running toward the safety of his men's spears. Then spears flew on both sides and the two forces had collided, were mixing, were swirling, were fighting savagely.

Hadon released Phebha inside the room. She raged mightily for several minutes then, as if water had been thrown in her face, became calm. "My men will die; they are outnumbered," she said. She summoned a trumpeter, who at her orders loudly blew the call for retreat. In a moment many of the Queen's men broke loose from the melee. About twenty made it into the chamber; the others stayed behind as corpses.

Phebha gave another order and a portcullis was dropped over the huge entrance. A solid iron door followed this, blocking off Gamori's men even if they had been willing to enter the temple.

"It's open war from this moment on!" Phebha shouted. "We will act at once!" She glared around, saw Klyhy coming to her and asked, "What is it?"

"The woman of Hadon, the Witch-from-the-Sea," Klyhy said. "She has been taken to the Chamber of the Moon. But her labor pains have stopped. They were false."

"Keep her there anyway," the high priestess said. "The prophecy will be fulfilled." She looked at Hadon. "Welcome home, tall one! Though it is a sad and grisly homecoming! Not unexpected, however! Well, Gamori has revealed his true ambition, which I knew all along. One who would exalt the Flaming God above the Mother of All. And one who would, not incidentally, exalt himself above the Queen. You see, Hadon, his agents have heard about the prophecy too, and Gamori fears the child. He also fears that you, though deprived of your emperor's throne, may wish to claim his as king. And he is afraid, justly so, that I might try to depose him and make you king."

"I? King?" Hadon asked.

"You won the Great Games," she said, "and you should be king. You are a true worshiper of Kho and so should replace that miserable hyena Gamori. And then there is the prophecy. If your child is to attain the glories promised her, she must be protected. How better can she be protected than if her father is king? And her mother queen?"

"My Queen—" Hadon began.

"I am sick and do not have long to live," Phebha went on. "If I should die soon, Gamori and the worshipers of Resu will have a great advantage. Klyhy is a capable woman, a strong one, but she needs a good man to lead her forces. You are the man. You can't marry her, since you are the husband of the violet-eyed woman from beyond the Ringing Sea of whom there is a prophecy. And you are the father of the child to be born. So I will proclaim you the new king, to take Gamori's throne by the dictates of mighty Kho. And your wife will become the new queen. Do not worry about Klyhy. She expects this and is glad. She has no ambitions to be high priestess and queen."

"That is true," Klyhy said. She had appeared by Hadon's side a moment before. "But there is a big difference between proclaiming Hadon and Lalila as rulers of Opar and actually being able to seat them on the throne. Gamori stands in the way."

Phebha looked around and said, "There are too many here to discuss affairs of state." She beckoned to a priestess and said, "Hala, take care of the girl Abeth and the boy Kohr, and see to the comfort of Hadon's men. Kumin, you come with us."

Phebha conducted them through many rooms. All were splendid, some offering even more magnificence and beauty than could be found in the palace of the Empress of Khokarsa. One room contained seven towering pillars of gold, and another was floored with a single sheet of gold said to be three feet thick.

Opar was rich indeed, but the pride of her citizens was tempered with the awareness that she was the object of envy and greed. She was safe when the Empire was strong, but now that civil war weakened it, Opar was vulnerable to attack. The raid by the Mikawuru pirates had only been a probe, designed to test the defenses. And suddenly Opar was herself being rent with war among her own citizens.

They ascended three flights of granite staircases and went down a long hall of polished mica into Phebha's apartments. These were luxurious indeed, but she took them through to a small room that was almost bare and bade them sit down at a plain wooden table. While wine and food were being brought in, she outlined her plan of attack. Hadon was amazed. Apparently she had been expecting this situation for a long time.

Before she could finish, however, she was forced to sit down in a chair. Her cheeks were red, her eyes feverish, her breathing heavy. The pendulous breasts rose and fell swiftly.

"It's the fever," she said, though no explanation was needed. "There is no way to overcome it. I have a strong will, but I cannot make my flesh ignore the fire that weakens it. But you, Hadon, and you, Klyhy, you know what to do. As for you, Kumin, you know the way. You have not forgotten the ancient tunnels, the old traps. You can lead your son to the battle."

"More than that!" Kumin said. "I may have only one arm, and I may have spent many years in sweeping floors and dusting statues, but I am a *numatenu*! I can wield a sword with only one hand and I can give a good account of myself!"

Phebha closed her eyes, smiled and said, "Good! You will do that."

Kumin looked excited. He was two inches shorter than his son, but at six feet he was still a tall man in Opar. His hair was gray, though when he was Hadon's age it had been as black as the wing of Kagaga the raven. He had picked up some fat and a paunch, but he was still massively built and he looked very strong. Indeed, having been forced to use one arm for twenty years, he had developed extraordinary strength in it.

"I gave my sword Karken to my son, but that does not mean I cannot swing another!"

"Then you must do it tonight, Hadon," Phebha said. "Pick out several other men; Klyhy will tell you the names of the best. And may Kho give you the stealth and the courage to rid us of this hyena Gamori."

A knock sounded on the door. A servant opened it, and a priestess entered. She bent down and whispered into Phebha's ear, looking up now and then at Hadon and Kumin, then she walked out. Phebha was silent for a minute.

"I have some bad news," she finally said. "Kumin, your son Methsuh has been captured by Gamori's men. He is being held just outside the Door of the Nine. My husband, the swine, has sent word that he wants to talk to you, Hadon."

Kumin swore. Hadon said, "What would he want with...?" He stopped, frowning, and said, "I suppose he wants a trade. If I deliver myself to him, he will release Methsuh unharmed."

"I imagine that is exactly what he will propose," Phebha said. "But you cannot do that, Hadon, even if you wish to. Lalila needs you; your unborn child will need you; Opar needs you. I am sorry for Methsuh, but you cannot sacrifice yourself for your brother."

"Let us go down and hear what Gamori has to say first," Kumin said. He looked pale but determined.

Phebha directed servants to bring in a litter. She was placed in it and carried after Hadon and his father. On the way, Hadon asked about his sister.

"Dedar is married now," Kumin said. "She went with her husband Nanquth—you remember him—to the new settlement of Kartenkloe. That was a year ago. I've heard from her six times. She's happy, though she says it's a hard life. She's pregnant, so I am happy. She is about to give me another grandchild, though Kho knows if I'll ever get to see it."

"You will live to see many more grandchildren, Father," Hadon said.

Again the crowd in front of the doorway had to be cleared so Phebha, Hadon and the others could look outside. The solid iron door had been pulled up; the portcullis was still down. After she had exchanged the litter for a chair, the Queen said, "Draw up the portcullis."

Men picked up her chair and carried her in it to the very doorway. Hadon did not think this was wise, since it made her very vulnerable, but evidently she believed that not even Gamori would dare attack her.

The marketplace was filled with about a thousand of the King's men, Hadon estimated, all in formation. By peering around the doorway, he could see down the street past the masses of bronze-armored, bronze-armed men. On both sides was a mob of citizens. Facing them were three ranks of spearmen. The citizens were not particularly noisy, but there were some shouts now and then soaring out from the sullen murmur.

They would tend to make Gamori discreet, Hadon thought. He would not want to enrage them by threatening the high priestess herself.

On the other hand, Gamori might be rash enough to force

186

a showdown. He might believe that a massacre of the citizens in the street would cow the rest of the population. And he could be right.

Trumpets blew. The troops on the right opened, and six soldiers and a prisoner came through the narrow avenue.

Hadon cried "Methsuh!" and heard the name echoed despairingly by his father.

Methsuh, looking much like Hadon, his hands behind him, his face bloody and puffed, was thrown down on the pavement. Gamori gestured and the trumpets and drums were loud. The crowd became silent. Gamori roared, "A trade, Phebha! A trade! One traitor for another!"

Her voice was clear but weak. "What is this, Gamori? Who is a traitor? *You* are the only one *I* see!"

"Not I!" Gamori bellowed. "I am not conducting warfare against you, wife! I am only asserting the right of Resu to primacy, the order of things as they should be! But I am not here to debate with you! I want that traitor, Hadon! Our Emperor has informed me that he should be arrested and sent back to Khokarsa!"

"There is no legal Emperor!" Phebha said. "Our Empress, High Priestess Awineth, has declared Minruth a traitor and blasphemer and profaner! So, Gamori, you have no legal basis for your claim! In fact, by pressing the rebel Minruth's claim, you proclaim for all to hear that *you* are a rebel and a blasphemer and a profaner! And so great Kho frowns on you, Gamori! And She frowns on all who support you! Death and destruction will visit those on whom Kho frowns!"

"Silence, you mangy lying bitch!" Gamori bellowed. His face was very red, but the faces of the soldiers near him were pale. "I am not here to discuss religion or politics or indeed anything except an exchange of traitors. I want Hadon! And if he refuses to surrender himself, or if you refuse to throw him out of the temple, then I will execute his brother! Now! Before his eyes and yours! And before the eyes of the dieties! Methsuh's blood will be on Hadon's hands, on your hands!"

"You do not order the high priestess of Kho to be silent, nor do you insult her—and thus Kho—without retaliation!"

Phebha said. Her voice was louder now, her anger having overcome her weakness for a moment.

Kumin, standing by Hadon, groaned. He said, "Great Kho, do not do this to me! I have lost my wife only two days ago, and now I will lose one or the other of my only sons!"

Methsuh was on his knees only twenty feet from the doorway. Two officers stood with drawn swords behind him. Gamori was to one side and about ten feet behind them. The nearest ranks of spearmen were about thirty feet from each side of the doorway.

Hadon wondered if the spacing had been arranged to tempt him to dash out and try to rescue his brother. Probably.

There was silence for a moment. Gamori, still red-faced, his lips open and his teeth clamped together, paced back and forth. Then he shouted, "Well, Hadon! I will not wait long!"

"You will, of course, do no such thing," Phebha said to Hadon. "It would be a brave and noble deed if you gave your life for your brother's. Also, an extremely stupid and selfish deed. The fate of Opar and the course of true religion in Opar depend on you. No one else can rally the worshipers of Kho as you can. You are a hero, winner of the Great Games—"

"I know all that!" Hadon said loudly, daring in his anger and grief to interrupt her. "I know that Gamori does not really expect me to sacrifice myself for Methsuh! What profit would there be in that except for Gamori and the cause of Resu?"

Kumin said, "It is cruelty which inspires Gamori to do this. He cannot violate sanctuary, so he is killing Methsuh to hurt us! He hopes that one of us will not be able to endure witnessing Methsuh's death and so will run out to save him!"

"You will not do that!" Phebha said sharply.

Kumin shouted, tore Karken from Hadon's hand and was out of the doorway before Hadon could grab him. Hadon started after him then, but a soldier by the Queen's chair thrust his spear between his legs and Hadon sprawled out of the doorway. Spears were instantly hurled toward him. He rolled back into the doorway. Two spears passed over him, one so close its shaft banged against his ribs. A third struck the pavement just in front of him, its tip digging into the cement. He scrambled to the protection of the wall beyond the doorway, and no more spears were thrown.

He bounded back three second later, determined to see what was happening even if it meant dodging more missiles. He saw the two officers who had been guarding Methsuh lying on the street, their throats gashed. Methsuh was on his side, but struggling to get up. Gamori was defending himself with his sword against Kumin's bloody weapon. Though Kumin had only one arm, he was using Karken as if he held its hilt with two hands. And then the inevitable occurred. Spears thunked into Kumin from both sides and from behind. He staggered and fell, though still swinging at Gamori.

The King stepped up and brought his sword down against Kumin's neck. Blood spouted, washing Gamori's feet, and Gamori leaned down and picked up the head by the hair and held it aloft, crying exultantly.

Hadon, shouting, seized a spear from a soldier and cast it at Gamori.

It flew almost true, catching Gamori in the shoulder. He dropped the head and fell into the pool of blood, clutching at the shaft.

A soldier thrust his spear through Methsuh. Other soldiers, forgetting in their rage and excitement that they were committing sacrilege, threw their spears at the doorway. Several just missed Phebha and Hadon; one struck a priestess in the stomach. A second later the portcullis dropped and the door was slammed shut.

Observers in the windows of the upper stories of the temple reported later that Gamori was carried away at once. The spear did not seem to have inflicted a fatal wound, unless infection set in. But Gamori had given an order before he left, and it was carried out with ruthlessness: the civilian witnesses were massacred, though a number escaped. And civil war began in earnest throughout Opar.

26

Phebha said, "I have just come from the Chamber of the Moon. Lalila's labor pangs have started again. She is now an ordained priestess, and I have ordered that the news be spread that she will be our new queen. And that you will be the new king."

"How can you do that?" Hadon said. "No public criers will venture into the street. They would be killed."

"We have our ways," she said. "Lalila will have to learn them; she has much to learn, in fact. I will teach her what I can before I die. After that, Klyhy and Hala and the others will teach her."

"It is too soon to talk about that," Hadon said. "First we have to get rid of Gamori."

"Which shall be done before the night is over, Kho willing," she said. "In two hours it will be midnight. I have sacrificed a cock and found the omens good, if somewhat ambiguous. But aren't they always? Midnight is the best time to start. Klyhy will be your guide, since your father is no longer available."

Hadon tried not to think of Kumin or his brother. There was no time for grief now. There was only time for thoughts of vengeance.

He walked to the window and looked out. It was a cloudy night, when the city would normally have been dark except for the torches of patrols. But now the flames from the burning tenements of the freemen to the north and the slaves' quarters to the south and some large buildings in the city itself lit up the night. The clouds were red, reflecting the fires below. Here and there torches bobbed, looking at this distance like fireflies. Most of the fighting had died down for the night, if the reports were to be believed. The majority of the population had fled the city itself, avoiding being ground between the Queen's men and the King's. Many civilians, however, had either joined one side or the other or had plunged into looting. The wooden areas outside the walls were destined to burn completely. No one was trying to quench the flames; all fire fighting was confined inside the walls.

Since most of the city was built of massive stone, the fires there were limited. Much furniture had been carried out to the streets and set up as barricades, however, and these had been torched. Hangings and furniture in many buildings had also been heaped and set on fire in order to create diversions.

Gamori had surrounded the vast temple, leaving about a hundred men at each entrance. Then he had started the city-wide slaughter which had sent the civilians into a panic. The stream of refugees had kept the Queen's men from fighting through to the temple for a long time. They could make no headway against the mass headed for the riverfront and the jungle behind the city.

Gamori had been taken to his quarters in the Temple of Resu and treated there. According to Phebha's spies, he had not left his apartment, but he was conducting operations through his general, Likapoeth. If the report could be believed, Gamori would be on his feet by late tomorrow morning. Meanwhile, Likapoeth had twice stormed the Door of the Nine, battering it with heavy bronze rams. At the same time soldiers had tried to get into the windows of the second stories. Flaming oil had been poured on them; the ladders, pushed aside or out, had fallen with their shrieking burdens. The rams had failed to beat in the double barrier of portcullis and door, and oil from the windows above had discouraged the attackers.

Then the portcullis and door had been opened, and Hadon had led a sally outside. This had resulted in his forces being driven back with heavy losses. He had suffered several minor wounds and once almost been captured.

Later, a force of about three hundred of the Queen's men

191

had fought their way through to the doorway. Hadon had again led his men out to help them, and two hundred of the reinforcements had gotten into the temple.

Phebha had sent messengers to the port to order at least half the troops there, six hundred men, to come to Opar. But it would be several days before the messenger could get there, even if he traveled night and day. And it would take heavily armed men four days to get to Opar with forced paddling. Moreover, Gamori was sure to have the river watched so there was no guarantee that the messengers would get through.

There were about five hundred soldiers inside the temple now. Unfortunately at least half of them were casualties. After eating the soup from the great kettles in the kitchen, two hundred and fifty had gotten very sick. Within an hour, almost a hundred had died in agony. The others had survived, but they were too sick to be of any use. Phebha started an investigation within half an hour after the first dozen became ill. By then the culprits, two chief cooks, had disappeared. Ropes dangling from third-story windows revealed their escape route.

"Gamori is not as stupid as I had thought him, though he is even more vile," Phebha said. "Well, he has hit us hard. But if you succeed tonight, Gamori and all his ambitions will go up in his funeral pyre."

Hadon was shocked. "You are going to burn him?"

"Why not? He deserves the fate of a traitor and blasphemer. Would you have me give him a hero's burial and erect a pylon over him just because he once sat on a throne and was my husband?"

"It's just that it's seldom done," he said.

"If you are to be a good king, you will do many things that are seldom done."

"I have been learning to do such things," Hadon said.

He excused himself and went to his apartment. Abeth and Kohr were asleep in an inner chamber, watched by an elderly priestess. She looked up as Hadon stuck his head into the room. She smiled and made a sign that all was well with the children. He went to his own bed but was unable to sleep at all. After tossing and turning, he rose and drank several cups of hibiscus-tea. Then he paced. After a long, long time the water clock indicated it was time to leave.

Klyhy met him outside the door of Phebha's quarters. "She is asleep," she said. "There is no need to wake her; we know what to do."

Klyhy's slave was carrying a large jar of some black stuff. She opened it, and Hadon and Klyhy stripped and smeared themselves with the ointment. Then they dressed, though there was not much to that. Each wore a tight black loin-cloth, antelope-skin moccasins and a belt holding several sheaths and metal hooks. Pouches dangled from some of the hooks. A loop in Hadon's belt held a curious T-shaped device of iron. During this time four men, all also covered with black ointment, entered. They carried coils of rope over their shoulders, and their sheaths held knives and short-handled axes. Pouches hanging from the hooks held lead double-coned missiles. Their leather slings were secured through loops on their belts.

Hadon had met these four that afternoon. He had gone over the diagrams with them and Klyhy until all could re-draw them from memory. Like the other men, Hadon had sworn an oath never to reveal what he had learned from the diagrams. He had also sworn not to allow himself to fall alive into the hands of the enemy.

Fully accoutred, Hadon and Klyhy led the others down the hall, past a sentry around the corner and down a small side hall. At its end Klyhy drew a large iron key from a pouch and unlocked a small iron door. Inside the room, she groped around until she found torches in brackets. Using a flint and iron and some tinder, she got a tiny fire going and then dumped the tinder on the oil-soaked torch. Two others also lit torches.

The room was ostensibly used for storage. The priestess went around behind a pile of wooden boxes, the others following. There was a space between the pile and a single large box set against the stone wall. The wall itself was com-posed of stone blocks, each a three-foot square. Klyhy opened the lid of the box, revealing that it was half filled with rolls of papyrus. Klyhy told them to remove these, which they did. On the bottom was an ingot of lead weighing about forty pounds. They lifted that out and a plate of bronze rose a few inches from the bottom.

"The lead block holds the plate down," she said. "Lift it and the plate comes up, and counterweights behind the wall start to work. Quickly! Into the opening!"

A section of the wall had swung open and out. The others quickly moved through it into a tunnel beyond. Hadon, at her orders, pushed up on a huge wooden lever within the opening. Klyhy replaced the weight, threw in the papyrus rolls, closed the box lid and went through the opening. Hadon took the pressure off the lever and the stone section pivoted back.

"Only the Queen has the key to the storage room," Klyhy said. "Only she and two priestesses at any one time know the secret of this room. Now you men know because this is an extreme emergency. But Kho will blast you if you should talk about it. If we can use it to get at our enemies, they can use it to get at us."

The tunnel was about ten feet wide and eight feet high. It was well ventilated, though the source of the air was not visible. The torch flames bent toward the far end of the tunnel. Klyhy went first, turning to the left. There was no need for them to know where the right passage led, so they had not been told. The left was a lower, narrower passage. It ran for about a hundred yards, turning often, apparently going between the walls of rooms and corridors. Occasionally there were niches in the walls, some of which held skulls.

"They are supposed to belong to the slaves who built these secret passages," she said. "I doubt that, though, since they would be seven hundred years old, and I think a skull would rot in that time. The walls are thick, but they are damp. Personally, I think they're the relics of enemies of the high priestesses of the past few generations. But if that's true, where are the skeletons?"

Those who could answer her questions were also dead.

The men made a sign to ward off evil spirits as they passed each skull.

Occupied with his own thoughts about the skulls, Hadon trailed Klyhy. All of a sudden he bumped into her, causing her to gasp and then curse.

"You clumsy hulk!" she said. "Watch where you're going! You almost knocked me down that!"

She pointed at the open well just below her feet.

Hadon said nothing. She was right. He should have been paying more attention. If he did not forget everything except the work at hand, he was likely to forget everything for all time.

The torchlight struck water far down. It also showed a bronze ladder affixed to the stone. Klyhy lowered herself over the edge and went down it swiftly. A man called Wemqardo held her touch out so she could see all the way to the bottom. Reaching it, she swung around the ladder and disappeared into an opening. Wemqardo lowered the torch to her at the end of a rope and then went down himself. Within a few minutes all six were inside another tunnel. This one curved rapidly to the left, taking them for a quarter of a mile in a path like a snake's. On coming to what seemed the end of the passage, the priestess pushed against one side of the wall close to the corner. It pivoted ponderously, requiring Hadon's weight to move it. The bronze pins squeaked loudly, causing Klyhy to curse.

Cold, wet air struck them. They advanced through the opening on to a curving piece of granite which held a boat just large enough to accommodate six adults uncomfortably. Though small, the boat took up almost all the room on the projection. A river, dark and greasy, lapped a few inches below the surface of the stone. Hadon lifted his torch to get a better view. The other side was at least three hundred feet away. The ceiling and walls formed an arch which glittered in the light; there were many veins of quartz in the granite. The highest part of the ceiling was about thirty feet above the water, though its height would vary further along.

Wemqardo said, "I have heard of this river deep under the city. It is said that the Cold Snake dwells at its bottom in the thick mud, and when—"

"Quiet, fool!" Klyhy demanded. "Would you scare everybody to death!"

Wemqardo said nothing more, but he had started a series of thoughts in the minds of the others. Hadon thought of creepy tales he had heard when a child, horrifying stories of the demons of the rock, the things, half-gorilla, half-worm, which were supposed to haunt these tunnels. It was said that the slaves who dug for gold in these deeps often unaccountably disappeared. Or their fellows saw them being dragged away by things dark and misshapen.... It was good not to think about such monsters, but how did you *not* think about something?

They got the boat into the water and themselves into the boat, though they came close to overturning it. They drove it downstream with the short-handled paddles stored in the craft. Brackets on the prow and stern held torches; the third had been extinguished. Their flickering light revealed niches carved into the walls, each of which held a skull. It also showed, now and then, a sudden boiling of the water when a paddle dipped in. Hadon, in a low voice, asked Klyhy what caused this phenomenon.

"It's a small fish which infests these waters," she said. "They're blind and colorless and only about four inches long. But they have a big head and many sharp teeth and they occur in great numbers. So it won't do to fall into the river. You'd be stripped of flesh within ten minutes."

"Why didn't you tell us about them earlier?" Hadon said somewhat angrily.

"You have enough to worry about."

Hadon lifted his paddle and held it in the torchlight for a moment. The wooden blade was pitted in many places.

"If there are so many of them, how do they get enough to eat in this sterile environment?" he asked. "Are there many other kinds of fish here? What do these eat?"

"There are some other types of fish," she said, "though not many. Not enough to account for the swarms of those devil-fish."

"Then what do they eat?"

"I wish I knew," she replied. "Though perhaps it is better for my peace of mind that I do not."

Hadon wished he had not been so curious.

After passing two aprons of stone, presumably opening to pivoted sections also, she told them to head for the third. They got onto the tiny dock without mishap, and she and Hadon pushed open the section. This, like the last one, squeaked loudly. The boat had to be left on the apron, since it was a little too large to get through the opening. Hadon did not like this. What if the King's men patrolled this area—as the priestess said they sometimes did—and saw the boat? They might take it with them, leaving Hadon and his group stranded.

"They don't come around very often," she said. "And since Gamori needs all the men he can get for the fighting, I doubt he'll spare any for this area. Besides, the King's men don't know anything about the secret passages. They might suspect we have them, but they don't know where they are."

"Won't they think it peculiar when they find a boat all by itself, up against a wall?"

"I suppose so," she said. "Occasionally a boat does disappear, and we figure that a patrol found it and took it along with them, although a rising of the river could account for it. Whatever the reason for the disappearances, the King's men seem never to have pushed on the wall sections. They might have thought the boats were being used by demons of the rock or some other things even more unpleasant. I don't think the patrols like to linger down here."

"One more thing to worry about," Wemqardo muttered.

Hadon, in turn, would have worried about Wemqardo, but he had been assured by Phebha that the man was a very dependable veteran. Wemqardo might grumble and appear apprehensive, but when the time for action came he would be very active indeed.

They proceeded down a narrow tunnel so low that Hadon had to duck down a little. Then the ceiling suddenly became quite high. After three hundred feet, Klyhy halted. Hadon expected her to push on the wall section ending the passage, but she held her torch high. Looking up, he saw a square opening about three feet across the ceiling. She handed her torch to him, removed and uncoiled the rope from her shoulder. Its end held a three-pronged grapple of iron. She tossed it up through the hole three times before it caught. After pulling on it to make sure it was secure, she braced her feet against the wall and hauled herself up to the opening.

Hadon's torch showed that the rope had caught on the rung of a bronze ladder set into the stone. Klyhy was now climbing on up it.

He followed her with the torch. Within five minutes, all were climbing up the rungs after the priestess. At the top they went along a tunnel so narrow they went single file and so low they had to crouch or crawl. Reaching the end of this, they descended another bronze ladder, at least fifty feet down, then they took a tunnel which led directly below the river.

Klyhy stopped again after more winding. She pointed to a sign carved in the rock on her right, about five feet above the floor. It was a simple, single vertical line crossed by two horizontal lines near its top.

"It means a trap," she said, though they had all been instructed in the use of the secret signs by Phebha.

She walked up to the oblong stone set in the floor just beyond the sign. It was five feet across, an easy standing jump. She leaped across and went on down to make room for the others. They hopped across, taking care to land at least a foot beyond the crack.

"The last time I was here—the last time anyone was here—was six years ago," Klyhy said, "I opened the trapdoor at the orders of my superior—she's dead now—to check it. There were two skeletons down at the bottom which had not been there before, according to my superior. You see, the stone does not give way immediately. There is a delay which allows several people to get on the stone before it drops. Apparently at least two of the King's soldiers had found this passage. Their armor identified them. But they had fallen in, and if anyone else was with them, they decided not to explore any further."

"What keeps the King from setting traps too?" Wemqardo said.

"Nothing at all," she said, not very cheerfully.

Wemqardo grunted. Klyhy turned and led them for about fifty yards in a straight line. Then she cast her grapple again, and after a while they were going along another horizontal passage. Once she stopped to point out another incised sign, a horizontal line just below a circle. A foot from it was a recess carved into the rock. This was large enough to admit a big man's hand. She put her fingers within it, gripping the raised edge.

"Pull hard on this stone and it comes out, causing the ceiling blocks for a hundred feet that way"—she pointed ahead—"to fall in. Don't forget that."

"Has this device been tested?" Wemqardo said.

"Well, no," she said. "At least not as far as I know. It was built Kho only knows how many years—perhaps centuries—ago."

"Then it may not work," Wemqardo said.

"Just hope you don't have to use it," she said. "Or, if you do, that it does work. There are about two dozen such devices in this complex. If you're pursued, keep your eye out for this sign. The recess grip will be near it."

"Just my luck not to have a torch," Wemqardo said.

"Talking about bad luck brings bad luck," one of the other men commented.

"Quiet now," Hadon ordered. "We're getting near the shaft to the roof of the temple, aren't we?"

"Yes," Klyhy agreed.

A minute later they came to another seeming end to the tunnel. Klyhy worked this device to swing it on its pivot. The group went through to an extension of the tunnel with a hole in the floor about six feet ahead. Above the hole was a shaft going upward and holding a bronze ladder. The hole went down, Hadon found out when he leaned over it, about thirty feet.

"The underground river," Klyhy explained. "It was King's men who sank this shaft," she went on, "old King Madymeth, Gamori's great-great-grandfather. He wanted an escape route to the river in case of revolt or invasion. He did not inform his wife about it, but she found out, of course, and had the necessary shafts and tunnels carved to come out here. Thus the vicars of Kho have long had a secret passage into the Temple of Resu, though it has never been used until now. The original bronze ladder was also set there by Madymeth. About fifty years ago an earthquake tumbled part of it down into the river, and the present one was set into the stone."

"I hope the men who did it were good artisans," Wemqardo whispered.

"We'll find out," Hadon said. He leaped out across the hole and caught one bar with his two hands while a foot scraped down the wall and then against a rung. The bronze seemed to give a little, but that was probably only his imagination. He climbed up until there was room for the next jumper. Klyhy grabbed a rung, but her foot slipped and she dangled, swearing, no doubt sweating, for a moment until she had found a foothold.

A torch was tossed to Hadon, who knotted his rope around it and carried it up that way, out to one side so the torch would not drip on those below. When he reached the sign—incised there how many decades or centuries ago?—he stopped. He drew the torch up and tied it two rungs above his head.

The last man had tied the second torch to the ladder at the level of the tunnel. Now they had light from above and below and were unencumbered. Far up, a pale oval indicated the top of the shaft. The light came from the reflection of fires against the clouds.

The sign was an inverted arrow on a horizontal line, the character of the syllabary which meant, among other things, sun, sungod, eagle. In this case it indicated the entrance to the apartment of the chief vicar of Resu, the Flaming God.

According to Phebha, the wall here was very thin. It was in fact a stone plate, a shell. It would operate like a drawbridge, its upper part describing an arc inward toward the floor. Originally it was operable only from the interior of the apartment. Madymeth had not wanted anyone coming *in* from the shaft, of course. It was accessible from the roof, however, which was why there were always twelve guards at the top of the shaft.

Madymeth had not reckoned, of course, with the silent and enduring cunning of the high priestesses, who knew there might be a showdown some day between Resu and Kho. The priestesses had cut and drilled and scraped passageways through the solid granite, taking perhaps fifty years or more, and at last attained their objective.

The final stage had involved drilling a hole in the stone

near the plate, giving access to the equipment which lowered the wall section. Now Hadon removed from his belt the long instrument of iron curiously fashioned centuries before. It had been waiting for its single occasion of service all this time. It would not be used again.

He inserted the swelling end of the iron device into the hole and then pushed in two-thirds of the stem. The capped end slid smoothly over the nine-sided end of a crank. Then, making sure that it was on securely, he twisted the T-shaped handle. Nine times he turned it completely, grimacing at the squeals issuing from the hole.

Something bellowed from above. He was so startled that he almost lost his hold on the rung. He jerked his head back, looking upward. The faint light from the clouds was gone now, replaced by bright torchlight. And then a section of the light fell off and was hurtling down toward them.

Fortunately the flaming torch only came close. If it had been on target, he would have had to let loose and drop, which he certainly could not do, or else let it strike him.

Klyhy cried out in horrified protest. Wemqardo swore and said, "I knew it! I knew it!" The others voiced their terror in their own fashions, but Hadon could not distinguish what was said. Nor was he concerned about that. How had they been found? Surely those on guard had not seen the torchlights? The shaft was too far up, and there would be too much glare from the great fires and reflections from the clouds.

Perhaps somebody long ago had detected the additions of the Queen's men to the wall-opening mechanism and, instead of removing them, had attached an alarm to them. Thus, when Hadon had turned the crank, he had triggered a notice to the King's men that someone was out in the shaft.

Whatever had caused the alerting of the sentinels, it was too late to get into the apartment. In fact, there would be no getting into it in any event. The wall section was not responding, was not beginning to move down inward as it was supposed to do.

In fact, and here he began to feel more than just a little alarm, the top of the wall was coming outward!

Hadon just had time to note that his idea was correct: the

mechanism had been found long ago. The wall was fixed now so that it would open out to the shaft. And anyone clinging to the ladder would be hanging upside down from it unless he could get to the rungs immediately below.

Hadon yelled at Klyhy to get down, but she was already on her way, dropping after the others, who fortunately had not frozen with fear. His hands were on the rung just below the bottom of the wall section when it fell outward, its upper part banging to a stop against the far side of the shaft.

At least the section would act as a shield, Hadon thought frenziedly. It would prevent the guards at the top of the shaft and in the apartment from dropping things on them. The damn fools in the apartment wouldn't be able to pursue them. Didn't they realize their own trap would stop them from getting out into the shaft?

Yes, they had considered that. They weren't such damn fools. The wall section continued to lower itself with a screech, flattening straight toward Hadon along the length of the ladder.

27

Since the wall would not miss him, it forced him to take the only action possible. He released his grip on the rung and jumped back, falling down the shaft, holding himself upright as long as he could.

Above him, men shrieked as the wall section struck them.

Everything outside him was a blur and he was frozen internally, not even wondering what had happened to Klyhy, nor why she was silent.

Then he was past the area of light of the torch on the lowest rung. He was in darkness and falling, falling, though still upright. Perhaps the water at the bottom of the shaft would be deep enough so that he might survive the impact if he entered it feetfirst.

Then he was out of the shaft—a very brief sensation of suddenly expanding space around him, a coolness—and he hit the river.

The force of the blow was enough to stun him a little, though he had entered it cleanly, presenting a minimum of surface. He went down, down, slowing. His toes were suddenly in cold ooze. His knees had bent and for a few seconds he was crouching on the bottom like the godling of the river, that often described but seldom seen monster. He too squats at the bottom and looks upward, waiting for victims, usually a young girl, squats huge and misshapen, breathing water slowly, waiting, waiting, patient as only immortals can be patient.

With such thoughts, Hadon rose to the surface. The current had carried him away from the shaft, or at least he supposed it had. He could see nothing and he could feel only the cold water and a far more numbing terror. He was not thinking of the godling of the river now, but of the little blind fish with the big heads and teeth. He expected to feel something rip out a piece of flesh at any moment, then a hundred jaws fastening onto him, then—his outflung hand struck something—flesh—and he almost cried out.

Though he had pushed himself away from it, he swam back and ran his hands over it. It was the corpse of a man. The head was split open. A coil of rope was still over its shoulders. One of his men.

There was little sound except for the lap of water against the walls and some gurglings here and there. Hadon swam toward his right and within a minute felt cold stone. He dog-paddled then, feeling the stone now and then, hoping that he would bump into one of the projections leading to a passage. So far, there was nothing except rather smooth stone. He did not really have any strong expectation of finding a projection: the number of passages must be very limited in number and restricted to a certain area. For all he knew, he was past that area. After a while he would be past the city above, borne only Kho and the deities and demons of the dark underground knew where. He would become too tired to swim and would sink. Or the ceiling would get lower and lower until it dived beneath the surface, taking him with it. Or the blind little fish . . .

The scream was so unexpected, so close, so shrill with utter terror, that it almost stopped his heart.

He knew, however, that it had to be Klyhy.

"Help! Help! Oh, Kho, help me! They're eating me alive!"

Hadon treaded water, turning, straining his ears to determine her direction.

He shouted, "Klyhy! It's Hadon! Where are you!"

The screams and his shout bounced off the walls of the tunnel and reverberated. He could not tell where she was, though he thought she was to his left.

"Oh, Kho!" Klyhy screamed. "Help me! I'm being torn apart!"

Hadon swam toward the voice. She stopped screaming for

a moment. He heard a thrashing and swam toward that, sure now that he knew approximately where she was. And then something touched his right leg. A second later a number of somethings were biting into his calf, fastening down on his toes, on his Achilles tendon. At first there was no pain, only numbness. Then fire struck in a dozen places.

His left hand struck soft flesh. Klyhy screamed in his ear. His right hand struck the wall, slid along it, stopped against a shelf of stone perhaps five inches thick. His fingers locked around it; the fingers of his other hand seized Klyhy's shoulder. In her agony she tore away from his grip, but his fingers clenched around her long hair.

Yelling at her to quit fighting him, he pulled her close to him. She struck at his face; fingernails tore at his eyes and nose. And now his left leg was being attacked. Pain shot through it. And then more pain, this time in his buttocks, then a tearing and plucking at his loincloth.

It was this last attack that gave him superhuman strength. He pulled himself up on the apron with one hand, afraid to let go of Klyhy with the other. While the upper part of his body was on the apron, his legs and groin area still undergoing attack, he pulled Klyhy on to the little tongue of stone. He struck her in the shoulder with his fist, felt to her face and struck her jaw. She collapsed, screaming no more.

He pulled himself completely up on the stone, gibbering in a frenzy of loathing and fear, and hacked the fish off his legs with the edges of his palms. The teeth came loose reluctantly, taking more flesh with them. He bent down then and dragged Klyhy further along the apron and repeated the dislodging process. Some of the writhing greasy things were knocked off easily; others clung, forcing him to grab them by their heads and rip them off, causing Klyhy to scream. And though he could not see the blood, he could feel it.

He turned then and groped around the apron, hoping to find a boat on it. There was none, so he felt around the wall, traced the thin line of partition with a finger and pushed on one side of the section. It swung slowly, groaning, requiring a great effort from him. Apparently this section had not been used for a long, long time.

The air inside was musty and heavy and surprisingly dry,

but cooler and wetter air from the river quickly replaced it. He felt along the wall to his left, raising and lowering his hand. When he found a large recess, he stopped. His fingers detected several torches—rather dry—some flints, irons and a box. The latter contained some tinder, also surprisingly dry. Within a few minutes he had the torch lit; he had never been so glad to see light in his life.

His legs and buttocks were bleeding, though fortunately the wounds were not deep. They were painful enough, however.

He went out to the apron and stood aghast for a moment. Klyhy's body was a bloody ruin. Chunks of flesh had been torn out everywhere, and it was a wonder that she could live after having lost so much blood.

He lifted her and carried her into the tunnel. When he put her down, he saw that she had lost several toes and a nipple, and the bones of a little finger were bare.

She moaned and looked at him with glazed eyes. "I hurt Hadon!"

"I know, Klyhy," he said. "But you are not dead yet. You will live."

He removed her loincloth and his, wrung them out and tied them around her worst wounds. But the blood continued to run.

"Oh, great Kho, I hurt!" she said, moaning. Then, looking down at herself, she asked, "Why should I live? Like this? Who would ever want to lie with me again?"

"There's more to living than lying with lovers," he said. "Besides, the wounds will heal."

"You're a liar," she said in an even weaker voice. "Hadon..."

He bent down so he could place an ear close to her lips.

"Take care of Khor. Tell him..."

"Yes?"

"I hurt, only..."

"What is it?" he said.

"I don't feel pain now. It's getting dark..."

She mumbled something, and with a sigh she had gone.

Hadon muttered the ritual words and made the necessary signs; he promised Kho and Sisisken to sacrifice a fine bull and a fine cock to them for the sake of Klyhy. He also promised her ghost that she would be honored as a heroine of Opar. He would erect a pointed monolith over her body after it had been suitably buried, and he would see to it that one of the gold tablets in the Temple of Kho bore her name and her deeds. Her tablet would be next to his.

At that moment he became aware of a very faint light coming from down the river. He rose painfully, noting almost unconsciously that his wounds had mostly stopped bleeding now; only a few still trickled. He stuck the torch in the recess, so its light would not shine directly out through the mouth of the tunnel. Then he pushed the wall section until only an inch-wide gap remained between the wall and the side of the section. Putting his eye to this, he looked up the river. A longboat had just come into view.

It held about thirty men. Four torches, two at the prow, two at the stern, lit up the bronze helmets and cuirasses of the paddlers and the two officers. There were no spears in sight, but these, he supposed, were placed on the deck.

He shut the section and removed the torch. He took Klyhy's dagger and stuck it through his belt. He was entirely on his own now, intent only on escape. His mission had failed, and the King's men were out looking for him. Not exactly for him, since they would not know the identity of the invaders—nor would they know if any had survived the fall—but search parties were out, looking. The men in the longboat would see the blood on the apron and would stop to investigate. They would push on the wall section and in a short time would be on his trail.

For all he knew, other men would be coming along the tunnels ahead of him. They would have the advantage, since presumably some of them would know these passages or at least have diagrams of them. He didn't have the slightest idea where any of them led.

Hadon walked for several hundred feet until he came to what seemed to be the end of the passage. After passing the torch slowly along the wall to check for warning signs, he pushed the section open. It gave to a round room which was the bottom of a vertical shaft. A series of bronze rungs set into the stone enabled him to climb for about fifty feet upward. The shaft ended in the center of a horizontal tunnel.

Hadon hesitated, not knowing which direction to take. Suddenly he heard a noise behind him. He looked down the shaft and saw men below. Ten were coming up the rungs, while others were crowding into the round room. Those on the rungs were making slow progress, since the lead man was holding a torch in one hand. He was forced to hook his right wrist over a rung instead of seizing it firmly.

Hadon thought it best to slow them down as much as possible. He went down the tunnel to his right—the clean or good-luck side—until he came to a bend. He placed the torch on its side and returned, guided by the light of the torches in the shaft. He lay down by the lip of the shaft and waited. Presently the light grew very bright and he could smell a strong resinous odor. The face of the lead man appeared.

Hadon ripped the torch from the man's hand. He flung it behind him and seized the man's throat. His dagger's point went through the man's eye, into his brain. The man ceased his cries.

Hadon dropped the dagger and grabbed the man's neck with his other hand. He pulled the body over the lip and into the tunnel. Below, men shouted. They did not know what was happening, but the cries of the lead man had alarmed them. Hadon removed the sword-belt of the corpse and strapped it around his waist. Then he took the helmet and the cuirass off, and leaned over the lip with the helmet in one hand and the heavy cuirass in the other. The man now on top looked up and cried out. His face was only five feet below Hadon, who hurled the bronze cuirass into it. The man gave a choked cry and fell back, missing those on the rungs. But his body struck the crowd at the bottom, hurling most of them to the floor.

Hadon threw the helmet into the face of the next man, also causing him to fall and injure or kill more.

Hadon lifted the corpse above his head with both hands, the effort causing some of his wounds to start bleeding again. He hurled the body down. It struck the first man and dislodged him, both falling on the man just below; the three fell, two screaming. Four more men were knocked down, all crashing into the heap of dead and disabled on the bottom.

That still left two men on the rungs. Besides, despite the

groaning tangle on the bottom, more soldiers were coming out from the tunnel into the shaft. Hadon counted eight. So he had immobilized all but ten of the thirty. Not bad for one man, he thought.

The survivors were either fools or very brave or both. They were coming up the rungs after him, ignoring the calls for help from the bloody mess on the bottom.

Hadon decided the climbers were stupid. They were in a helpless position if he stayed where he was, and he would be crazy to leave now. Once they were on the level, he would be outnumbered.

Hadon waited by the lip. After a while he heard the heavy breathing of the first man. He sat up then and when the bronze helmet slowly appeared—the man was cautious—he brought the sword's edge down on top of the helmet. Not, however, hard enough to split it or knock the soldier unconscious. The man cried out but clung to the rungs. Hadon stood up and leaned down, unloosening the chin strap and removing the man's helmet. The soldier stared at him with crossed eyes. Hadon grabbed the long hair and yanked the fellow on up. As he came over the edge, Hadon brought his knee up under the man's chin. The fellow sprawled out senseless.

Leaning over the edge, Hadon hurled the helmet into the upturned face of the next man, who was climbing up swiftly and desperately. The force of the blow broke the man's nose, but he did not let go of the rungs.

Hadon removed the sword and dagger from the man on the floor beside him. He rolled the groaning man over the edge. There were two cries, one from the falling man, who had just regained sufficient consciousness to realize what was happening; the other was from the man beneath the body. His grip broken, he fell with the other on top of him, and three others were scraped off.

Which left three.

These men became very wise very suddenly and retreated. Hadon did not want anybody able to follow him, however. He hurled a sword down and it went point first, striking the lead man on top of his helmet. He fell with a scream into the man below him, and both smashed into the heap at the bottom of the shaft. The sole survivor went down swiftly, too swiftly in his panic. He lost his hold and fell twenty-five feet on his side. Hadon thought he had been killed but, no, he was up on his feet and climbing over the tangled bodies.

Hadon threw a dagger at him. It missed, sinking instead into the neck of a man lying facedown on top of several bodies. The soldier got through the doorway and, though Hadon waited for five minutes, he did not show his face again.

Hadon speculated about going back down the ladder and killing the man. But that would accomplish nothing. The man was trapped there, since he could not handle the heavy longboat by himself. He would not dare to come back up the shaft again for a long, long time. He would want to make sure that Hadon had left the area.

Which was just what Hadon was doing. He walked away, holding a torch, a dagger and a sword in their sheaths. There was no doubt now which one of the two tunnels to take. Down the one to his right was a faint light, a murmur of voices. And then a blood-stopping sound, a sudden outburst of barking! Dogs!

28

Hadon walked or trotted for what must have been hours. He went down and up and along, confused and thirsty. Once he came out onto another apron by the river, where he drank deeply. But there was no boat so he retraced his steps until he found another branch and went down it. Several times he heard the barking of dogs and the shouts of men, but he got away each time. At least he put a lot of distance between them and himself. Though the hounds had his scent, they could not climb the shafts. They had to be lowered or raised by ropes, so his pursuers lost much time at these places.

They would surely catch up with him in the end, unless he could find a way out of this three-dimensional labyrinth.

He went down a shaft about thirty feet deep which ended in the ceiling of a tunnel. He dropped from the bottom rung to the stone floor. Five feet away was a seeming dead end, a wall composed of granite slabs, ten inches wide and six inches high, set in concrete. He went to it and pushed on both ends but it resisted his hardest shoves. Either the bronze pivot mechanism was not operating or else it was truly what it looked like.

Ten feet the other way was a shaft. He went to it and looked down. His torchlight glittered on water, either the river or a well. A faint red light glowed at the top of the shaft— the open air. The great fires outside the city were reflecting from the clouds, providing a flickering light up there, a dim tawny oval.

But there were no rungs in the sides of the shaft. And the walls sloped slightly in from this point up.

The tunnel continued fifteen feet away at the other side of the well. He could not figure out why there was no bridge here. Did the carvers of the passage intend the wayfarer to jump the gap? Or had there once been a wooden bridge here, now rotten? Or a winch for a well?

He did not know what the situation had been. He did know what it was now.

He heard far-off barking and returned to the shaft he'd come down on. Torches flared at its head and several faces looked down at him. Frantic barking drowned out their cries, though their open mouths made it evident they were announcing his presence.

Hadon stepped quickly back out of sight. He turned and, holding the torch to one side, retreated to the wall of masonry. There he crouched, then ran as swiftly as he could; on reaching the lip of the well, he leaped.

He landed easily enough and with inches to spare on the other side. Fifteen feet was not much of a long jump for him. His pursuers were going to be stopped for a while, though. He doubted that the dogs would dare the jump. And the soldiers would have to shed their heavy bronze helmets and cuirasses before they made the attempt. As it was, only the most daring and agile would attempt it.

For a moment he thought about waiting on the other side of the gap to knock the jumpers back down the well. But the idea, though attractive, was not workable. The soldiers could throw spears at him, or sling missiles he couldn't dodge. No, he could only hurry on, hoping that the leap over the abyss would make them hesitate for a while.

The tunnel across the well was about fifteen feet wide. This side of it was narrower, only seven feet wide. He went along it for about a hundred feet, coming to a flight of steps cut into the stone and leading downward. The bottom landing was about twenty feet below, from which the tunnel continued. A few minutes later he came to a heavy wooden door secured by two enormous bars.

He shot the bars and opened the door. Its iron hinges screamed. Hoping there was no one on the other side to be warned by the noise, he passed through the entrance. He was in a large room, about sixty feet long, thirty wide and fifty high. It was empty except for three ingots of gold. Hadon thought this must once have been a storeroom, emptied except for the three ingots. Or pehaps it was being refilled and the three ingots were the first to be placed here.

That did not matter. What did was that near the door, on the sweating stone wall, was an incised sign, the same Klyhy had pointed out, a horizontal line just below a circle. Near it was a carved recess with the handgrip.

Hadon went across the chamber to the other side. There was another door here but this was unbolted. Just outside the doorway, another sign and recess with handgrip were revealed in the torchlight.

Past the door the tunnel ran straight as a sword for as far as he could see.

Hadon went back to the chamber, trying to figure out the peculiar placing of the bars on the doors.

Why bar the doors at all?

Was it to keep someone else from coming this way?

Hadon had a hunch that the long straight tunnel led to a place outside the city walls. And since there were outlaws, runaway slaves, wild Gokako and even Nukaar, the hairy halfmen of the woods, out there, the doors might be barred against them.

Well, he would find out what this meant later on. Or perhaps he would not. It was of no immediate importance.

He looked through the door he had entered by. A light shone far down the tunnel, so somebody had made the jump—more probably somebodies, from the speed at which the light was advancing. One or two men would not proceed so boldly. Not when they knew he might be waiting in ambush.

Hadon ran back to the other door. He stopped just past it and put his fingers inside the recessed grip. He leaned back and pulled with all his strength. The stone section slid groaning out, then suddenly it was free and he had to stagger backward to keep from falling. Then he was running, while behind him the ceiling, which was made of bricks and cement for about thirty feet, fell in. The crash was loud, booming down the tunnel, echoing. There was no dust, since the moisture was too heavy on the stones for that.

He heard or saw nothing of pursuit after that. Even if the bricks had not filled the tunnel completely, they would have given pause to the King's men. They would wonder how many more such traps lay ahead of them. But Hadon did not think the passage would be cleared for some time. The mechanism of the ancient priestesses had worked quite well.

At the end of about thirty minutes he came to a narrow flight of steps. He went up this spiral, coming suddenly into a cleft just wide enough for his shoulders between two granite walls. The clouds shone redly above him. The steps had disappeared, replaced by a steep incline of polished granite. He went up it to find himself in the open air. He was standing on top of a huge boulder.

Below him was a tiny round temple of marble, shining whitely in the light of a big fire. It was more of a shrine than a temple, consisting of a circle of white marble pillars with a conical gold-plated roof. The floor was a mosaic of varicolored stones with a great statue in its center. Just in front of the statue was a fire, burning in a vast bronze box.

Hadon had been confused at first. Now he knew where he was. He was on the Isle of Lupoeth. There, a mile west across the lake, was the city of Opar. Its towers and domes and walls shone in the fires still blazing on both sides of it.

The tunnel had gone under the river beneath the city and led to this islet—this islet sacred to the demigoddess Lupoeth and forbidden to the human male. He had committed sacrilege, though unknowingly.

The deed could not be hidden from Kho, he knew. But perhaps, since he had come here while in Her service and he had not known what he was doing, he might be forgiven. If he could get away before the three priestesses discovered him, he might be able to get through this without harmful consequences. Since he could cover the whole islet with one sweep of his eyes, and since he could not see the three women, he knew they would be in their tiny quarters right below him, in the hollowed-out part of the boulder. One would be awake, since the fire had to be tended at all times.

He went down the back of the boulder, which was like a small cliff here. The river lapped the foot of the great rock, so he had to wade around the vertical shore. Once he slipped into some deep water and swam around until his feet touched bottom again. He rounded the whole body of land in five minutes, failing to find a boat.

The three priestesses had their food and firewood brought to them, probably by water, since the tunnel would be used only for emergencies or secret messages.

There was only one thing to do. He would have to swim the river to get back to Opar. But the current was strong in its middle, and he was exhausted from the emotional and physical stresses of the day and night.

He might make it to the shore, but he would be far past Opar when he got there.

On the other hand, he thought, why not swim to the eastern, the near, shore? There would be fishermen or hunters along the strip of land between the river and the eastern cliffs. They would have boats, and he would just borrow one.

That was the sensible thing to do.

Hadon sat in water up to his waist and rested a moment. The temple looked eerie in this strange light from the clouds and the fire within the bronze box. The giant figure of Lupoeth, three times life-size, towered in the midst of the marble pillars. It was in the stiff, graceless style of the ancients, of marble painted with flesh tones and hair and eye colors. As was still common in those days, the body from the waist down was theriomorphic, in this case a crocodile's hindquarters. Her breasts were huge and rounded, each marked with the stylized head of a crocodile, Lupoeth's totem. Her eyes were painted blue. Her hair was long and black, crowned by a triple tier of gold set with diamonds. In her right hand she held an immense spear of gold.

Through the pillars Hadon could see the dark opening carved into the foot of the boulder. Where was the priestess who tended the sacred fire?

This question was answered suddenly and startlingly. A white figure rose from behind a small boulder to his right. It advanced toward him, becoming somewhat more distinct as it neared the light from the fire in the bronze box. It was not a ghost, as he had thought for a moment when he had first seen it. It was a woman in a white robe with a hood.

Apparently the light was strong enough to distinguish Hadon. The priestess stopped at the edge of the solid rock shore and stood still, looking at him for a long time. Finally, nervous from the prolonged inspection and the silence, he said, "Guardian of the Temple of Lupoeth! I am Hadon, son of Pheneth and Kumin the *numatenu,* and I am the victor of the Lesser Games of Khokarsa. I am a refugee..."

The woman threw her hood back, revealing a middle-aged face. She said, "I know you, Hadon. Do you not remember Neqokla, keeper of the Chamber of the Moon for many years? I used to give you sweets now and then and a hug and a kiss too. I expected great things of you, Hadon, though I also predicted that you would get into much trouble."

"Neqokla!" Hadon said joyfully. "Now I remember! You were sent here about twelve years ago! I have not seen you since! And yes, I cherish the memories of your kind deeds and words. You were very good to a small boy who was only the son of poor parents."

"How did you get there?" she said. Then, "Of course, you came up through the tunnel to the river! I thought I felt a shaking of the earth some time ago, but I had been dozing off and I told myself that I had dreamed it. Or Lupoeth was making the earth shake to wake me up and remind me of my duty."

"The quivering of the earth was caused by the collapse of part of the tunnel outside the great chamber which contains three gold ingots," Hadon said. "I set off the trap to escape from the King's men. I did not know the tunnel led here. I committed sacrilege unknowingly."

"We only know what happened in the city up to late yesterday evening," Neqokla said. "The supply-boat captain gave us the news, saying he might not be able to return in the scheduled two days. We watched the fires for a long while and made some sacrifices to Lupoeth, asking her to guard the city she founded and aid the people of Kho in their battle against the heretics.

"As for the sacrilege, I am sure that some slight penance will satisfy Lupoeth. You are here in the service of Kho, her mother, Mother of All."

"In that case," Hadon said, "may I come ashore?"

"You may," she said, "but you may also have to take to the river again."

She pointed past him. He turned and saw an assemblage of torches moving out from the city toward the island.

Neqokla said, "They are coming this way. Those torches are fixed to a longboat manned by the King's soldiers. They must have guessed you would be here."

"How could they?" Hadon asked. Then, "I suppose the men blocked by the trapfall returned to the King to report. He must have determined from the location of the trapfall that it was under the river—then he would have also figured out that the tunnel was used by the priestesses to get to and from this islet. I have betrayed you!"

"It couldn't be helped," Neqokla said, "I'll rouse the others and we'll hear your story quickly so we can plan what to do."

She hastened toward the round doorway carved at the base of the immense boulder. Their voices must have awakened the two women, however, since they appeared in their ghostly white robes before she had reached the temple. She beckoned to them and they came swiftly. One was old, white-haired and bent-backed, crippled with arthritis. This was the chief, Awikloe. The other, Kemneth, was about twenty-five, a pretty girl who had been with Hadon at the temple school.

Neqokla explained quickly all she knew and Hadon filled in the missing data. Kemneth and Neqokla brought a great wooden chair from the quarters for the old woman. The chair was some twenty feet in front of the fire, which Neqokla replenished with fuel.

"Gamori is a desperate and a hard man," Awikloe said. "He has already sinned greatly by violating sanctuary and attacking and killing priestesses and worshipers of Kho. He will not hesitate to violate another taboo and set foot on this island. He may even plan to kill us, though that would be going far even for him. As for his men, they must be as conscienceless and greedy as he, otherwise he would never have gotten them into the boat."

"Pardon, Awikloe," Hadon said. "But you sound as if you think Gamori himself will be on that boat."

"I think he will be," she said, flexing her gnarled hands.

217

"He will want to make sure you are killed; he will want to witness your death himself. Besides, his men, no matter how hard they may be, would be reluctant to touch taboo soil unless they were led by the King himself. But we shall see whether or not I am right."

"If I am not here, then they will have no excuse to come ashore," Hadon said. "I can swim to the eastern shore."

"After what you have been through?" Awikloe said. "Be truthful, Hadon. Could you swim half a mile in your exhausted condition?"

"I might," Hadon said.

"And more likely you would not be able to," she said. "Anyway, this is too good a situation to abandon. This business could be settled once and for all. If you kill Gamori, the rebellion would fall apart."

"And how can I do that when he has a boatful of men?" Hadon said. "Providing, of course, that he is on the boat."

"That is up to you," she said. "From what I have heard, you have been tricky enough. You are a man of many turns, equal to every occasion of danger, improvising where needful, eluding death where others would have been caught."

"Even the king of foxes was caught in the duckhouse," Hadon said.

"Don't quote proverbs to me, young man."

"If I stand here boldly defying him, his men will cast spears at me until I am a human porcupine, bristling with quills," Hadon said. "No, I must not be seen at first, at least not recognized."

Hadon asked some questions and then explained what might be done. The three agreed to do as he proposed. They did not think it had a high chance of success, but it was better than nothing.

And so it was that Gamori and his men saw an impressive sight when they neared the islet of the Temple of Lupoeth. The fire was blazing high, its light illuminating the giant statue from below, causing highlights and deep shadows. Lupoeth looked grim and terrible, harshness forming around the eyes and mouth. The aged priestess sat huddled in her chair, her back to the fire, her hooded face in darkness. The middle-aged priestess stood by the great bronze box, ready to throw more fuel on the flames. She too was shrouded in white. The young priestess stood at the right of the old woman, but she had removed all her clothing and gashed her breasts and arms and legs with a small sharp knife. Her unbound hair moved without a wind. Presently, as the prow of the boat ground gently against the rocky shore, Gamori saw why the hair seemed to have a life of its own: a small flat head with a darting split tongue raised from the mass, its head turned toward Gamori.

"By the venom of this snake, I summon death!" the naked young woman cried out. "By *my* blood I summon *yours*!"

There was a murmur among the men, thirty paddlers, a steersman and an officer who stood behind Gamori at the prow. The paddlers had put their blades on the deck and had unsheathed their swords or gripped their spears. Gamori held an officer's stabbing sword in his left hand. He was helmeted and cuirassed and wore a long scarlet cloak, a scarlet kilt to which the feathers of the kingfisher were sewn and sandals of hippopotamus hide. A thick white bandage was around his arm, covering the wound inflicted by Hadon's spear. Since he was left-handed, he could still handle the sword effectively.

"Do not come ashore!" the old priestess said in a high quivering voice. "This is sacred soil, Gamori, and all males are forbidden to touch it!"

Something was wrong with the tableau, but Gamori could not grasp just what it was. Then the officer, a colonel, tugged at his cloak and said in a low voice, "Your Majesty! The golden spear of Lupoeth is missing!"

Gamori looked up past the white figure on the chair and through the pillars and he felt a sudden shock. It was true! The great golden spear was gone! The hand of the idol was still bent, but it held only air.

"Where is it?" he said, looking wildly around the island. The fire lit up the white pillars and the white shrouds of the two priestesses and the white, darkly stained figure of the young priestess. It burnished the statue of Lupoeth, who seemed to be glaring at him, and the towering face of the gigantic boulder, said to have fallen from heaven shortly before Lupoeth and her expedition came to this river valley.

The chief priestess cried, "The spear of the goddess is with

219

me, Gamori! The goddess has delivered it to me, her vicar, to use against the first man who violates this isle, who soils it, who mocks Lupoeth and mighty Kho! You have committed enough crimes against the Goddess, against your wife and Queen, the high priestess, Gamori! You will soon pay for these! But do not add to your heinous deeds by touching an area which the deities have forbidden you. Go away, Gamori, before the angry spear of Lupoeth exacts vengeance!"

The men in the boat murmured again. The officer shouted at them to be quiet, but his voice lacked authority.

Gamori, however, though he must have been just as frightened, could not back down. To show fear now after having attacked the Temple of Kho and slain priestesses, having slaughtered a quarter of the population in the name of the Flaming God and the superior rights of the King—to back down would weaken his cause, even fatally. It would not take much to reverse the flow of victory. Though he had driven his men to commit sacrilege, he had not eradicated all anxieties from them. Deep down, though they lusted after the treasures and the power promised them, they were still fearful of the Goddess. This unease had driven them to hysteria, a frenzied attack on all they had been taught to revere and honor since childhood. It was this hysteria which had caused them to slay where there had been no need to slay, to profane beyond their orders.

For Gamori to show the slightest weakness now was to weaken his believers too. They would wonder why Gamori had not trespassed when his greatest enemy, Hadon, was within his grasp. Hadon was somewhere on this tiny place, probably hiding in the carved-out chambers inside the boulder. And their wonder would lead to a great loss of confidence in him. If he hesitated now, perhaps he was having second thoughts. Perhaps he really believed, under his pretense, that Resu was not supreme, that Kho was the greatest of the dieties.

Gamori's face was haggard in the firelight, deeply scored with fatigue, worry and dread. But he was not going to back down. He turned to his men and shouted, "I am going ashore! All of you follow me and search every inch of the island! And if the priestesses oppose you, slay them!"

He let himself down over the high prow, assisted by the officer. The river came to his waist at this point, but he held his sword up with his left hand, his right trailing in the water. He put his head down like a bull and thrust against the river. Soon he was standing on the shore, water running from his cloak and kilt.

The aged woman in the chair seemed to grow taller and straighter. She shrilled, "You have delivered yourself to the house of dread Sisisken! Do not follow him, you soldiers who are traitors to your Queen and your Goddess! You may yet escape the wrath of Lupoeth! Take yourselves and this boat away now! Report to Phebha and beg for mercy, saying that Awikloe sent you."

The colonel, who had been about to leap down from the boat, paused.

Gamori turned to the boat and yelled, "Obey me!"

The colonel did not move. Some of the soldiers had stood up, but now they sat down.

"They wait to see what you will do, Gamori!" the crone said, a definite jeer in her voice.

Gamori whirled, snarling, and said, "I will kill you, you wrinkled old bag! And then they will see that your Lupoeth is powerless to protect her own chief priestess! And if that is not enough, I will slay the other two!"

The young priestess gashed herself again on her arms and thighs, shouting, "*My* blood summons *your* blood, Gamori!" The snake slid out from her hair and down her neck, coiling itself around her bloody shoulder.

Gamori walked swiftly toward the chief priestess, his sword raised.

The priestess near the bronze box threw a bundle of split sticks on it and then cast a handful of green powder over the flames. A green cloud whooshed out and upward, covering her for the moment, then expanding to veil the old woman on the chair. The men in the boat gasped or moaned, and Gamori stopped.

The green cloud quickly thinned, revealing Awikloe standing straight and tall, magically tall, behind the chair. In her right hand she held the mighty golden spear, holding it above her head, though no man could have lifted that weight of gold in one hand.

"Behold!" she cried. "Lupoeth has given me stature and strength to slay her enemy and the Queen's enemy and my enemy!"

It may be that Gamori, who was much nearer than the men in the boat, saw the features under the hood. He may also have considered that the spear was not made of solid gold after all.

Whatever he thought, he had no chance to express it.

The spear went back and up as the priestess readied for the cast, then it flew to its target.

Gamori gave a cry and turned, but the point drove into his neck and through his windpipe. Choking, clutching the heavy shaft dragging on the ground, he staggered backward. The old priestess went around the chair and sat down, seeming to shrink back to her normal small size.

Gamori fell backward into the water, which covered his face. The golden spear disappeared under the surface, holding his body down, keeping it from moving with the current.

The priestesses were as still as the idol. They said nothing, nor did anything more need to be said. The colonel gave a sign and the soldiers seized their paddles and backed the boat out and around. They sped for the city of Opar, lurid in the flames.

Not until the boat was halfway to the city did the priestess arise from her chair. Then the robe was removed, revealing the grinning face and tall body of Hadon. The old woman came hobbling out from the round doorway. Hadon went to the body, drew the huge weapon out and threw it on the ground. Then he pulled the King's corpse ashore, because it would have to be shown to the people of Opar to convince them that he was really dead.

Neqokla, using a blanket to cover the fire at the correct intervals, had sent signals to the watcher in the dome of the Temple of Kho. A longboat put out an hour later, returning with Hadon at dawn. He was greeted at the quay by Phebha, who conducted the rituals cleansing him of the guilt of regicide and of profanement of the Isle of Lupoeth. After this, surrounded by soldiers who kept off the cheering crowd, he was led to the temple, through the temple to the room where Lalila lay in bed.

Though she looked pale and haggard, she smiled on seeing him. He kissed her, then took into his arms the tiny blanketed form. He lifted the flap from over the face and saw the most beautiful newborn baby he had ever seen. Wide blue eyes stared at him, focusing with an ability infants that age just never had.

Phebha, sitting in her chair behind him, said, "Hadon, behold your daughter! La of Opar!"